THE $\mathcal{S}$PIRIT OF $\mathcal{S}$WEETGRASS

THE SPIRIT OF SWEETGRASS

a Novel

NICOLE SEITZ

INTEGRITY®
PUBLISHERS
Nashville

The Spirit of Sweetgrass

Published in association with Mark Gilroy Communications, Inc., 2000 Mallory Lane, Suite 130–229, Franklin, Tennessee 37067.

Unless otherwise indicated, Scripture quotations are taken from the King James Version. Public domain.

Cover Painting: Nicole A. Seitz
Cover Design: Chris Tobias, www.tobiasdesign.com
Interior Design: Inside Out Design & Typesetting

Library of Congress Cataloging-in-Publication Data
Seitz, Nicole A.
The spirit of sweetgrass / Nicole A. Seitz
    p.   cm.
    Summary: "Soul-soothing tale about strong family ties and the glorious magic of heaven"—Provided by publisher.
ISBN-13: 978-1-59145-506-6 (pbk.)
ISBN-10: 1-59145-506-5 (pbk.)

1. Domestic fiction.   I. Title.

PS3619.E426S65   2007
813'.6—dc22   2006030016

Printed in the United States of America
07 08 09 10 11 RRD 9 8 7 6 5 4 3 2 1

For Brian and Mimi,

my rock and my wings;

for Mama Jim and Daddy Jim,

the pillars of our family;

and for Bonnie Marie,

my muse.

Acknowledgments

I THANK GOD FOR CHOOSING ME to tell this story, for fueling my fingertips and putting Essie Mae's voice so clearly in my head. I thank Him for my husband, Brian, who gave me the courage to climb this mountain, lifting me along the way; and for my mother, Miriam Furr Lucas (Mimi), my tireless reader and greatest fan—she inspires me to reach for the stars and loans me her wings to get there; and for my children, Olivia and Coulter, my glorious distractions from writing—they bring me back to reality and keep me grounded, knowing what is truly important in life. I could not have written a word of this without each of you.

I am grateful for a supportive extended family and am so blessed to be a beneficiary of my grandmother's fervent prayers, Miriam Coulter Furr (Mama Jim). She embodies the faith, heart, and tenacity of my dear Essie Mae. To my grandfather, James Martin Furr (Daddy Jim), and my aunt, Bonnie Marie Furr Buck—I miss you both, I think of you often and thank you for your inspiration. You help keep my eyes upward and my thoughts on heaven.

So many have helped in the making of this book; I am both humbled and thankful. First, my sincere appreciation goes to Mark Gilroy, my agent, who believed in Essie Mae from the start. To my publisher, Joey Paul, I thank you for hearing my voice and for taking a chance on a new writer; and to everyone at Integrity, including Kris Bearss, Jennifer Day, Scott Harris, and Bobby Sagmiller, thank you for helping ease my transition into this new world of books. My deepest gratitude goes to Rachelle Gardner, my insightful and brilliant editor, for helping to make this a much better book and for making me a better writer along the way. Thank you.

To some talented authors of the South Carolina Lowcountry, especially Pat Conroy, Richard Coté and Harlan Greene, and to author/musician Michael Conner in California, thank you for your generous advice and direction. And to the Seacoast Christian Writers' Group, I'm so glad you were there when I was finally ready to take the plunge and share my work. I will always appreciate your enthusiasm and "loving critiques."

I appreciate the following people: Eartha Lee Washington for filling my head with her wonderful stories and voice at a time when I needed it most; Annie Scott at Boone Hall Plantation for teaching me to weave; and Thomasena Stokes-Marshall whose important work helps to protect and empower the sweetgrass community. There should be more like you.

Finally, a very special thank you goes to Queen Quet, Chieftess of the Gullah/Geechee Nation and to Alada Shinault-Small of the Avery Research Center at College of Charleston. I am forever grateful to you both for your support and your efforts in helping me to get my facts straight about the Gullah/Geechee culture.

I have tried to convey the richness and lyrical nature of the Gullah language, but it is based on oral traditions and as such, hard to do justice on paper. Therefore, I have taken quite a few liberties in my portrayal of the Gullah language and of the Mount Pleasant African-American vernacular so that this book will be accessible to readers from all regions and backgrounds. In saying this, I would like to encourage readers to visit the Lowcountry and experience the Gullah/Geechee culture and sweetgrass basket makers first-hand.

A few final notes: my portrayal of New Orleans voodoo is purely fiction and not intended as fact. Also, *The Spirit of Sweetgrass* was written before the Gulf Coast was ravaged by Hurricane Katrina in 2005. My thoughts and prayers remain with those affected and with those who are working so hard to rebuild the great city of New Orleans.

Peace!

"Ef hunnuh wan fa kno de tru ting wha kin hol hunnuh
toggeddah, e dey een de spirit ob sweetgrass."

*If you want to know the true thing that can hold us together,
it's there in the spirit of sweetgrass.*

~ QUEEN QUET,
Chieftess of the Gullah/Geechee Nation

Prologue

T HIS IS WHAT I REMEMBER ABOUT THAT NIGHT—my last night alive. After having me a fine meal of crispy cornbread and dipping it in buttermilk just like Daddy used to do, I headed on back to the bathroom. I turned on the water in the tub, not too hot, but good enough to get my blood moving. I wanted to feel the life tingling through my veins.

For being seventy-eight years old, I can't say as I ever felt more alive than I did that very night. It's a funny thing knowing you gonna die soon. I felt the air kiss my skin. The sound of water rushed in my ears like a river. And I seen colors like I was seeing 'em for the very first time—like I'd been blind up 'til then. I wanted to look back on my life and taste every speck of it, the good and the bad. It had been a good life, sure 'nough. I'd had me a fine mama and daddy, a sweet husband, and a beautiful grandbaby. My daughter had been my only real grief, seeing as she ain't loved me too much, but I done the best I could with her, and I had peace with that.

1

I lay there in the water feeling it tickle down over my shoulders. I remembered when Jim would touch me like that. *Oh, Jim, it won't be long now*, I thought. I was getting right excited about what I was gonna do. My blood was a-boiling and my fingers was itching to weave. By the grace of God, this was gonna be the finest basket I ever made. And everything that was bothering me—my house I was getting ready to lose, and the nursing home I was fixing to get stuck into, the stretch of highway I was gonna get kicked off of, and the tension 'tween my daughter and me—it was all gonna be over soon. Hallelujah, praise Jesus! Jim'd told me if I made one of my love baskets just one last time, that we'll be together forever—and I could touch his sweet face again and meet Jesus just like I always wanted.

I reached down and pulled the plug by my feet and watched as the water and bubbles and all the dirt that was on me just a-washed down the drain. My body sure ain't looked like it used to, no sir. My black skin was loose and not so pretty no more—not like it was when I met Jim and 'fore I had Henrietta. I was a good-looking woman back then if I do say so myself.

I grabbed on to the white porcelain and tried to pull myself up real slow. With all the water gone, my big ol' body was dead weight and not so easy to lift. I wrapped my towel around me and looked in the mirror above the sink—at my gray hair still in them cornrows I been wearing forever and my shoulders all drooped from carrying this extra weight. But my eyes was what struck me the most. It sure is a strange thing looking into your own eyes and seeing the life in there, knowing it'll all be gone soon.

I turned real quick and headed 'cross the hall to the bedroom, changing into my most comfortable nightgown, the one with the white lace 'round the hem like my wedding dress had. I stuck the cloth up close to my nose and breathed in real deep. I'll always remember that. I been using the same washing powder since forever, so it's the same smell Jim used to have when I'd hug him tight 'round the neck.

I'd already pulled my sweetgrass up onto the bed. I reached over and grabbed the picture frames propped up next to me and traced each and every face. There was Mama, God rest her soul. And Daddy right beside her. I guessed I'd be seeing 'em again real soon. I looked at the one of Henrietta and my sweet grandbaby, EJ. I sure was gonna be sad to leave my EJ, but he'd be all right without me. He was a fine young man and had his future to look after—ain't no need to waste time looking after me no more.

The last picture I seen was of my Auntie Leona with her hair pulled up tight. She looked back at me, and I swear I could hear her say, "You can do it, Essie Mae. You got a strong head and an even stronger heart. Girl, you can do anythin' you set your mind to." So I pulled out my big-print Bible and grabbed Jim's hair I'd stuck down in there. Then I used my free hand to reach 'round and pull one of my own hairs out my head. After twisting 'em up real tight, I closed my eyes and prayed, "I love You, sweet Jesus. Help me out now, Lord. Let this one work, please, and bring me on home. Sweet Jesus, go 'head and bring me on home."

I weaved all night long 'til my fingers and my back was sore. My mind was racing so much, I ain't felt it none 'til I was just about done. Once I realized it was almost finished, I said, "Whoa, now." Not sure what was gonna happen to me. I'd asked God not to hit me with a Mack truck, but ain't thought about what else might happen. Was it gonna hurt? Lord have mercy, all a sudden I was getting kinda scared. I decided to set my basket down and wait to finish it while sitting with Jim at my stand next morning. That way, I wouldn't be alone when the good Lord called me to heaven, however He decided to take me there.

PART I:

when trouble come to see me

Chapter 1

May

I RECKON THIS-HERE ROADSIDE STAND's a whole lot like my life—sometimes good folk stop and visit a while; other times, folks come by, seems like just to haggle and make my day long. All the time, there's these cars zipping by, one after the other after the other—can't stop 'em. Just like time. It keeps rolling on, don't care who I am or what I'm selling—just lets me bake here in the sun, getting older every minute.

Sweetest thing to ever happen to me out here was 'bout nine, ten years ago just after my husband, Jim, died. I was sitting here making a sweetgrass basket, and I looked up kinda sudden-like. Walking down the side of the road like he just got dropped off the CARTA bus was my sweet Jim, just a-smiling and grinning. I almost fell out my chair, sweet Jesus! Now, I'd heard 'bout dead folk coming back around and visiting, but I never expected to see Jim again. He come to me, though, sure 'nough, and he shows up every morning when I'm setting out my baskets. He sits with me every day in this here pink plastic chair I pull out for him. He's a-sitting here right this very minute—"Ain't you, Jim?"—just like he was bright and early this morning when trouble come to see me.

There we are, Jim and me, sitting here talking 'bout nothing much with traffic kicking up dust. The air's so humid, we know it's fixing to rain. Got no idea how bad a storm it's really gonna be.

'Round nine o'clock we see a car fixing to pull in. I get to praising Jesus for the business He's bringing when all a sudden, my heart 'bout stops. There's my daughter, Henrietta, pulling over to the side of the road, and I know she ain't bringing me nothing but heartache.

"Henrietta, what you doin' here?" I ask her, pushing up from my seat.

"Hey, Mama," she says, real sweet-like when she rolls the window down. "I'm here to pick you up!"

"Pick me up? What you talkin' about?"

"I got the day off, so I thought we could spend some time together," she says. "It'll be a girls' day out."

Well then, that's when I know it, and it ain't good. There ain't no way Henrietta's coming to spend time with me. No sir. Last time she did anything friendly with me a'tall was when she hauled me over to the Belk store few years back to find me some bigger brassieres to wear. And she only done that 'cause she was embarrassed my bosoms was popping out my blouse at her Christmas Eve supper.

My daughter Henrietta's what I call uppity. Now, I know it's a sin to talk like that—'specially when it's your own flesh and blood—but sweet Jesus, that girl ain't got a tender spot on her body. Like she was

8

born with a thorn in her side, makes her mad as all get-out at the world. Matter fact, I can remember her screaming bloody murder from the time she was born. It must be hard having an angry spirit like Retta's. Ever now and again, she tries to be sweet, but it wears her out fast, and she goes back to mean. All I can do is love her how she is, I reckon. She don't make it easy, though, I tell you what. Henrietta's got a strange way of showing love for people. Most times, it comes out like she don't like you much a'tall. But sometimes, like this morning, she can be downright scary.

"I can't go nowhere, Retta. I'm sittin' at my stand now," I tell her. "I can't leave my baskets."

"Well sure you can," she says. "Nancy's right there." Miss Nancy's stand is over yonder 'bout thirty feet or so. She hollers over to her, "Miss Nancy, will you watch Mama's stand while we go out for a bit?"

Nancy look like she don't know what to say. I'm over there shaking my head *no*, but she must not see me 'cause she says, "I reckon I can. How long you gonna be?"

"Not too long, Nancy. And we might just bring you back something. An ice cream cone maybe?"

An ice cream cone? Well now that seems fishier than a shrimp net in summertime. *Oh sweet Jesus*, I pray, *please let us just be goin' out for ice cream, hear?*

"Mama, you sure look nice today," says Henrietta, grabbing my arm and trying to pull me on up into her SUV. She's wearing pressed pants and a nice red blouse, and her hair's straightened and smooth and perfect—just like she always has it. I look down at my walking shoes and my long gray skirt and orange blouse with the top two buttons missing. My heart sinks plumb down to my shoes 'cause I know she lying 'bout my looks. That girl sure is up to something.

"Henrietta, listen here—where we goin'?" I say, eyeing her hard.

"It's a surprise," she says.

"I don't like surprises."

She don't say nothing back.

"I said, I want to know where you takin' me, Retta. I got my baskets to tend to."

Still nothing.

"Henrietta! Take me back now. I ain't playin' your games."

"All right!" she says, not so cool no more. "All right. We're going over to James Island."

"James Island? What in heaven for?"

"It's a beautiful day, Mama."

"Retta, we ain't never gone to James Island together in all my memory. Tell me right now, what we gonna do over there?"

Retta seems to be heating up, and she pulls the car to a stoplight and holds her breath. When she lets it out again she tells me, "There's a lovely place on James Island called Sunnydale Farms."

"Sunnydale Farms? What they got—collards? Strawberries? 'Cause I can get me all I need over to Boone Hall," I say, relieved. "Come on. Let's turn on back and get us some greens."

"It's not that kind of farm, Mama."

"Not that kind? Then what they got? Onions? Snap beans?"

"It's not for food, Mama." She squeezes the wheel tight. Sounds like her fingers gonna rub the leather plumb off. Then she says real slow and careful-like, "Sunnydale Farms is a very nice retirement community."

"Retirement? You takin' me to a nursin' home? Oh Lord have mercy! I ain't retirin'! Sweet Jesus, help me outta here!" I'm grabbing for the handle and scratching at the door.

"Don't get so upset, Mama." She punches the pedal again. "We're just going for a little visit. A *visit*, okay? It's just to see if you like it, that's all."

"Oh God in heaven, my life is over! Retta, no you can't, I'm your mama, child! Stop the car this minute!"

"I promise!" she yells, 'bout breaking my eardrums. "I'll take you back to your stand in a couple hours, Mama." Then quieting down to a real low voice she says, "Now come on. I thought we could have a nice time, but I suppose we cannot."

"You ain't gonna leave me there, Retta. Child, you just try it, and I'll go kickin' and screamin'. You'll be mighty embarrassed, yes ma'am—mighty embarrassed! You'll wish you ain't never hauled me over there. I—"

"Mama, stop talking crazy." A scowl I seen a hundred or more times spreads over her face. I can tell it even though she staring 'head at the road. "Let's just take a look. Nothing more than that. All right?"

Well, I drop it, sure 'nough. But I got to keep my guard up— less Henrietta try something funny.

Chapter 2

AFTER WHILE, ALL WE HEAR IS THE ROLLING OF THE WHEELS as we drive through Mount Pleasant and then on up that skinny little bridge to downtown Charleston. Lord have mercy, I hate that bridge. Makes me wanna bring my food up when we's on it 'cause the cars is so close, you just know you gonna get hit. And Lord help you if you look down, is all I can say.

I used to drive over that bridge, but one time got to the top and there was all these cars just a-honking at me. My foot done froze up like a rooster in December. After while, this police fella come up the wrong way to bring my wagon down, 'cause I weren't moving. I swore it'd be the last time I ever drive up on the Cooper River Bridge.

Now Henrietta's dragging me back over it.

Retta holds on to that wheel real tight and tries to keep us going straight over them shaky little metal grates. I just cover up my eyes 'cause my stomach is acting up. All I can hear is the *ta-dum, ta-dum* of the wheels scraping over the seams in the road. Once we get to the other side, I open my eyes. Think I'm gonna have a chance to relax my fists, too, 'til Henrietta opens her big mouth.

"Now what's this I hear about your house taxes not being paid for *ten* years, Mama?" she asks, shocking the living daylights out of me. "Is there something you want to tell me?"

Oh, Lord! *EJ, baby, can't you keep your mouth shut?* For some dang-stupid reason he must 'a told her about it, 'cause Henrietta knows all 'bout my tax problem, sure 'nough. I'm hoping if I don't answer her back, she might forget all about it.

"Mama. Tell me what happened. I already know you're in trouble."

Lord have mercy, my taxes is all she can think about. We're done with the Cooper River Bridge, thank You Jesus, but getting right close to James Island. Too close. Now I know it's true—Retta's gonna lock me up in that Sunnydale Farms and throw 'way the key!

My forehead's starting to sweat, and my heart's having palpitations when she says, "Spill it, Mama."

Lord help me, I figure it can't get no worse so I open up and flat tell her the truth.

"There I was, sitting in my kitchen, Retta," I say, "having me a cup of whole milk and reading the obituaries—just to see if there was anybody I knew."

She looks over at me, waiting for more.

"Put your eyes back on the road!" I tell her. "So this shiny black car pulled up and out come this tall skinny fella dressed in a black suit and sunglasses, looking all serious-like. He was eyeing my baskets 'neath the magnolia tree real hard. I figured he wanted one and walked out to meet him."

"Well, were you nice to him, Mama?"

"'Course I was nice, Retta! I was sweet as I could be. But 'fore I knew it, there was this paper stuck smack dab on my door saying they was having a 'tax sale' on my house. *My* house, Retta! I tell you what, made me sick, what it done. The milk in my belly curdled and wanted to come right back up." I grab my stomach for effect, but she don't pay me no attention, just keeps a-driving and listening hard at me like a hawk. After a few seconds she lights into me.

"Mama, how could you do this? *Ten years*, Mama!"

"I swanny, I ain't never got a bill, Retta! I told him they been sendin' mine to some other house, all I can figure, 'cause I ain't got *nothin'* askin' for money all this time." I shake my head, feeling low as all get-out. "I just don't know what happened, Retta. Jim's the one used to pay all our bills."

I decide not to tell her how much I owe—figuring she already knows. But Lord have mercy, I ain't got that kind of money. Only one who's got that much is Henrietta, but I ain't gonna ask her for it, no sir. I just know she won't give it to me even if I did.

"Why didn't you come to me?" Retta asks, touching my knee with her hand. It's a real sweet touch, tell the truth, and I might enjoy it 'cept my skin beneath her fingers gets to burning when we turn down this long drive. There's a sign up ahead says THIS WAY TO SUNNYDALE FARMS.

"Why in tar-nation would I come to you?" I ask her. "You sayin' you gonna give me ten thousand dollars?"

"Ten thousand dollars?! Mama!" The car swerves off the road when she swings her head to me.

"Eyes on the road, Retta! Eyes on the road! Now see? That's 'xactly why I ain't told you in the first place!" My arms is folded up tight, and I'm staring at the weeds growing up 'longside the road, wishing I was out there 'stead of in this here car.

It takes her a minute to calm down, I reckon. Then Henrietta tells me, "Mama, I'm worried about you. I think that money might be better spent on a nice *new* place where you can get the care that you need."

"Care? What care I need?! I don't need no care!"

"You can't even pay your bills properly, Mama," she says.

Lord have mercy, she might as well slapped me upside the head. I grit my teeth and turn real serious on her, the wheels slowing beneath us.

"Child, I carried you for nine, count 'em, *nine* hard months and nearly died bringin' you into this world."

"Don't do this, Mama."

"And your daddy, God rest his sweet soul, and me—we raised you in that very house, Retta! What you doin' ain't right, child. You don't just throw your mama in a home 'cause you ain't got no better use for me."

"Mama. Don't say that. You know that's not how I feel."

"Oh no? Hmmph!" I'm so mad, think my head might pop, but I just bite my lip the rest of the way. Talking to Henrietta ain't gonna do me no good.

We pull in to the parking lot of the old folks' home and I sit like a lump, ain't moving. Retta finally comes round and drags me out the car. But my heart's broke and ain't nothing I can do.

Chapter 3

WELL, WE GO UP TO THE ENTRANCE OF THAT OLD FOLK'S HOME, and there's palm trees 'bout everywhere and the color pink. Lots of it. My stomach feels ill the second I step in the door Retta's holding open for me. I cut my eyes at her sideways-like—*Don't you mess with me, missy*—and then we walk on up to the desk.

While we wait for this lady to get off the telephone, I'm looking for the quickest way out. I make note of all the red exit signs and keep my legs jiggling and loose in case I need to make a run for it.

The first place we go is the cafeteria which ain't good a'tall. I can't eat, but I stick some biscuits and gravy on my plate and push 'em around to keep Retta quiet. They ain't nothing like how I can make 'em at home. Retta tries to buy me an ice cream cone, too, but I tell her no. Then this white lady in a pink uniform walks us 'round the place, pointing to all the stuff there is to do.

We come to a room with a couple television sets and board games set out—and a baby gate in the doorframe! I ain't lying! "Here's where we have arts and crafts classes every Tuesday and Thursday," she says. She's yelling and just a-waving her arms at me like I'm deaf or something. There's wheelchairs every which-away and they's all lined up, eyes on that gate. The lady slips us through that gate and half of 'em try to escape, rolling this way and that and scrapping with each other. When I slip back out fast as I can this one lady gets to cursing me like a sailor. Child, I ain't never seen nothing like this old folks' jail!

We go outside in the fresh air and the lady says, "Out here's the courtyard where you can take a nice stroll or sit under the oak tree and read a nice book." An old glassy-eyed man looks up at me real slow from the bench he's sitting on. Has his hand resting on his walker, and it seems like he just woke up. I tell you the truth, there's a piece of drool 'bout to slip right out o' his mouth! And if that white woman says one more thing is "nice" 'bout this place, now I know I'm gonna have me a fit!

After while we finish up the tour, and boy am I surprised when Henrietta lets me leave. Just like that. Real quiet-like. She don't try to hold me there or nothing, 'course I figure that's coming later. She drives me on back to Mount Pleasant just like she said she would, but it's plain as day to me: Henrietta don't want to help her old mama. She's just ready to get me out the way.

"EJ's got his own life now," she says. "He's a young man and needs to be spending time with people his own age instead of hauling you back and forth to your little stand every day." My ears are getting hot like fire. Think steam might be coming out any time now, but I hold my tongue just so I can get back faster.

Three, four years ago I gave EJ that old brown station wagon I was driving, the same one Daddy Jim used to crawl around town in and carry back the fish he caught over there in Shem Creek. EJ was real grateful. Comes over every morning to pick me up and then carries me home every night too. He even picks up groceries for me when the milk and eggs is low, seeing as it's right on his way. Oh sure now, he complains some just like any twenty-year-old's gonna with prettier people to see and better things to do, but deep down EJ's a good boy. Don't know how he come from his mama, no sir. 'Course, as far as that goes, don't know how she come from me neither.

Henrietta tells him he a-wasting his time—that I can find somebody else to come and do my bidding for me. He don't tell me that, but I know that's what she says to him. She offered to buy him a nice little sports car, too, if he'd quit shuffling me around town. Can you believe that? Now I know EJ wanted that car bad, but he must 'a said something smarty to her 'bout me 'cause he's still driving that sad ol' wagon this very day. He tells me it's all right though. Says it makes him feel close to his granddaddy, 'cause Jim used to take him fishing in it most every weekend he was alive. Jim and EJ, they was real tight, but I still see him eyeing them pretty cars whizzing by us all the time. Makes me sad what that boy give up for me.

EJ's short for Edmund James; he's named after his daddy. By the grace of God, Retta married a pretty nice man, one of them White brothers from West Ashley. Not white like white folk but White like his name is: Edmund White. Yes sir, Eddie's a nice enough fella—I like to call him Eddie, anyways—Henrietta says, "His name is Edmund, Mother," and she's all higher-than-me when she says it too.

Henrietta and Eddie live over there west of the Ashley River in a real fine house. Got two stories and a whole lot of space—more than enough for a big ol' family, even though it's just the three of 'em living there. I imagine if she really wanted, she'd find a spare room for me there too.

Eddie's mama and daddy are pretty well off so I s'pose that's why he is. Henrietta likes to spend Christmas and Thanksgiving and such over at the White house with the big turkey and all the trimmings. Can't say as I blame her much for that. There ain't enough space at my house for a big get-together, what with my two bedrooms, living room, and little ol' kitchen.

When EJ was just a young'un, Henrietta got herself a job working in an office. That just made her even harder to be around. I reckon she figures she's all high-fallootin' now with some big job, thinking she's all better than everybody else and treating 'em that way too. 'Specially me, her own mama.

"I just can't believe you go out and sit on the side of the road in that—that shack!" she told me after EJ built my stand for me and was so proud and all.

"Now listen here," I told her, "don't you talk to your mama like that! Basket makin's in my blood. It's in yours, too, and you'd know it if you weren't so ashamed of where you come from. I may not have me a lot of money like you White folks do, but I got everything I need, sure 'nough. The good Lord done provided for me, yes ma'am. Just can't figure out how come He give me a ungrateful daughter like you, is all."

Henrietta says that Sunnydale Farms is "a nice new place to

make some friends my own age," but I ain't born yesterday. I know better. There ain't an able-bodied soul living there, what with the wheelchairs crawling up and down the hallway and the smell o' alcohol everywhere. And when she brings me back to my stand, I ain't never been so happy to see my baskets in all my life.

Or Daddy Jim.

I don't know why, but Jim don't like to come home with me to our house on Rifle Range Road. Not sure if it's the window trims painted blue to keep the haints out or not. Don't see why that would matter none, seeing as he ain't no haint. Probably a good thing he don't come home, come to think of it, 'cause they's lots of days I just feel like staying in bed when my rheumatism starts acting up. Thinking about seeing Daddy Jim's what makes me get out of bed.

Sitting there with the traffic rolling by, I'm telling Jim all about my trip to the old folks' home and trying to keep from tearing up.

"Jim, what I'm gonna do?" I ask him. "Things is fallin' in all over me. I got a heap of money I can't pay which means I'm gonna lose our house—the very house you and me lived in—and I can't do nothin' about it. And Henrietta's just itchin' to stick me in that nursin' home. You should a' seen her all 'Mama look at this' and 'Ain't this nice, Mama.'"

Jim don't say nothing. He just looks out at the cars flying by.

"Jim," I say. "Jim, say somethin'. You know what this means? I ain't gonna be able to come out here and weave no more. You just gonna have to come to Sunnydale Farms with me."

He don't say nothing again.

"James Furlow Jenkins, you *are* gonna come with me, right?" My stomach's knotting up 'cause he stays real quiet. If he was solid, I'd a-pop him on the leg. But since he ain't, I just got to wait for him to feel like talking again.

"What you doin', Mama?" he asks me finally. Now I'm the quiet one 'cause I'm holding my breath, wondering what he's gonna say. "What are you really doin' anymore, Mama? Henrietta ain't got the time of day for you, and pretty soon, EJ ain't gonna have time for you neither. And what you gonna do in a nursin' home? You can't do your baskets no more."

"But I'll still have you, Daddy, right? 'Cause you gonna be with me. You ain't gonna make me go to the home all alone, are you?"

"I ain't goin'," he says, just like that. "You gonna have to go on alone."

Telling you this now probably don't hit you like it hit me, but hearing Jim say he ain't gonna be with me no more was too much for me to stand. I done lost him once, and I can't do it again. Jim's my life—all of it, pretty much, 'cept for EJ and my sweetgrass baskets. Without Jim here with me, I just don't see how I can take one more day on God's green earth.

Chapter 4

WHEN JIM COME DOWN WITH THAT CANCER IN HIS LUNGS from smoking all them years—cigars and cigarettes and such—he woke up coughing and feeling sick one morning and was gone just three months later. That sure was something. You go through life riding along fine, and then, wham! The good Lord decides to up and change things on you. Right when life's all nice and cozy like this here pair of walking shoes I got on my feet—they just now getting all nice and roomy.

Ever since Jim died, Henrietta's even more ornery to me, if you can imagine that. She tried to be kind when I was grieving so bad over him, but after while she pretty much washed her hands of me. Tell the truth, I reckon she blames me for not noticing Jim's cancer sooner than I did. Don't see how I could, though, seeing as Jim worked out in the yard every day and was just as happy and feeling good as he could be. No sir, first time I knew he was sick, he was coughing up blood—liked to scare me to death.

When Daddy Jim died, my whole life just flip-flopped like a catfish dying on the dock. Right about then's when I took up basket making again. My friends at church said it would lower my blood pressure. Said it'd be good therapy 'cause it soothes a restless spirit. Well, I reckon that's just what I had 'cause I couldn't sleep no more. I'd just sit up and think about my sweet Daddy Jim being gone and me all alone in that empty house. So, I started coiling and weaving to pass the time. I'd go on and on sometimes right through the night.

Before Daddy Jim passed I was working as a nanny for some white folks who live in one of them fancy neighborhoods with white picket fences over on the Wando River. I was a nanny for a lot of folks over the years, got to see the babies turn out good when they growed up and all. Well, for about two years I'd been looking after these two little adopted babies, Mason and Leah. Leah come from South America, I think, and Mason, he's from around here in Charleston but got mixed blood in him—half black, half white. I wonder if that got something to do with his being up for adoption. No matter though. I got to loving those children, I surely did. You just can't be with a child for eight, ten hours a day and not get to feeling for 'em.

Well, when Daddy Jim died, I guess my head was just up in the clouds. I weren't playing too well with the babies and kinda keeping to myself. Then one day, I made some grits for Mason and must 'a left the stove on. Nothing happened, though. Not like the whole house caught on fire or nothing, but you'd never know it the way Miz Price made on about it. Next day when I showed up for work, both the Mister and the Misses was there. I knew that ain't good.

"Are you having a problem with your memory, Essie Mae?" Miz Price said. "Have you seen a doctor?"

"Well no, I ain't, but—"

"Essie Mae, I hate to do this, I really do," she said and then started blubbering. That lady boo-hoo'd and carried on so much, Mister Price finally told me they was putting the babies in day-care school, and they weren't gonna need me no more. And that's all there was to it.

That's when I really got to weaving again. It'd been a good fifty, sixty years since I learned how, but when I picked up that sweetgrass and started sewing, it felt just like I'd been doing it all my life. I'd sit there late at night, just listening to the crickets talk about their day, and the way my fingers moved made it so I didn't have to think no more about missing Daddy Jim or Leah or Mason. With the help of a cut-off silver spoon handle I call my "nail bone," my hands just looped that palmetto leaf in and over, in and over, and after a while of feeding my rows with more sweetgrass and pine needles, I had me a whole heap of baskets just sitting all over the house. When there weren't a place to sit no more, my grandson EJ offered to build me this here roadside stand. Did a fine job too—painted it key lime green just like my house on Rifle Range Road.

This morning, I right near tore into EJ when he come to pick me up. "In all that's holy, what in heaven's name were you thinkin', tellin' Henrietta 'bout my tax problem?"

He said he was just trying to help, and I know he was. I felt bad yelling at him like that. Said there was no way his mama was gonna stick me into a nursing home, no sir. "I'll find a way to help you keep your house, I mean it!" I know he means well. EJ sure is a sweet boy.

I'm right fumed at Jim for saying he won't go with me to no nursing home, so I ain't said much to him all day. Finally I say, "Daddy, look at that lady over there tryin' to stop. 'Bout ran Miss Georgia right over. You'd think people could slow down a bit when they pullin' over to the side of the road. Good Lord better watch over all of us."

"Mm hmm, that's right." He smiles at me but I'm still mad, so I push myself up from my chair and walk over to Miss Nancy's stand. Hers is real nice. Her son's a contractor—works for builders over in those fancy new neighborhoods close to the bridge. He used real good wood to put Miss Nancy's stand together, and it's as straight as can be—and sturdy, whooee! You can try and shake on the frame, but it just stands there real solid. Nancy even got a little covered room with carpet right behind the boards covered in nails where the baskets is hanging. When it rains, I get up and go sit with Miss Nancy in her nice, dry room. It ain't so easy for me to get around these days, but I'd rather hurt a little walking a few steps than sit here sopping in the mud.

I'm trying to keep my mind off yesterday. Don't wanna think about no nursing home or Henrietta or nothing. So even though Nancy's good at yapping her mouth, I'm happy when I see a car fixing to stop. I run back over to my stand and out steps this pretty little thing—has fine blonde hair pulled up in one of them smart-looking dos, and her face is sweet as a little girl's. She's dressed in high heels and a fancy little dark suit with a bright yella scarf tucked 'round her neck.

"Hello," she says. She smiles and walks 'round my stand, looking at each and every basket like they's gold or something. "How much for this?" She picks up a nice round one good for holding muffins and cornbread.

"That depends," I say. "Is it for you?" See, I always like to know where my baskets is going—what kind of life they's gonna have when they leave Mount Pleasant. I ain't never been outside South Carolina, so it's right exciting when my baskets get to go plumb 'round the country.

"No, actually, I promised my mother I'd bring her back something from Charleston. She's been dying to come down with me, but got sick right before the trip." She puts the basket to her nose and breathes in that sweet smell. "I'm here for a conference, and I kept meaning to pick one up for her at the market downtown but just ran out of time. I'm so glad I saw you!"

"Oh, you're here on a conference? What do you do?"

"Nothing exciting, really. I work for a marketing company up in Massachusetts."

"Oooh, now that sounds pretty nice, I'd say." I use an old spoon handle and a palmetto leaf to sew some rows I'm making while we talk.

"Well, I guess it can be, but it can also be pretty stressful some-times."

"Mm hmm. Are you married?"

26

"Uh . . . no . . ."

"What? Pretty young lady like you and nobody done snatched you up?"

The lady's face blushes bright red as a beet. "Well, I guess I just haven't found the right person yet. Um, how much for this basket again?"

Daddy Jim whispers in my ear. "Oh, go on and give it to her, Mama. You know you want to."

"Well," I say, "you seem nice enough, bein' from up north and all. You just go on and take it. I don't need nothin' in return. But now you be sure and tell your mama Miss Essie Mae says 'Hello from Mount Pleasant,' you hear?" I push the basket on her like I'm shooing a fly.

"Oh, no! I can't let you do that! Here, how about fifty dollars?" she says, setting her bag on Jim's lap and pulling out her wallet. "I insist."

"Well, I don't know . . ."

"Please, take it. Your work is beautiful. It wouldn't be right."

I don't have the heart to tell her I can get twice as much for that very same basket. "Well, you are too kind Miss . . . what's your name again?"

"Susanne. Susanne Maybree."

"Well then, Miss Susanne Maybree, you have a very safe trip back home to Massachusetts. And if you're ever in Mount Pleasant again, stop by, you hear?"

"Oh, I will, I promise." She smiles a nice big smile and then leans over to my chair. Next thing I know, this little bitty thing's wrapped her arms around my shoulders and's giving me a big bear hug. Now see, that's what I'm gonna miss if I can't sit out here no more! I smile back at her, and when she pulls away, I say, "Now Daddy, give Miss Susanne her pretty purse back so she can be on her way." Lady looks at the pink chair, then back at me and winks.

I wave as I watch her get in her car and pull off onto the highway and go on up north.

"Sweet girl, don't you think, Daddy?"

"Oh, she's a good one, now. Pretty too. Gonna make somebody a lucky man some day, mm hmm. Just like you did me."

"Well, what in heaven's name is a sweet pretty thing like her not found herself nobody to love yet? It's a shame, what it is," I tell him. "Why, I was seventeen when I found you Jim, 'member?"

"Oh I remember, Mama. I sure do."

Jim and me was both born and raised in Mount Pleasant, and I can remember seeing him around, but I didn't really know him. Not 'til the day Mama sent me to Barker's Feed 'n Seed to fetch her some cornmeal for a whole heap of cornbread she was fixing to make.

I'd just come from church, so I was wearing this pretty white dress with frills around the bottom. That was my nicest dress, sure 'nough. Had little pearl buttons that liked to gone clean up to my neck, and a two-inch sash that showed off my tiny waist I had back then. Well, I walked right into that feed 'n seed in my white patent leather shoes and see-through white hat with the daisies on it. God knew to put me in my finest that day—He sure did want me to look pretty, seeing as I was about to meet the man I was gonna marry!

Well, Jim was there sweeping up in the back of the store, and when I walked in the door, a little bell went off.

"When I looked up I liked to drop my broom!" Jim's telling me. "I was just a-staring at you 'cause the breeze done carried your hem up 'round your knees."

"Oh Jim. Cut it out now."

"No really, Mama. Thought an angel done walked in to carry me home."

"Mm hmm, we was married just five short weeks after that day."

"When it's love, you just know it, I reckon," says Jim, sweet-talking me.

"'Course things was a lot more simple back then." I say it all ornery but then I look over at Jim and give him that smile I always do. He knows now I forgive him and how much I still love him— even if he *is* gonna leave me again.

Chapter 5

EJ COME AND HELPED ME PUT AWAY MY BASKETS and carried me home this afternoon. It's a real nice evening with a west wind blowing in, so I been weaving under the magnolia tree out front after a supper of beans and cornbread. I had me two helpings 'cause my mind's carrying on so—sopped it right up in my buttermilk just like my daddy used to do.

After a while of sitting here, I look down and see this dainty little blonde hair just a-staring up at me from my gray knit top. I pick it up real careful-like and all a sudden, a big idea comes to me—out from nowhere! I run fast as I can back into the house with that little bitty hair 'tween my fingers—I'm real careful not to drop it—and I go and find a piece of tape I got left over from wrapping Christmas presents a few months back. I open up the little drawer in my night table next to the bed, pull out my big leather Bible Miss Nancy got me, and I tape that blonde hair of Miss Susanne's just as tight as I can get it to the first page what has my name on it: Essie Mae Laveau Jenkins. Then, I shut the drawer and sit on my bed just to think.

See, ever since Jim died, and he weren't there to take care of anymore, and ever since Mister and Miz Price said I weren't fit to care for their young'uns anymore, and ever since yesterday now that Retta wants to put me away, I'm feeling downright useless. Don't nobody need me no more, and what good am I anyway, and that sort of thing. Yes sir, this old black lady's 'bout as blue as can be. So, now I got this little hair, I'm getting right excited thinking I can actually do something important with the short life I got left in me. Sure 'nough, I'm gonna find Miss Susanne Maybree of Massachusetts a good man to love!

Now all I got to do is remember the magic I growed up hearing all about. Lord have mercy, Mama would have my hide if she knew I was thinking 'bout doing hoodoo. Even though it's what brought my mama and daddy together, sure 'nough.

Mama was born and raised here in the Lowcountry, just like me. She's what you call a true Gullah. Gullahs are the black folks who the white folks brought from West Africa, oh, about two or three hundred years ago. They knew how to pick cotton and handle rice and such and was used to the heat, so the white folks, thinking they was real smart, knew they'd get a lot of use out of 'em— brought 'em here for slaves, you know. Down there in the market on Chalmers Street just over the Cooper River Bridge, they'd buy 'em and sell 'em just like cattle, I reckon, with chains on and such. It's a cryin' shame, what it is.

Well, them black folks out on the Sea Islands, they kept a little bit of the language and songs and food and such from Africa and kept their own culture 'cause they was cut off from the mainland. Weren't no bridges back then, no sir. The Gullahs still 'round today, they link us African-Americans to our true heritage, and that's mighty important. These days, people 'round here get pretty excited about studying Gullah culture 'cause there ain't too many of 'em left. Big developments done pushed 'em out their homes mostly, but some of 'em are still out on the Sea Islands, and some are scattered about. You can tell a true Gullah by the way he talks. Got pretty much a whole different language, you know. It's pretty too. Sounds like the waves rolling up on the ocean and the marsh grass blowing in the wind. I grew up around Gullahs, seeing as Mama was one, so I can understand most of it—what little is said these days.

"Ef hunnuh ain kno whey hunnuh dey frum, hunnuh ain gwine kno whey hunnuh da gwine." That's what Mama used to tell me. It's Gullah for, "You need to know where you come from in order to know where you goin'." I believe it, too, sure as I got these gray hairs up all over my head. See, lots of folks is lost. You might be stumbling 'round life just itching to find whatever you s'posed to be doing. But the answer's there if you look for it, sure 'nough. You got the place that you was raised, and the people you gonna meet along the way. Mix that up with the gifts the good Lord give you, and if you look real hard, you gonna see what He put you here on Earth to do.

I'm pretty sure Mama was put here on Earth to cook. That's one of the gifts the good Lord give her. She made the best pot of okra soup you'd ever eat—stuffed with okra and shrimp and just enough hot stuff to make your top lip sweat. Whooee! And she always made a pot big enough for everybody in the neighborhood to throw over rice. There was cornbread too. Made just right with that buttery hard crust on the bottom you can only get from a cast-iron skillet. That skillet belongs to me now, seeing as Mama died about thirty years back. And to this day, it still makes the best cornbread I ever tasted.

Mama weren't no more than a teenager, I think, when she started cooking her cornbread and okra soup for everybody. Used to have big neighborhood parties; fact, that's how Mama and Daddy got together—with the help of my Auntie Leona's meddling, that is.

See, most of my roots are in South Carolina—right here in these pretty oak trees hanging over the road. But I got a little mix in me too. Makes me interesting, I think. See, my daddy was born and raised in New Orleans. That's over there in Louisiana. I ain't ever been, but I heard a lot of stories about it. Daddy and my Auntie Leona were what you call Creole folk down in New Orleans. They growed up Catholic and all and had pretty Creole accents. My daddy could speak French just as plain as day. I know a little bit of that, too, but nobody ever speaks French 'round here in Mount Pleasant.

Now the black folk in New Orleans, they come from West Africa, too, but lots of 'em come through a place call Haiti and brought old beliefs and the Vodoun religion too. Over in Louisiana, they call Vodoun "voodoo." 'Round these parts here, we call Vodoun "the root" or "root work" and the folks who know what they doing with it "root doctors." But over the years, from what I understand, it sort of got mixed up and watered down with the Catholic religion in Louisiana or with Protestant influences here. And most of what's done today is just called hoodoo. That's real different—just the folk magic—it ain't the same as what come from Haiti or Africa and what folks who really know something 'bout Vodoun do.

So anyway, back in the 1920s Daddy come looking for work in Charleston. He'd been let go at the factory he was working at in Louisiana and needed to get out of town right quick. Auntie Leona was with him, too, 'cause she was the reason they had to leave New Orleans.

Now Auntie, God rest her soul, knew all about voodoo and studied the Vodoun religion back in her day. She was a practicing Catholic but also had these psychic powers. She knew how to make potions and gris-gris and all—that's those little bags of herbs and stones and such that bring folks good luck. Well, back in New Orleans, Auntie worked as a hairdresser and did the hair of a white lady named Mabel Gleeson every week. Mabel was married to the man who owned the shirt factory where Daddy worked. So one day, Miss Mabel got to asking my auntie a lot of questions about spells and things. Said she wanted to make herself more attractive to her husband. Right then and there, Auntie started chanting and praying, and Mabel started going along too. Next thing you knew, Miss Mabel was dancing in a trance just as naked as she could be right out in the middle of the road. A policeman up and arrested her, and when Daddy's boss bailed her out of jail, boy was he mad! The next day, he fired Daddy and threatened to kill him and Auntie Leona if he ever caught sight of 'em again. So, they packed their bags and caught a freight train in the middle of the night. Daddy said he wanted to stop in Savannah 'cause it was closer, but Auntie Leona had her heart set on Charleston.

Well, once they got here, folks in Mount Pleasant didn't know nothing about New Orleans-style voodoo 'cept to be scared of it. They knew plenty about "the root" though. They knew root doctors could bring people good things like love and luck and health and such. But folks here don't even like to talk 'bout that stuff less they conjure up trouble for themselves. Most black folks here is Baptist or Methodist—good God-fearing Christians in Mount Pleasant, sure 'nough—and when Auntie come she 'bout scared the pants off 'em, what with that crazy eye she'd get sometimes. They figured she was just like a root doctor or witch doctor—something they knew plenty about. So whenever bad things happened, folks would say, "Best stay away from that Leona. She gonna put another hex on you, she is."

So, after a couple years of them being here, Auntie got pretty tired of cooking and cleaning for Daddy. Felt just like a hired hand, she said. She decided it was high time he find himself a wife. Daddy was pretty set in his way, though. He liked things just like they was. That's where my mama come in.

She'd made a heap o' cornbread and okra soup for everybody, and Auntie never liked to miss a party, so she dragged my daddy over to Gran's house in Six Mile one Sunday afternoon. The whole neighborhood was there with music and such, but my daddy just sat there like a lump on a log, dipping his cornbread in buttermilk and not saying a word to nobody. Well, Auntie Leona got to talking to my mama, and she started thinking about what a good cook she was. Then she went in the house and seen how clean she and Gran kept it. That's when Auntie decided to go ahead and stick her finger in the pot and stir things up.

Like I was saying, Auntie knew everything about making a good gris-gris or love potion. She liked to dry sweetgrass and hang it across her door, or sometimes she'd burn it and say chants and such. Once in a while though, she put the hoodoo on somebody in a bad way, like the time Mister Wallace grabbed her in the hindquarters. Now Auntie was a pretty lady, yes she was, but don't nobody better mess with her if she don't want it. Mister Wallace sure did get what was coming to him when his arms swelled up the size of two watermelons. He couldn't work or eat or nothing for two weeks 'til finally, Auntie felt kinda sorry and took the hex off him.

Most times, Auntie used her magic to help folks. And that's just what she decided to do when she hugged my mama real tight after that cookout and plucked a hair right out the back of her head. She knew my stubborn ol' daddy would never get around to finding a woman to marry, and Auntie was tired of waiting.

So, one night on a full moon after she'd been doing laundry for most of the day, Auntie grabbed that ol' hair of my mama's that she'd set aside and put it with one of my daddy's she'd picked off of one of his dirty shirts. What she did with 'em next must 'a worked good 'cause within two months, my daddy was head over heels in love with Mama and acting like a fool. He asked her to marry him one night as they was walking back from Mama's church, and she said yes—so long as he would quit being a Catholic and start being a Baptist instead. I was born about a year after that.

Now, Auntie never told Mama and Daddy what she did to 'em that night. Said they were in love and wouldn't 'a cared anyways, but all the same, she kept it to herself. Auntie told me, though. She was always telling stories, and that one was my favorite. I kept my mouth tight as I could too. The only one what knows about Auntie Leona's meddling to this day is me—and Daddy Jim, of course. So now all I got to do is think back on the magic Auntie Leona used to tell me about. Hope I can 'member it. And first thing tomorrow I'm gonna keep my eyes open. Got to find us a good man for putting together with Miss Susanne Maybree from Massachusetts.

Chapter 6

Tell you the truth, I been looking all this morning for a nice fella for Miss Susanne. But had me just three old ladies stop by and a young man what didn't buy nothing from me.

"No, he can't be the one," I told Jim, even though he was right nice-looking. "He don't know a good basket when he sees it."

I'm starting to think this might be harder than I 'magined.

Then I see a pickup truck pull in. I know that truck, belongs to Mister Jeffrey Lowes. Today's Thursday, middle of May; every middle of the month he comes a-calling to pick up his big order of baskets for selling at the flower shop he got in downtown Charleston. Now, Mister Jeffrey, he's right close to my heart. I was Jeffrey's nanny when he was just a little ol' thing with brown hair all curly and scruffy and feet so big he had to grow into 'em like a puppy do. Few years back, Jeffrey opened this little flower shop down on East Bay Street called La Belle Fleur. And I know that means *pretty flower*, seeing as I got some French left in me from when Daddy was alive. It's a fine name for a flower shop, if you ask me.

"Morning, Miss Essie Mae," Jeffrey says when he steps out of his truck. He walks over to me and grabs my hand, squeezing. He's wearing good-fitting blue jeans with his middle nice and trim, and his hair's cropped close so I can't see no curl. His eyes are caramel-colored with long eyelashes, like to give me shivers when I see 'em. "Got some baskets for me today?"

"Oh, I sure do, Jeffrey. Got 'em all stacked up for you right behind there."

"And how's Mr. Jim these days?" he asks me, looking over at the pink plastic chair where Jim sits.

"Oh, he's just fine. Just fine, thanks for askin'." Jeffrey always was a fine boy with real nice manners and such. When he walks around to grab them baskets, Jim says, "Essie Mae, do you know what we got here?"

"No, Jim," I say. "What we got?"

"We got ourselves a man for Miss Susanne Maybree."

Praise God, Jim sure is right! Mister Jeffrey's never been married, and he has himself a good job, and he's real respectful. Never did quite understand why he ain't found nobody yet.

"Jeffrey, honey, tell me how long you and me know'd each other."

"Oh, about thirty years, I guess."

"Well now, in all them years you ain't once brought a special young lady to meet me. Why is that?" Jeffrey shifts in his shoes like the ground's too hot all a sudden.

39

"Well, it's just not every day that a person finds a love like you and Mr. Jim here," he tells me. "I date a lot, I guess, but there just hasn't been anyone I want to spend the rest of my life with yet. Tell you what though, I'll be sure and bring that person around to meet you as soon as I do."

"Oh, that'd be real nice, real nice," I say. "Now come on over here and give Essie Mae a hug, you hear?" And Jeffrey comes over and leans down real far, bending his knees and everything and gives me a real sweet hug.

"Ouch!" He jumps up real quick.

"Oh, sorry, baby. Had a bug in your head. They bad this time o' day." I look over to Daddy Jim's chair. He's just a-grinning and a-laughing. It's hard for me not to chuckle myself as I stick Jeffrey's hair nice and tight down under my brassiere strap.

Jeffrey pays me the money he owes and then loads up his truck bed all nice and full of baskets.

"You come and see me again real soon," I tell him. "Next time I see you, I'm gonna have a real special basket made just for you."

"Oh, you don't need to do that, Essie Mae."

"I want to, you hear? You kinda like a son to me, Jeffrey. Yes sir, you're a real good boy." And he *is* like a son to me. And I'm like his mama. Jeffrey's real mama was always nice enough, but I can't remember her one time telling him she loved him. I never seen her hug him or love on him one bit a'tall. Poor boy only got that from me, his nanny. It's a shame, what it is.

I swanny, Jeffrey looks 'bout to cry. His bottom lip gets to sticking out, and he comes back over and gives me another hug. I don't yank no hairs out this time.

"How about Monday, then?" he asks. "Are you and Jim going to be here on Monday?"

"You know we will," I say. "Be right here a-weavin' and waitin'." We smile at each other, and then Mister Jeffrey drives off in that silver pickup truck of his 'til I can't see it no more.

"Well, we found Susanne a fella, Jim. And found Jeffrey a girl. How 'bout that!" I slap my knee 'cause I'm getting real excited. If I ain't got much time left making my baskets and being with Jim, I sure as anything want it to be time worth *something*. I'm seventy-seven years old for heaven's sake. I got to do me something good with the time I got left.

I look on back behind me and realize my supplies are running low. "There's only one problem, Jim," I tell him, sad as all get-out.

"What's that, Mama?"

"Dad-gum. I'm plumb out of sweetgrass!"

"You and everybody else out here," he says, looking on up the road.

Lord have mercy, ain't that the truth.

Chapter 7

THEM TWO HAIRS OF MISS SUSANNE'S AND JEFFREY'S been burning a hole in my pocket. But my grandson, EJ, come by this morning to haul me to church, and he brung me a good surprise. Now EJ, he's a fine young man. Gonna be somebody big some day—maybe a doctor or a lawyer. Right now he's studying something called "political science." Not sure what he's gonna do with that, but he goes to that college they got downtown, the one that's spreading every which-a-way like Confederate Jasmine.

EJ dragged me outside the house and showed me the back of that wagon just as full as it could be with a whole heap of palmetto leaves, pine needles, and real nice sweetgrass—already dry, too, 'cause he left it in the sun a couple weeks. Being May, it's a good time to start pulling sweetgrass, if you can find it that is. EJ gets mine near the marsh off Highway 41 still, even though Miss Nancy's son says he got to go plumb all the way to Georgia to find his. Sweetgrass is fixing to run out, I reckon, what with all the big developers coming in and clearing it all out to make room for big buildings and houses and such. It's a crying shame, what it is.

Well, I sure was happy to see that mess of grass he brung me 'cause I had me a real special basket I was fixing to make.

EJ waited for me in the living room while I fixed my hair and put on a nice blue skirt and blouse. I grabbed me a banana and a swig of whole milk, same as I always do when we's heading out the door. EJ likes to visit my church over here in Mount Pleasant better than the one his mama and daddy go to ever now and then. Says he likes the singing a heap more and the preacher is better at preaching. I reckon Henrietta don't like hearing about that.

We drove over to the Mt. Zion AME Church up yonder, and I was just a-singing and a-grinning the whole way there. "Take my hand, Lord, take my hand. Lead me on to the promised land . . ." I know, I know. I said my mama was Baptist, and I was raised that way, too, but I like the singing and all more at Mt. Zion. Anyway, I don't think God cares much where you worship, so long as you do it.

I took us a seat near the back 'cause I needed some space to do my thinking. Inside, the stained-glass windows was steaming up since we ain't got good air conditioning, and the Reverend Jefferson was preaching on the virtues of a godly man. "Praise God!" I shouted, thinking about my sweet Jim. "Hallelujah!"

"You sure is in a good mood, Essie Mae," said Bertice Brown when the dancing stopped for a minute. She looked like she was just itching for some gossip. Bertice is the one who always knows everything 'bout everybody else's business. I think every church got a Bertice Brown. Sure 'nough, that woman got a mouth bigger than a bass on a hook.

"I'm just feelin' good, is all, Bertice," I told her. "God is good, praise Jesus!" She was hoping I'd go on more about my life, but I just smiled and grabbed EJ's arm. It was all I could do to make it through the service, but I sang my hymns and thanked God for my new sweetgrass. I asked Him, *Please, can You find me the money so I can save my house? Please don't make me go live in no nursin' home.* I asked Him a couple times, and I hope He heard me. I reckon we'll see about that.

EJ drops me off back at the house after church and gives me a big hug.

"See you tomorrow morning bright and early," he tells me. "You make sure and get some sleep now. I don't want you staying up all night sewing with this new grass."

I just smile at him and nod 'cause I don't wanna lie to him, what with it being the Lord's day and all.

Walking back to my bedroom, I'm 'bout to start skipping 'cause I'm so happy with the love basket I'm fixing to make. I ain't ever made a love basket before. Never done no magic myself come to think of it—just let Auntie Leona take care of all that. I pull out the drawer in my night table and lift that big ol' Bible up onto the bed. Opening up the cover, I see them two little hairs I done grabbed still taped up next to my name—one belonging to Miss Susanne Maybree, the other to Mister Jeffrey Lowes.

I reach over 'cross the bed to another little table full of pictures and stuff and grab me a good one of Auntie Leona—the one where her hair's all pulled up in a fancy do. God rest her soul, looking in her eyes I can hear her say just as plain as can be, "Now Essie Mae? What I taught you is some powerful magic. Don't ever let your Auntie find out you used it for bad. Only use it for good, you hear?"

I say to myself and Leona too, "Well, if this ain't for good, I don't know what is." I grab them two hairs and twist 'em up together 'til I can't see which one's which no more. Then, I hold that little bitty hair braid real careful and carry it out front to the magnolia tree where my sweetgrass is waiting for me. After I set it in my bosom for safekeeping, I make a nice, tight coil to use for the coaster bottom and stick that hair braid right down in the middle of it.

The dad-gummest thing happens next. I'm 'bout ready to start saying a love chant over 'em just like Auntie Leona used to, but ain't nothing comes to mind—not one silly word! I close my eyes tight as I can and brace myself on the edge of my chair. I hold my breath, and I can see Auntie just as clear as day. Can hear her voice too—just can't hear a dad-gum thing she's saying. Well, it comes to me then, real natural-like. The only thing I can do is get down on my knees and start to praying.

"Oh, sweet Jesus, let these two souls come together. Don't let them be 'lone no more. Lord Jesus, rest Your hand on 'em and bring 'em together. Yes, Jesus! All things through You, Lord. All things through You." I keep praying and praying, and I'm right near frenzied, so I know He done heard me—I can feel it in my bones.

Chapter 8

EJ COME BY 'BOUT EIGHT O'CLOCK TO GET ME THIS MORNING, like he always do. He hollers to me while I'm getting dressed in my bedroom. "Grandmama, this sure is a nice basket you got here, but it wasn't here yesterday—I know you didn't stay up all night making this."

"Oh, honey, ain't no big thing," I say, walking into the living room trying to zip my skirt up on the side of my hip. "I'm an old lady, EJ. Don't need much sleep these days."

Sure enough, I stayed up all night weaving. 'Course once it got dark, I took my basket on up in the bed and kept working with my lamp on. I ain't never finished a basket all in one night before, but when Mister Simmons' rooster next door got to cock-a-doodle-dooing this Monday morning, it was done.

The basket sits about two and a half foot tall and has a right nice lid to go with it—got a little ball I sewed right on top, good for lifting.

Besides that, I used some pretty red bulrush in some of the rows giving it a real nice stripe all the way up. Yes sir, Mister Jeffrey sure is gonna be tickled to get this!

EJ looks at me like I'm a young'un what ate too much sugar. "I just don't want you falling asleep on the side of the road, is all."

"Well now, that's a fine place to snooze," I tell him. "No use watchin' the cars go by. They's gonna stop if they want to no matter if I'm awake, or if I ain't."

"I suppose so," he says. "This is a real nice basket, though. You'll probably be able to get two hundred or two fifty for it! Whatcha think?"

"Oh, no, baby. That one's not for sale," I say, shaking my head. EJ looks at me kinda funny.

"Grandmama, haven't we talked about this?" he fusses. "You can't give your baskets away for free. You're not made of money, you know."

I just smile at him 'cause he knows I'm gonna do what I'm gonna do anyway.

"All right then, how are you going to pay your taxes if you keep giving baskets away?"

I cut my eyes at him. "I made that one special for Mister Jeffrey down to the flower shop," I say, my voice letting him know I can handle my own business, thank you very much. "He's comin' for a visit today."

EJ softens up like butter. "You always did get attached to the kids you raised, didn't you, Grandmama? They sure were lucky to have somebody like you, real lucky if you ask me."

"What a nice thing to say, EJ." I ain't grumpy with him no more. "You gonna make your old grandmama cry is what you gonna do." EJ come over and give me a big hug, 'cept my cheek is in his belly, seeing as he's so tall. His granddaddy, my Jim, was tall like that too. Made me have to step up on my toes just to get me a kiss.

EJ set me up at my basket stand and I had a right quiet morning. Got to get some good sleep in, seeing as most folks ain't looking to buy baskets first thing on a Monday morning. Jim said he'd keep watch for me and let me know if somebody was stopping, so I could rest my eyes.

I wake up when I hear a car slowing down. An older fella and his Misses pull their Cadillac over and get out to look at Miss Nancy's stand. Then the Misses wanders over to me and spots that big ol' basket I just made.

"How much for that one?" she asks me, her eyes getting real big. I can always tell when a body's really interested 'cause their eyes can't hide it a'tall.

"Oh, that's not for sale," I tell her, "but this one here's a real cute basket too. You like this one?"

"Well, actually, I really like this basket," she says, running her fingers over the coils. "The colors are perfect, and I have just the right spot for it in my dining room. Sure I can't talk you into selling it to me?" She gives me a sugary sweet grin lining cotton candy lips.

"Sorry," I say. "But I'll give you a real good deal on this other one." The Misses sighs, but then agrees with me and goes over to grab her husband who's still standing there chit-chatting to Miss Nancy. They buy the basket from me, and then pop back in the Cadillac and pull out into traffic. I sure am hoping Mister Jeffrey drives up soon. Can't wait to see his face when I give him his basket.

After a few minutes of wondering what's taking him so long, I see that pretty silver truck pull on up beside me.

"Hey there!" I say, pushing up to greet him.

"Miss Essie Mae, you sure do look beautiful today. How are you doing?" Jeffrey gets out the truck just a-grinning big as he can. "I brought you something," he says.

He pulls his arm out from behind his back and there's the prettiest bunch of flowers I ever did see! Even prettier than the ones I held at my own wedding just a-walking down the aisle.

"For me?" I fan myself with my hand, almost blushing.

"For you, Essie Mae, 'cause you're so special to me." I take hold of them flowers and breathe 'em in real deep. Then I find a nice basket to set 'em in 'til I can get 'em home and stick 'em in water. Right now, I'm feeling faint and my heart's a-fluttering. I'm 'bout close to crying as I ever been.

Walking around to the back of my stand, I tell him, "Wait here a minute." When I come back out, I'm carrying that great big basket I made for him and Miss Maybree in my arms. Jeffrey's eyes like to pop right out his head! He puts his hand over his heart and backs up a couple steps.

"This here's a special basket I made just for you, Jeffrey," I hand it to him real gentle. "See? The lid comes off and everythin'!" Feels just like Christmas, it does.

49

"I . . . I don't know what to say. I can't believe you did this for me."

"You're a real sweet boy," I tell him. "Now this basket's just for you, hear? No sellin' it down at the flower shop."

"I wouldn't dare," he says. "In fact, I've got just the right spot for it. I'm going to put it on a pedestal right next to the fireplace, so I can see it every day." He runs his fingers along the stripes and lifts the lid on and off, peeking inside.

"That sounds real nice. Real nice. And who knows? Maybe somebody special's gonna sit next to you whiles you look at it one of these days."

"We'll see," Jeffrey says, grinning.

We'll see, sure 'nough.

Jeffrey and I talk a while longer 'fore I get me some more customers stopping to take a look.

"I'd better be getting back to my shop. I'll see you real soon though," he says when these folks is fixing to buy a basket from me. "Thank you so much for the basket, Essie Mae. You really made my day."

"And you made mine, Jeffrey. You sure did make mine."

Chapter 9

July

LET ME TELL YOU, IF YOU GONNA BE IN MOUNT PLEASANT the month of July, you might as well roast in oyster steam and save yourself the trip. The sun's so hot and the air so sticky, you wanna bathe three, four times a day. But that ain't something I can do, now is it, sitting on the side of the highway. Nobody's pushed us off this stretch of 17 just yet, but Miss Nancy and me seen plenty of folks poking 'round here lately. We know it ain't gonna be long now. I've been selling baskets left and right but I swanny, my due date on my taxes is coming up quick, end of August. I hate to say it but I'm still over eight thousand dollars short. I'm doing the best I can though, and that's all a body can do.

The only good thing 'bout the last couple months is I've been able to sit with Jim every day and been weaving so much I don't have time to think 'bout my troubles. I'm mighty good at weaving, if you ask me—almost as good as Miss Georgia over there across the street.

Miss Georgia's baskets is always perfectly round, and her stripes just so. She's been making baskets all her life, so she's got a good fifty years on me—I should hope hers'd be better than mine. Better than Nancy's too—don't tell I said that—but tourist folk stopping on the side of the road, they don't know the difference. And if they do, that don't matter neither. There's plenty enough business for all of us out here.

Mama's the one taught me what I do best—making sweetgrass baskets. Let's see, I was, oh, 'bout eight years old the day I sat down with Mama under that old pecan tree we had out back. It was a hot day—hot enough to dry the linens just as soon as you hung 'em on the line. But under that pecan tree, it was real shady and right near cool. That's where Mama liked to weave.

I sat there watching Mama make perfect rows out of that sweet-smelling dried grass, then they'd stack up one on top of another 'til the next thing I knew, it actually looked like it could hold something. Sometimes Mama'd make great big fancy baskets to sell to the white ladies in town. They didn't use 'em—just liked to prop 'em up in their houses for decoration and such. Other times, she'd make little bitty ones for holding bread or fresh shucked corn.

I'd seen Mama sew baskets maybe a hundred times or so, but this day was different. That's when Mama let me make my first basket ever. I still got it, too, sitting right up on top of the fireplace mantel next to the picture of my mama and daddy. It's a sad-looking little basket with the rows all different sizes and the sides all lopsided. But Mama told me it was good, anyway. She said, "Essie Mae? Das da bes' one I ebuh see. Now lissen, chile. You had git da Gullah blood een you an' da gift ob sewin' yo grammy had. Jus' keep weavin', Essie Mae, 'cause Gawd done give you dat gif'; an' eed be a sin ta waste um." Well, I reckon I musta sinned a whole lot over the years, seeing as I didn't make another basket 'til I was just about sixty-eight years old.

Some ladies like to put lots of dark brown bulrush in their baskets to make 'em pretty. I do that, too, sometimes when the mood strikes me right. Miss Georgia likes to use fresh green sweetgrass in hers. Rows of green mixed in there do look kind of nice and fancy, I reckon. Besides, some people like that kind of stuff—pretty little pine needle buttons and fancy dyed colors and all—but I been adding something real special in my baskets lately too. Something none of these ladies knows about. Only Jim and me knows 'bout my love baskets.

Now, some folks is lucky. They find the calling early on in life. I guess I weren't so lucky 'cause I just figured mine out. Mama used to say, "Essie Mae? Yo body full'up yo ansestah blood." I believe it, too, 'cause I got me some sweet-smelling sweetgrass and powerful magic running though my veins.

"Come on over here, Nancy!" I holler. I got me an extra Coke-cola for her from the General Store, and things been pretty quiet for a while. I figure Miss Nancy can use some company.

She's moving on over to me, bringing her own chair, I reckon so she won't have to sit on Daddy Jim, when we see a car fixing to stop. Miss Nancy turns around real quick, chair and all, and hurries on back to her own stand. A woman gets out the car and comes to see me, so Nancy plops down, picks up a basket, and gets to sewing.

All a sudden, I think my eyes is playing tricks on me! The prettiest little blonde lady comes over and leans down to give me a hug. When she gets real close, I 'bout fall out my seat! Sure 'nough, there's Miss Susanne Maybree all the way from Massachusetts. She's dressed more casual than the last time I seen her. Wearing a white top with blue jeans and her hair's pulled back in a ponytail.

"Well, I'll be," I say, "if it ain't Miss Susanne Maybree."

"You remembered my name!"

" 'Course I did, honey. I'd never forget a sweet face like yours. What you doin' back here in Charleston so soon? It's only been—what? Couple months?

"Well," she says, "it's kind of a funny story." She goes to sit down in Jim's pink chair, and then thinks twice about it.

"Oh, go right ahead and have a seat," I tell her. "Jim don't mind. He's used to folks sitting a spell to watch me weave." Miss Susanne sits down and then looks at me all serious-like.

"Well, I really enjoyed myself when I came down to Charleston for that conference. I really did. And I had a long time to think about things as I was driving back home." She shifts in her seat and crosses her legs. "I got to thinking about my life and work and, well, everything. Then I started feeling like something was missing. I can't really explain it, but when I got home and went back to work, I just got this overwhelming feeling that I was in the wrong place. I'd never felt like that before."

I'm sitting here listening to Miss Susanne talk and trying to act like all this is coming as a surprise. 'Course by now, I'm just as tickled as I can be, seeing that my love basket's working like a charm. I swanny, I might just bust my britches.

"My mother just loved that sweetgrass basket I bought from you. She said to tell you thank you if I saw you again."

"Well now, tell her 'you're welcome' right back for me, hear?"

"I will," she says. "Actually, it was Mother's idea for me to come down here."

"Really?"

"Yes! We were having coffee last week and staring at your basket. I was going on and on about how much I loved Charleston and griping about work every other word. Well she finally said, 'Susanne, you have one life to live. So live it! Move to Charleston!' Can you imagine?"

"No!"

"Of course, she might have had ulterior motives," Susanne says, looking kinda iffy. "Mother's going to join me here once I get all settled in."

"Well, I'll be. How 'bout that! So you just up and quit your job?"

"Just like that," she tells me. "None of my clients wanted to see me go, so I've actually got quite a few of them sending their work to me now instead of the firm. Can you believe it? I'll actually be making more money freelancing!"

"Whoooeee, child! That sure is somethin'. Don't God work in mysterious ways," I say, shaking my head.

"Yes, He does, Essie Mae. Anyway, I'm meeting with a real estate agent in just a little bit. I'm so excited!"

"Miss Susanne, I'm mighty happy for you, mm hmm. Got a

good feelin' about this move too. Now you stop back by and let me know where you move to, you hear?"

"Oh, I will. Why, you're my only friend here so far."

"Now listen here," I tell her, thinking real quick-like. "You get a chance, hop on over to La Belle Fleur flower shop downtown. Young man what owns it's a good friend of mine, Jeffrey Lowes. Tell him Essie Mae sent you and 'fore you know it, you got two friends in Charleston already!"

"La Belle Fleur? Thank you, Essie Mae. I'll do it. I need all the friends I can get."

"I hear that."

Miss Susanne waves at me and then drives off with the biggest grin on her face.

"How about that, Jim!" I say, slapping my knee hard enough to leave a mark. "It's workin'! My love basket's workin', praise God." I had a pretty good idea that my love basket would work, but seeing as I ain't actually done magic before, it's hard to believe it's working so fast!

I tell you the truth, Auntie Leona sure would be proud right about now. For the first time in my entire life, I feel power glowing in my fingertips. I can feel it coursing through my veins like a long swig o' whiskey. I ain't had nothing to look forward to in the longest time, 'cept now I can sit and watch what happens with Miss Maybree and Jeffrey Lowes.

"Girl's got a lot to look forward to, don't she, Mama?" Jim asks me with a cute little smile on his lips.

"She sure do, Daddy," I say. "She sure 'nough do."

Chapter 10

TODAY'S MONDAY. HAD ME A PRETTY LONG DAY of nobody buying nothing and Miss Nancy talking my ears off. I sold just one little piece to a young man who ain't had much money to spend. He was looking for something for his girlfriend's mama and ended up getting a potholder.

"Essie Mae, you seen that sign they put up behind that old oak tree over yonder?" Miss Nancy asks me, pointing to the woods.

"I seen it, sure 'nough," I tell her. "Looks like some developer's bound to come on in here and push us out."

We stare at that big For Sale sign for the longest time not even speaking a word to each other. Both of us been sitting on this part of the highway for the better part of ten years. Miss Nancy was here 'fore I was, though. She's been sewing a lot longer than me, and used to sell her baskets farther down south on Highway 17 'til somebody bought the land she was on to put up a gas station.

"What you reckon they gonna build here?" she asks. "A restaurant or a car wash, maybe?"

"Can't rightly say. Only God knows for sure."

"Well, what you gonna do if they push us outta here?" Miss Nancy's face scrunches up just like Queenie, her ugly ol' pug dog. "I like this spot, and I'm too tired to move. They gonna have to pick me up and move me themselves then. I'm just gonna sit right here 'til they haul me off. They done pushed us halfway to Awendaw already!"

"Don't know what I would do," I tell her. "Might have to set me up a stand out in front of my house on Rifle Range." 'Course I'm thinking, *if'n I can keep my house, that is.*

"Essie Mae Jenkins, you know you wouldn't get good tourist traffic out there, no two ways about it!"

"You're right about that," I say, shaking my head. "Sure are right about that."

My eyes is starting to glaze over just looking south down the highway when I see the strangest sight I think I ever seen in my life. Traffic's coming up real slow, like a tractor done got up in everybody's way. But when the cars get closer to me, I see it ain't no tractor a'tall. Riding down the road just as wobbly as you can imagine is an old white man on a rickety red motorcycle. But the doggone-est thing about it is that sitting right behind him, not tied down or holding on to nothing, is the shabbiest yella dog on the face of this earth!

"Lord Jesus, don't let that dog fall off," I say when they slow down even more than the twenty miles an hour they's probably going. They start to veer off the road and heading right for me. Problem is, they's in the wrong lane and all these cars is just a-honking and cursing. That man and his dog finally make it over into the dirt by the grace of God and sputter on up to me sitting in my chair.

"What can I do for you?" I ask him, standing up. When the man comes to a full stop and the motorcycle tips a little, that poor ol' dog falls plumb off and kinda lays there, looking sad. He can't be more than ten pounds if an ounce, and he got more hair on his head than anywhere else. That ain't saying much, neither, seeing as he's just about bald.

"My dog is thirsty," the scruffy old man says, wiping the dust off his face, "and I just need me a place to sit a while if that's all right with you."

"Sit! Sit," I tell him, pulling out Daddy Jim's pink chair and patting it real nice. "I'll fetch you some water from Miss Nancy over there. She keeps a jug of it in her back room. You just sit and wait for me 'til I get back, you hear?" The old man smiles at me when he sits down and shows me the biggest mouth full o' no teeth I ever seen. Looks like he got two of 'em on the side, but they's all rotted and probably ain't much good to him, I reckon. Miss Nancy comes back over with me to carry the water jug 'cause she just got to see this man and his dog. Neither one of us can believe they's able to ride on a motorcycle and stay upright.

The old man pours out some water from the jug into his hand and bends down real slow to stick it under his dog's mouth. Poor ol' thing can hardly lift its head up. "Riding's getting hard on her," the man says. "She hasn't been feeling well the past few months or so. Lost a lot of weight too."

59

"I reckon so!" I tell him, watching the bones in its ribcage move in and out when it breathes.

"How long have you two been ridin' together?" asks Nancy.

"About six years now, I guess," says the man, rubbing his knee bones and then his shoulders. He's almost as skinny as the dog and as dirty as a chicken coop.

"Well, where'd you come from?" I ask him.

"Oh, here and there, West Virginia, California, Louisiana. I was in the military, so they moved me around a lot."

"Louisiana? You don't say!" I tell him. "My daddy was from over there in Louisiana. You ever been to New Orleans?"

"Boy, have I," he says with a smile coming over his lips. "Had me a fine time down in New Orleans. Met my ex-wife down there as a matter-of-fact."

"Well, what brings you and your dog all the way to Charleston?" Miss Nancy asks him. "Don't you get tired of ridin'?"

"Well, my body does, but my mind doesn't," he says. "Now that the cancer in my bones is back. Don't know how much longer I got neither. I'd just go ahead and die, though, if something were to happen to Happy here." He points to that poor ol' dog and shakes his head. "Happy and me have been together for as long as I can remember now. She's as good a dog as there ever was. Saved me from a fistfight one night in Richmond. I kid you not. I hadn't ever seen her before, but after I'd taken a few good licks, she walked right up next to me like she belonged to me. Came out of nowhere just like an angel. Man took one look at her snarling teeth and decided he didn't want anything to do with me after that. Yep, me and Happy's been together ever since."

"What's gonna happen to Happy if you die?" I 'bout fall out my seat when Nancy asks him that!

"Nancy!" I fuss at her. "What kind o' fool thing to say is that?"

"Oh, don't worry," says the man. "Trust me, I think about that too. There ain't nobody around who's going to love that dog like I do. I don't know which one would be worse, me going first or Happy."

When that yella dog hears him say its name, it opens its eyes up as wide as it can and looks up at its daddy. I can see it's trying to lift its tail to wag it, but it just sits there, twitching a little. Miss Nancy's got a customer pulling up to her stand so she leaves me and the old man and Happy all alone. 'Course Jim's here, too, 'cause the old man's sitting in his lap.

"Take a good look at this fella, Mama," Jim says to me real quiet. Happy seems to perk its ears up. "'Bout the saddest state of things I ever seen. Why don't you go on ahead and pet that dog now, you hear? And then, make sure you hug that man when he gets up to leave." Jim winks at me, but for the life of me, I can't figure out what in Jesus' name he talking about. This ain't like Miss Susanne Maybree and Jeffrey; this is an old man and his dog! They sure ain't gonna fall in love, and they already love each other, anyhow! Jim ain't never led me wrong, though, so I go on over and bend down on my knees. That yella dog is sleeping just as hard as it can and don't even move when I rub its little head. "There you go, Happy," I say. "You just rest now. There you go." I stand up again, not so easy, and slip some of the dog hairs right down in my bosoms 'fore I sit down again.

"Can I get you some water too?" I ask the man, handing him the jug.

"Please," he says, real polite. His hands shake when he pours some water in his palm then slurps it out real careful.

"My husband, Jim, died of cancer," I tell him, and then like to die when I realize what done popped out my mouth!

The old man looks at me real sad and says, "I'm so sorry." At least, that's what I'm pretty sure he says 'cause a man with no teeth ain't really got the use of his s's, I reckon.

It's more than an hour or so that the man and me talk. He seems like a real good man too. Name's Clayton, and he tells me he fought in the Korean War then the Vietnam War. Shows me a scar on his back from where he got shot down in a helicopter. He says he had a family once but lost everything when he started drinking. Turns out he's the kinda man who can't stop it once he starts.

"I've been sober for almost twenty years," he tells me, and I believe him too. Says he started riding that motorcycle when his wife left him 'cause it was the only thing what kept his mind off the pain of his loss. I sure do understand about all that, yes sir. Ain't no surprise to me why he keeps on riding even though he ain't got nowhere to go.

After a while, Happy the dog starts stirring again and sits up. "Well, we better be going," says the man. "Got to take advantage of the driving time we have when Happy's feeling good."

He thanks me for the water and the nice conversation, and I stand up with him when he walks over to get up on that motorcycle. He picks up Happy real gentle-like and presses her down on the seat behind him. I got to say, I feel like crying a little and don't rightly know why. I reach over and give the man a hug and pull off a gray hair sitting there on his leather jacket.

"Ain't you got a helmet?" I ask him.

"Don't need one," he tells me. "The good Lord takes care of us."

I smile at him, and he smiles back. Then, I stand there a-watching and waving as he and Happy wobble back onto the highway, like a great big slow bumblebee trying to ease on into a mean ol' stream of hornets.

Chapter 11

DADDY JIM TOLD ME TO MAKE A SPECIAL BASKET for that old man, Clayton, and his yella dog. By the grace of God, that's just what I'm gonna do too. Only problem is, I already used up the sweetgrass EJ brought me, and I'm running right low again. When EJ comes by this morning to carry me to my stand, I'll ask if he can get me some more.

"Come on, Grandmama," he says once we in the car. "I want to take you somewhere."

So me and EJ ride on down past my stand and turn onto Highway 41. It's a real nice day, and I close my eyes with the wind blowing in my window. We pass that Colonnade neighborhood and Horlbeck Creek and go on down past Cousin Leroy and Mavis' house. Then he turns down a dirt road I ain't never noticed before. As we bump on down the road, some dust kicks up and blows in my nose, and I sneeze 'bout the whole way. We wind up out by the water. EJ comes 'round and pulls me out the car door and walks me up to marsh. There's fiddler crabs running around my feet and jumping into little holes in the ground.

"You see that?" he asks me, pointing to a nice long patch of sweet-grass.

"I see it, baby."

"This is where I've been pulling your sweetgrass from all these years."

"Oh, that's real nice, honey, real nice," I say, squeezing him on the arm.

"But you see that over there?" EJ points to a For Sale sign somebody planted in the ground about a stone's throw away. "Looks like this land's going to be bought up pretty soon."

I ain't sure what he's getting at, so I just look at him like, *Well now, go on and tell me the rest of the story.*

"What I'm saying is, when somebody buys this land, they're going to build on it—a bunch of houses, most likely. And that means it'll be somebody's private property. I won't be able to come out here anymore and get you your grass. This is the last patch of sweetgrass I know of in Charleston."

I look up at him for a second, and then we just stand there staring out over the marsh. There's two big white egrets walking back and forth in the grass and crickets chirping all around. I take in a real deep breath and feel the salty air clean the dirt out my lungs.

EJ puts his arm around me and says, "Don't worry, Grandmama. I'll get some grass somewhere, even if I got to go down to Savannah or further to find it. I just think it's a shame, though, that there's hardly a public place around here anymore, and the sweetgrass is dying out fast. No one's really looking out for you basket ladies, that's for sure."

"The good Lord above does," I tell him, squeezing his hand and thinking about that old man and his dog just a-wobbling down the highway. "And you do too. That's what counts. Now get this old lady on back to my stand so I can earn me a livin'."

I had me a real busy day today. Made close to five hundred dollars, if you can imagine that. Still ain't nowhere close to having 'nough to pay my taxes. EJ come back to get me this afternoon with a trunk full of pretty sweetgrass he been storing up. He drives me on back to Rifle Range Road and makes sure I'm set up inside for weaving 'cause it looks like it's gonna rain.

"EJ, sit here with me while I make us some supper, you hear?" I pull out a chair for him, and he sticks his long legs up under the table. "Sweet Jesus, you sure do look like your granddaddy. Got his eyes and his smile too."

EJ fidgets with his fingernails for a while, and then he says, "Grandmama?"

"Yes, baby?" I almost got my corn all the way shucked, and I'm looking 'round for my frying pan so I can fix us some pork chops. EJ sure does love my pork chops.

"When you and Daddy Jim met," EJ stares at the wall like it's gonna answer him back, "would you say that was love at first sight? I mean, that *does* happen. Love can happen that way, don't you think?"

"Well, you might say that." I put my ears of corn down and take me a seat next to him at the table. "Daddy Jim says he fell head over heels when I walked in to that feed 'n seed. But I'd say it probably took me a few weeks, even though I can remember this funny feeling I got in my stomach first time he looked at me hard. But even when he asked me to marry him, I don't know that I was completely flipped over him."

"You weren't?" You ought to see the look on EJ's face. Looks like he done swallowed something raw. "Well, why'd you marry him then?"

"Oh, that's easy. I knew he was a good man," I tell him. "A woman got to be careful, you know, but I knew who his mama and daddy were and ain't never heard of a bad thing he'd done to nobody. There ain't too many men like that out there. Not only that, but he was as sweet to me as sugar on a cane." I can't help but grinning, remembering sweet Jim's kisses and the way he smiles at me every time he sees me.

"And his eyes were clear and honest. You can't hide what's in your eyes, baby. A person's eyes look right back into the soul. So, when he asked me to marry him, I knew I'd end up loving him soon enough. Faith's got a lot to do with love, baby. If you ain't got faith, you ain't got nothin' a'tall."

"Well, maybe you were in love with him, but you just didn't know it yet."

"Well, maybe so, but . . . baby, why're you askin' me all these questions?" I sit up straight and look him square in the face. "There ain't nothin' you want to tell me, now, is there?"

"Well, I don't know," he says, staring down at his untied shoelaces. Looks like he's thinking about tying 'em up again. "There's a girl at school, is all."

"A girl! Well, how about that!" I slap him on the arm. "Tell me about her! What's her name?"

"Her name's Felicia. She's a junior." If that boy could blush through his dark skin, he'd be red as a cherry pie!

"Well now, you two been seein' each other? Have you met her mama and daddy?"

"Not yet," he says. "We've been seeing each other for almost eight months now, and I . . ."

"Eight months! And you ain't never brought her 'round to meet me?" I fuss at him. "You ain't embarrassed of me, are you? Oh, Lord have mercy, my own grandbaby's ashamed of me. Oh, sweet Jesus, what's your mama drilled into your head, boy?"

"No, no, it's nothing like that," he says. "I haven't even brought her home to meet Mom and Dad yet either. It's just that she's, well, different."

"What you mean, different?" I ask him. "She Presbyterian? Catholic? Oh, she from up there in Summerville? What?" EJ gets up from his chair and walks over to the window. "EJ? Tell me what's goin' on."

"She's white, Grandmama, okay? She's white."

As God as my witness, I mean to say something right quick, but nothing comes out of my silly old mouth. I ain't got a problem with that girl being white, I'm just taken aback is all.

"Well say something, Grandmama," EJ says all defeated, putting his face in his hands. "Can't you say something?"

I stand up from my chair and walk on over to him. I wrap my arms around his waist as hard as I can and look up in his dark brown eyes. They's getting all glassy and it 'bout breaks my heart.

"EJ, get that child on the telephone," I tell him. "We got too many pork chops to eat for two people, and I'll be mad as a chicken in a cock fight come Sunday if I got spoiled meat in the icebox."

EJ smiles just a little at first, but when he sees I mean it for real, he shoots up like fireworks and grabs his coat off the back of the sofa.

"Wait here," he says. "She doesn't live too far." EJ comes back to me and bends over so he can hug me. Then he kisses my cheek so hard I think his whiskers might tear my skin plumb off.

"Now hurry up, you hear? I got sewin' to do tonight." I pop him on the hind end, and that boy runs faster than Brer Rabbit into the brier patch.

I see EJ and Felicia walking up the drive 'cause I been peeking out the window every few minutes. EJ's 'bout twice as tall as that little bitty girl. She's cute, I reckon, with brown hair tucked behind her ears. She's dressed nice for a college student in a long summer dress. I open the door 'fore he can turn the knob, and EJ just stands there a-grinning like he might fall over silly.

"Well, hey there," I tell her, throwing out my hand. She takes it in hers and pats it real nice.

"I've heard so much about you," she says. "Thank you for having me over."

I look up at EJ who's eyeing me hard, waiting. I smile at him and wink so he knows it's all right. "Come on in now. Supper's almost ready."

We sit down nice and proper at the table and both of 'em got backs so straight I could iron on 'em if I wanted. Things is quiet in the beginning. Lots of little talk. I notice after while, EJ leaning in closer to her. Great God in heaven, the look on his face, I ain't never seen this one. I'm praying I like this child.

"What you wanna be?" I ask her, talking 'bout when she gets out of school.

"Well, that's a good question," she says, pushing her finished plate away and sticking her elbows on the table. "My degree will be in social work, and I'm doing an internship now with the Department of Social Services. I work with child abuse cases right now."

"Mercy. How you do that? Can't imagine how sad that is. Takes a mighty special person to deal with other folks' heartaches, I reckon."

"It is sad," she tells me. "I don't ever think I'll get to the point where it doesn't bother me."

"Tell her about your painting, Felicia," EJ says all proud. "She's an unbelievable artist too, Grandmama. You ought to see her work. She can paint anything, really."

Felicia blushes and touches his arm. "I guess I'm an artist at heart, but I'm not showing anywhere yet. No galleries or anything. I'd like to someday."

Well we go on like that for a while, me asking her questions and her answering every one. I have me a fine time meeting EJ's girl, yes sir. EJ can't stop grinning from ear to ear the whole time. Felicia sure is as nice as she can be, and I can see why he's smitten. She even helps me clean

70

THE SPIRIT OF SWEETGRASS

the dishes after supper and goes on and on about my cornbread. A girl who knows good cornbread can't be too bad.

Now, I'd be lying to you if I said something like, "After a while, I forgot she was even white," 'cause that just ain't the truth. In my day and age, a black man best not be seen with a white woman if he know'd what was good for him. But, I s'pose times are different now, and two people's got a right to be with each other no matter what color skin they got. Lord help him, though, when EJ takes that girl home to Henrietta. I got me a sneaky feeling she'll be trying to put a stop to that relationship real quick.

After EJ and his girlfriend leave, I lock up and go on back to the bedroom. I sit down for a spell in my rocking chair and just listen to the rain hitting my tin roof. I always did love that sound, even as a little girl. Makes me feel all nice and warm-like. *Thank God, I sure am glad I ain't stuck out in the rain.*

All a sudden, my eyes pop open and I can see that poor old man and his dog just a-shivering out in the wet somewhere. It's more than I can stand. I don't know for sure what making a basket's gonna do for 'em, but I get the itching to. What's it gonna do? Make Mister Clayton wanna stop riding and settle down so him and that dog can relax? Or maybe make him well, or the dog, or both? I ain't sure, but I set out to making it right quick.

I pull out that yella dog hair and that old gray hair from my Bible and twist 'em up real tight. I pray over 'em real good, and once I got a coaster made with that hair braid tucked down in it, the basket pretty much makes itself.

By morning, I've had me a couple hours sleep and the basket's

71

almost done. Just got to make me a lid and finish tying off the top, and I figure I can do that sitting at my basket stand. I can't wait to go and tell Jim all about EJ's girlfriend, not to mention I got me something else to look forward to. Today is Thursday, middle of July. Jeffrey Lowes' gonna come calling to pick up his stack of baskets, and I ain't talked to him since Miss Maybree come back to town.

Chapter 12

SOMETIMES, LIFE IS FUNNY. You might be rolling along just slow as molasses and wondering if you gonna fall asleep. All a sudden, things start happening all at the same time. I think the Lord helps us that way. He gives us good things along with the bad. You can't get too high on life that you don't need Him, but He don't let you get too low neither.

I'm sitting here talking to Jim this morning. He's right tickled at the fact EJ got himself a white girlfriend and seems mighty smitten, at that.

"In heaven, Mama, ain't no such thing as black and white folks," he tells me. "If somebody's done made it up to heaven, they get to glowin' like a rainbow full of all sorts of colors. Ain't no black and white here, Mama, no ma'am."

That sure do make me feel good, him saying that. "'Course, down here on Earth," I tell him, "things ain't quite like they's in heaven, now are they? Even though times is different, lots of folks is gonna have a problem with seein' a mixed couple, and that's all there is to it. Don't get me wrong, I want our grandbaby to be happy, I sure do. I just hope he ain't settin' himself up for too much heartache."

Jim don't seem to be worried about EJ, so I decide to just drop it with him. I'm pulling the last palmetto leaf over and in, over and in, to tie up the lid for my basket when I see Jeffrey's pickup truck pulling on in next to me. I stand up to greet him with a hug.

"Hey, Jeffrey, how you doin' today?"

"Just fine, Essie Mae," he says. "Just fine. Can't wait to see what baskets you got for me."

"Oh, got some good ones, 'though I'm runnin' kinda low. I just got me some good sweetgrass yesterday. I can make you some more pretty soon."

"These will do just fine," he says, picking up the stack and laying 'em in the back of the truck. He hands me his money, and I tuck it down in my cash pocket.

"Now, sit, sit," I tell him, patting Daddy Jim's lap. "Tell Essie Mae what's been goin' on in your life these days. Anythin' new?" I'm grinning.

"Can't say as anything's new, really. Daddy's been feeling poorly. He just hasn't been himself since Mama passed away."

"Oh, I'm sorry to hear that," I tell him, touching his knee. "You tell your Daddy I'm prayin' for him, you hear?"

"I will. That's real sweet of you. He doesn't even get out of his room any more. Just sits there in his rocking chair looking out the window. The nurses at the home say he's not eating much either."

"Home? Your daddy's living in a home now?"

"Yes, didn't I tell you? After he broke his hip, I had to do something," he says. "I just can't be with him all day long. We looked all over but Sunnydale Farms is a real nice place."

If I could swallow my tongue, I think I probably would. Sunnydale Farms! Great God in heaven!

"Lord have mercy, Sunnydale Farms?" My heart's a-pounding. I can't believe I forgot Jeffrey's daddy was in a home. He must a' told me so, but I reckon I don't think much 'bout it happening to other old folks. Just don't wanna see it happening to me. "I think it's been right near twenty years since I seen your daddy. He's over to James Island, you say?" I swallow hard.

"That's the one." There's new lines in the corners of Jeffrey's eyes I ain't seen before. Looks like worrying 'bout his daddy's beginning to age him, sure 'nough. "Hey, I have an idea," he says, brightening up. "I'm heading over there tomorrow afternoon. You want to come with me? I know he'd love to see an old friend."

"Well no, I don't think so—"

"Oh please, Essie Mae. It'll do him a world of good. He never gets any visitors but me."

"I can't, Jeffrey."

"Oh please will you do it? For me?" Always could beg like a puppy. Jeffrey bats his eyelashes all silly-like, and dad-gum, I don't have the heart to tell him no.

"I reckon," I say, dreading every minute of it. He smiles and looks like a weight done lifted off him. If I can't make an old man and his boy happy, what good am I? That's what I figure.

I pick up my basket and sew a little bit. My fingers are nervous all a sudden. "So what else is new?" I ask him, trying hard to change the subject. "You got any new customers lately?"

"No, just the usuals."

Hmmm. I thought for sure Miss Maybree'd have been in there by now. Maybe things ain't happening fast as I thought.

"You ain't met nobody new?" I press him.

"Well, let me see. No, I did meet one lady, now that you mention it. Said she was a friend of yours. Sarah? Susanne maybe?"

"Susanne Maybree!" I shout, perking up. "That's my girl from Massachusetts. I told her to go by and see my sweetie pie down to the flower shop."

"Well she did. Seems like a real nice girl. She bought some gladiolas for her new apartment."

"Oh she found one? Where she livin'?"

"I think she said over near Shem Creek."

"Well, I'll be. Ain't she a looker? And smart, too, I tell you. Do me somethin', hear? Take her round town, baby. She don't know a soul but you and me."

"Then consider it done. I'll look her up." He gives me a big toothy smile. "Hey, now, this isn't the same basket you made for me, is it?" He touches the one I'm working on. "I thought I had me an Essie Mae o-riginal!"

"Oh, no. This one is different, Jeffrey. Real different. You see them pine straw buttons? Yours don't have none. And there ain't no bulrush stripe on this one, neither. That basket was special, just for you."

Jeffrey winks and let's me know he's just a-fooling with me. "Hey, why don't I show Miss Susanne the basket you made for me? I haven't been able to show it off yet."

"Oh that'd be real nice," I say. Jim's just a-chuckling, sitting under Jeffrey.

After a few more minutes of talking, I hold up my basket and say, "Well now, I done give birth to another one. I do believe it's finished."

Jeffrey's oohing over my handiwork when he looks out north up 41, pointing.

"What in the world?" he asks, his arm still hanging out in the air. "You see that, Essie Mae?"

I turn and look and boy, wouldn't you know it, but here come that old man and his yella dog just a-crawling down the highway. I sit up straight and slap my knee. "Well, what do you know? There he is again."

"You know who that is? He's gonna kill himself driving that slow! And what's that on the back of him? Is that a dog? I don't believe it!"

Well, I'll be. Clayton's coming back to town. I throw up my hand to wave at the old man 'cross the highway.

"Yoo hoo! Hey there!" Not sure if he sees me or not, but it looks like he's trying to get on over. There go the horns and honks and people cursing at him again.

Lord help him, he's just a-veering off! Ain't even looking back! Great God Almighty, I can't take it!

"Mack truck comin'!" All a sudden, my ears hear and my eyes see the biggest commotion in my entire life! Seems a big ol' Mack truck was trying to pass all that slow-moving traffic. Now it squeals on the brakes—twists up like a jackknife!

Lord have mercy, sweet Jesus in heaven!

"He down! He down!"

Four, five other run smack into it all! Smoke! Fire! Screaming and crying!

"Lord have mercy! God have mercy! That sweet poor man and his dog! His daaawwg, oh Happy!" I say, wailing and Jeffrey too. He grabs me up and pulls me close.

"Why?" I holler. "Why, Lord?!" Holds me tighter still.

Police all over and sirens blaring. There's people hollering, going every which-a-way. I ain't never seen such ruckus in all my life! Look like hell done hit Highway 17, and I just can't take it!

After a while, Jeffrey sits me down careful, and we watch the goings on 'cross the street. Ain't neither of us saying a word.

That poor sweet Clayton and his dog, Lord! Why this had to happen?

I'm still boo-hooing—don't think I'll ever stop. Jeffrey's got to go, but he makes sure I'm okay 'fore he gets up to leave. "I can stay if you want me to, Essie Mae," he says, his face all red. "How about you just let me take you on home?"

"That's okay, baby. You get on back to work now. I'm okay," I lie through my sniffles. "I really am."

Miss Nancy's been 'cross the street watching it all. Then she comes back and tells me what they done told her. "Ain't nobody else hurt bad, but that poor old man and his dog ain't even known what hit 'em. They was gone in half a second, what they said." She sets off to crying.

"Imagine that," Jim whispers to me. "They ain't even felt a thing, and they went exactly at the same time. Now neither one of 'em has to suffer no more. Ain't that wonderful, Mama? Don't that just beat all?"

Jim winks at me which ain't right a'tall. Not at a time like this, it ain't. Then he points to the special basket I made 'em still sitting at my feet. "Your love basket done put 'em together forever," he tells me.

Lord have mercy, I sure am having a hard time swallowing the fact my basket just killed them two sweet souls. I boo-hoo and carry on so. But after a while Jim tells me, "He says thank you, Mama."

"What?" I ask, drying my eyes with my shirt.

"Clayton says, 'Thank you for what you done.' Says it was mighty kind of you. Happy's here, too, just a wagglin' her tail. She wants to thank you too."

Oh Lord God. Can you stand it? That old man and his dog is just a-sitting there in heaven with my sweet Daddy Jim. Just like that. And my basket's what put 'em there! God help me, I know it sounds real strange, but it brings me comfort, what it does.

"They ain't gonna be sitting out in the rain no more, Mama. They ain't gonna be sick no more, neither, or living in pain."

Once I get that through my thick head, I praise the Lord Jesus for what He done through me. "Hallelujah!" I shout over and over, getting frenzied while the smoke's still rising 'cross the street. The Lord sure works in mysterious ways.

Chapter 13

IT'S 'BOUT FOUR O'CLOCK. Been a hard day at my stand, what with all I'm looking at. There's pieces of cars and bumpers and glass still out there on the highway and skid marks over where Mister Clayton went down yesterday. Lord have mercy, I s'pect he and Happy's doing fine there in heaven. Jim says so anyway.

I aim to keep my promise to Mister Jeffrey today, but I don't like it much. I told him I'd visit his daddy at the Sunnydale Farms, and I keep my word, so that's just what I'm gonna do. I figure I can just get in and out real quick without having to really see anybody. Don't want 'em to get a good look at this old black lady, or they gonna wanna keep me, sure 'nough.

I got my baskets all stacked up and ready. Daddy Jim's trying to tell me it ain't gonna be no big deal going back to that nursing home, but I don't feel right. All a sudden, my heart 'bout stops. Here comes Jeffrey now, pulling over to the side of the road.

We say "hey there" and all, and he loads up my baskets. Then we haul 'em back to my house on the way. Locking up my front door, I breathe in real deep. I don't wanna leave my house. There's too much of me and Jim in there. There's part of Retta too, my sweet baby, Retta. I still love her, God only knows how much. Makes it hurt worse, I reckon, her wanting to put me away and me loving her so much. Can't see how I can get through to her. Maybe she's right. I *am* old. 'Bout old as the hills. Could be time for me to pack it on up.

"This is real kind of you, Essie Mae," Jeffrey tells me as we're heading over the Cooper River Bridge again.

"Mm hmm," I say, my eyelids shut tight so I don't feel queasy. Jeffrey grabs my hand and holds it steady 'til our tires hit regular road again.

"Thank you, baby," I tell him. I'm real quiet rest the way.

"I called your friend Susanne," he says. "I promised you I would."

"Always were a good boy, Jeffrey."

"I'm taking her out for a drink tomorrow night."

"Really? Well I'll be." I wish I could be more excited, but I'm thinking too much 'bout that old folks' home. "You two gonna have a good time together. Nice young man, nice young woman. That's what it's all about now."

We get on over to the Sunnydale Farms and I firm myself. "You can do this, Essie Mae," I say under my breath. Jeffrey hears me, so I grin at him real big showing him everything's all right.

We walk up to the desk and there's that same lady what seen me here couple months ago. I look down. Don't think she knows it's me. Jeffrey signs in and says we're going to see his daddy. Then he tells me to go on myself while he waits here and reads a magazine.

"By myself? Oh, I don't know—"

"Go on, Essie Mae. He'll be so surprised. Just go right down there and knock on his door. I guarantee he's in there."

So I walk on down this long skinny hallway with pink wall coverings and silly looking drawings. Must 'a been done by children—least I hope so, anyway. I pass this white man shuffling on by me 'bout half mile an hour. I say, "Hey there," being polite as I can, and he looks up at me and smiles real big. Shows me he ain't wearing his teeth. Lord help me. Then tries to whistle at me, throwing spit everywhere! I glare at him, sure 'nough, and move a little faster. But I mean to tell you, that dirty ol' man plumb reaches for my rear when I pass him! I swanny, I ain't been goosed in forty-some-odd years! Ought to haul on over there and bop him upside his head good. Probably kill him though, so I won't. I'd like to anyhow. Dirty ol' man.

Not soon enough, I find Room 101 and knock real soft. When nobody answers, I knock louder and say, "Mister Lowes? It's me, Essie Mae. Essie Mae Jenkins. You in there?"

The knob jiggles, and then the door opens up real slow. Mister Lowes sure is looking poorly. Must 'a lost twenty, thirty pounds since I seen him last. He's using one of them walkers with the wheels on it. I lean in and give him a hug, and he gets to smiling.

"Essie Mae," he beams at me. "What a surprise! You sure are a sight for sore eyes. Come on in, come in." We walk over real slow to the bed. He sits down on it and gives me this purple chair next to him.

"Been a long time, ain't it?" I say.

"Goodness, it's been too long," he says. "You look wonderful. 'Course you always did."

"Oh stop it now. I'm bigger than two o' you put together! Hey now, 'member back in the day when I used to pull out Millie's blonde wigs and go all silly for Jeffrey?"

"Oh, I do! I nearly busted my side laughing so hard at you. Oh, and you remember that time we had that big oyster roast and got hold of those bad oysters from North Carolina?"

"Lord have mercy, child. Thought we was gonna up and die. The whole neighborhood too!"

We laugh real hard 'bout old times—a lot of "Remember this? And remember that?"

Then I tell him, "I sure was sorry to hear about Millie, Mister Lowes. I liked Miss Millie. Sweet lady, she was."

"Why, thank you, Essie Mae. She was mighty fond of you too. Maybe always didn't show it the best, but she trusted you like nobody else. I was real sorry to hear about Jim passing away too. How long's it been now? Nine, ten years?"

"Mm hmm, they was some rough times, I tell you what. Ain't easy losin' somebody you love so much."

"Well now that's the truth," he says.

"You holdin' up all right, Mister Lowes?" I look at his old worn-out self.

"I'm doing okay, I guess. I miss her though. Think about her every day." His eyes go off to some far away place. "I'm getting used to being alone now, I suppose."

Mister Lowes and me have us a real nice talk, 'course I'm a good bit distracted, looking around the room and thinking I might have to live here one day soon.

"I been seein' lots of Jeffrey lately," I tell him. "Lord, I love that boy. Love all the babies I cared for, but Jeffrey's just real special to me. Tell you what, I'm prayin' every night for him to find a sweet young girl to settle down with. Can't understand why he ain't done it yet."

That's when Mister Lowes' lips curl up. He looks me square in the eyes and says, "Essie Mae, it's about time you knew something." Mister Lowes pushes off the bed and grabs for that walker. Then he wheels on over to the window and looks out.

"What's wrong?" I ask him. "Something wrong with Jeffrey?" I'm panicking, thinking my boy's sick.

"There's nothing wrong, I don't guess," he says real slow. "It's just that—Essie Mae, Jeffrey's never had a girlfriend."

"Lord I know that. It's a shame, what it is. Fine-lookin' fella like him. And smart as a whip!"

Then he turns to me and says, "No, I mean—he's never gonna have a girlfriend, Essie Mae. Jeffrey's gay."

"He's what?"

"He likes men," he tells me. "Jeffrey's a homosexual."

Well, you could knock me over with a feather. My Jeffrey's a gay boy? Cat got my tongue sure 'nough, 'cause I don't know what to say.

"You sure?" I ask him. "Maybe he just ain't found the right person, is all."

"No," he says, sitting down again. "I'm sure. Told me himself after his mama died. He said he just couldn't keep it a secret anymore."

"Lord have mercy," I say. Me and Mister Lowes just sit there quiet, looking at each other. *What in tar-nation is my love basket gonna do now?* I wonder. Here I am trying to fix up little Miss Susanne with Jeffrey, and he winds up gay! Oh, Lord help us all.

I try not to say much more but promise Mister Lowes I'll come see him again someday soon. I'm just hoping and praying to God it ain't gonna be permanent, is all.

Chapter 14

"CAN YOU BELIEVE THAT, JIM? I swanny, I ain't known what to say to Jeffrey when he was takin' me home yesterday. My mind was spinnin' all this way and that. Don't know why he ain't told me himself he's gay. Why he ain't told me, Jim?"

"Reckon he thinks you can't handle it good."

"Well why not? I can handle it!" I jump up and pace back and forth in front of my baskets. They's rattling on my stand 'cause the wind's kicking up. "Shoot, ain't nothin' needs handlin' in my life 'cept for my sweet Jeffrey's gay, I'm 'bout to lose my house, and that ol' For Sale sign's stuck up over yonder. Oh that, and pretty soon I'm gonna be sippin' dad-gum skim milk, eatin' soggy collard greens and greasy catfish in that old folks' home called Sunnydale Farms! No, Jim. Ain't a thing in the world I can't handle!"

Whooee! I needed that—a woman got to let off steam ever now and then. Jim's always been real patient for me so he listens to me holler a while. Then tells me he done come up with a plan.

"You 'member how that old man and his dog got hit with the Mack truck?" he asks me.

"Gracious, Jim. You know I do." I'm wondering what in the world he's getting at.

"Well, your love basket's what put 'em together forever, ain't it?"

"Well I was thinkin' so, but how do I really know? That old man and his dog were just bound to get hit sometime, right?" I come back over and sit next to him to pout. "Shoot, I can't do no magic, Jim. I been thinkin' my love basket for Jeffrey and Susanne Maybree was workin', too, but come to find out he's a homo-sexual. Can't be too good of a magic basket if you ask me, 'cause that sure ain't gonna work. No sir."

"You just wait and see, Essie Mae. If you start to see it workin', will you believe me then?"

I tell him 'course I'm gonna believe him then, but what's that got to do with a thing?

So this is what he tells me: "You go on back home tonight and when you get there, go rifle through my closet. You're bound to find a hair of mine somewhere, seein' as you ain't had my clothes cleaned since the day I died."

"You want me to make us a love basket, Jim?" Lord have mercy, I'm getting kinda scared. "What you mean? What it gonna do?"

"Mama, if you make a love basket with my hair and your hair, it's gonna put us together forever. Wouldn't you like that?"

"Well 'course I'd like it, but—really Jim?"

"Jesus is here too, Mama," he says. "You wanna meet Jesus, now don't you?"

Well now, you know I do. If I could be with Jesus, I wouldn't have a care in the world, now would I? So I tell Daddy Jim that if I get to seeing Jeffrey's basket work, I'll make us a basket too. That way, I can leave all my troubles behind me and go on to be with him and Jesus in heaven. And won't have to set foot in that Sunnydale Farms.

"Lord better not hit me with a Mack truck, though," I say. "Lord, anythin' but a Mack truck."

Chapter 15

August

NASTY WEATHER WE HAVING THIS SUMMER. If the heat don't kill you, the rain surely will. Two weeks ago Friday, I was showing a man a basket and he was 'bout to buy it, too, when all a sudden the sky opened up, and rain pounded down on us. He screamed and I hollered and we both picked up and run—me over to Miss Nancy's back room and him back into his car. He honked a couple times when he drove off. Would 'a been a nice sale, sure 'nough.

Miss Nancy'd been eating fried onions 'fore I got there, so let's just say it weren't the most comfortable time, sitting and talking with her in that little room. "Got a mint, Nancy? Or some chewing gum? Whooeee!" I knew I was gonna be in there for a long time—least 'til the rain let up, and Boy, howdy, it looked like it'd be a good while at the rate it was coming down. In a second, I heard the gravel moving, and then a light hit us. Somebody was actually stopping in the rain!

"Essie Mae? Essie Mae Jenkins?" I heard my name, so I peeked on out the room.

"In here," I said. "Whoo-hoo, in here!"

A great big white lady eased on out of a big ol' blue wagon. Even through the rain, I could see it was stuffed full of lamps and boxes and clothes—looked like all her belongings. She had a big purple umbrella hovering over her head, and she shook it out when she bent down to squeeze in next to us. We ain't never had three people in there, let alone a big lady like that.

"You Essie Mae Jenkins?" she asked me.

"Sure am," I said.

"Oh, I'm so excited to meet you! I'm Clarice Maybree, Susanne's mother—from Massachusetts?"

I just looked at her 'cause I ain't seen no resemblance. None a'tall. Susanne is just as cute and tiny as she can be, and this lady—well, her hair was white and puffy, and her face was covered in age spots. There was a mole 'bout the size of my pinky nail up over her lip, peeking out from behind a thick dark mustache.

"You're Susanne's mother? Well, how do? It's so nice to finally meet you," I told her, putting out my hand. "Miss Susanne said you might be comin' down here soon. You here for good now?"

She just leaned on in and squeezed me tight. "I sure am," she said, smiling from ear to ear. "I'm just so excited to be here in Charleston. Can't wait to be away from that nasty weather we have up there. This rain is nothing to me, long as it's not cold out. Well, I promised Susanne I'd stop by and see you on my way into town. I almost passed you, though. You need a bigger sign!" She pushed me on my shoulder.

"You're the reason we're both down here. You were so nice to Susanne, and then that pretty basket you made me—well, people just aren't nice like that up north, you know?"

"Well, we sure are glad to have you," I told her. "You gonna be stayin' with Miss Susanne for a while?"

"Oh, yes. For as long as she'll have me."

We talked a bit more 'til the sunshine come out again. *Hallelujah*, I was thinking, 'cause I couldn't breathe no more in that tiny room what smelled like onions. She give me a big hug and told me she'd be seeing me again soon. I said to stop by anytime and good luck with the moving in and stuff. And that was it. I didn't think a thing more about it 'cept for figuring Miss Susanne's daddy must a' been one good-looking man with real bad eyes, all I can figure.

Well today's Thursday, middle of August. Mister Jeffrey pulls on up in his pickup truck. He gets out the car and waves at me, but then keeps on going 'til he's plumb on the other side of the truck. He reaches out and opens his passenger side door and pulls out—and I ain't kidding now—Miss Clarice Maybree!

"Well, hello there!" I say, getting up to greet the two of 'em.

"Hi, Essie Mae," Jeffrey leans down and kisses me on the cheek. "I believe you two have already met—Miss Essie Mae, Clarice. Clarice, Miss Essie Mae," he says, pointing to me and then her and then back at me again. Clarice leans in and gives me a big bear hug. 'Bout picks me up off my feet.

"I just had to come by and see you again," she says, scratching at her mustache. "And to thank you for introducing Susanne to Jeffrey here. He's just the sweetest thing!"

"Nice to see you two met," I say. "Where's Miss Susanne today?"

"Oh, she's busy with work," says Clarice. "I don't have anything to do, so Jeffrey's been nice enough to let me play in his shop." She leans over on him and loops her arm in his. "He's such a sweetheart—teaching me all about flower arranging. He's a wonderful teacher and just as chivalrous as he can be."

I watch as Clarice bats her eyelashes at Jeffrey and then look over at his face. What I see makes me go weak in the knees. Jeffrey Lowes is looking back at her the very same way! This ain't no friendly "welcome to the neighborhood" look, neither. This is a "boy, howdy, I'd like me to have some o' that" look! *Well now, what in tar-nation is going on?* Then, I see it. Miss Clarice is wearing a bright yella scarf 'round her neck. It's tied up in a little knot beneath her bosom and over her tank top.

"That's a beautiful scarf you got there," I tell her, feeling sick. "Did you borrow it from Miss Susanne? I seem to remember her wearin' that the first time I met her."

"Oh, no," she says, shaking her head and running the scarf through her big sausage fingers. "No, this is my scarf. I let Susanne borrow it for her trip down here a few months ago. It is pretty, isn't it?"

Well, now I got to go and sit down. I look over at Jim in that pink chair, and he's a-grinning like a sly cat. "It was her scarf, Mama," he tells me. "That hair you put with Jeffrey's? That was her hair, Mama—Clarice's hair—not Miss Susanne's."

I think I might suffocate. I thought for sure that little hair was blonde like Susanne. Clarice ain't blonde—she's white as a cotton ball. I swanny, my eyes ain't what they used to be.

Sweet Jesus! Is my love basket actually working? God Almighty, did I really join a gay man and an old lady with a mustache together forever? It can't be, Lord, can it? And if it's true, means my love baskets are working, and I done promised to make Jim and me one too. *Lord Jesus, can You hear me? Looks like You want me to come on up to heaven for sure now.*

"Are you all right, Essie Mae?" asks Jeffrey, walking over to me and grabbing my hand. "Can I get you some water? You don't look like you're feeling well."

"No, Jeffrey, I'm fine," I lie. "Now come sit over here with me." Clarice is walking 'round the stand handling every basket I got.

"Miss Essie Mae," he says, looking real serious. "Are you sure you're feeling okay?"

I look over at Clarice. She's leaned over holding her shoe and itching her big ol' foot. Then I see the look on Jeffrey's face. Great God in heaven, there's a light in his eyes I ain't never seen before. No two ways about it—I done made a mess of things, sure 'nough. But, good thing is, Jeffrey ain't feeling gay no more, and he's found himself somebody to love, even if she ain't what I would 'a picked out for him.

"I just want you to be happy, baby," I tell him, and I stroke the side of his face.

"I am happy, Essie Mae. Don't you worry about me."

Jeffrey pops out his chair and dances around my stand picking up the baskets I made for him and throwing 'em in the back of the truck. He and Clarice tell me bye and then roll on back down the highway.

"Well, it worked, Jim," I say, plopping down next to him. "It sure 'nough worked. Maybe not the way I thought it would, but it worked anyhow."

Jim's happy as all get-out now but he don't say, "See, I told you so." He ain't that way. No, Jim just tells me things that get my heart to racing. "Can't wait to see you Essie Mae. Can't wait to hold you 'gain."

Lord have mercy, my head feels like a wasp's nest.

When EJ comes to take me home, I'm real quiet.

"Grandmama, you okay?" he asks me. "You aren't saying much."

"Oh, I'm okay," I tell him. "Just got some things on my mind, is all."

"Now, Grandmama, if it's about your house taxes, I don't want you to worry about that anymore," he says, gripping the wheel real tight. "I'm not gonna let anybody take your house away from you. Maybe Mama won't put up the money, but I'm gonna figure something out, I swear I will."

I lean my hand over and touch the top of his head. I stroke his hair same way I used to do Jim's, and it feels real good. I close my eyes and take in a deep breath. I can't wait to see Jim again in the flesh and blood. And EJ's gonna be just fine without me. Fact, everything's gonna be just fine—I got a real sense of peace about me. When I open my eyes again, EJ's looking at me and not at the road.

"EJ! Get your eyes back on the road," I tell him. "You quit worryin' about your old grandmama and just pay attention to your own life, you hear? You got school and a girlfriend now—you got too much goin' on to spend your time on my problems. But I think you're sweet for tryin', you know. You sure are a good boy, EJ. Sweet Jesus blessed me good when He give me you."

EJ unloads my baskets and makes sure I'm in the house nice and safe. As soon as the door shuts, I turn the latch and then head to the back of the house—straight for Jim's closet to go rifling through his clothes. After I find one o' his hairs and tuck it away for safekeeping, I go through my clothes, too, 'cause tomorrow's my birthday—I got to look nice. Got to get clean and peaceful and look 'round at everything tonight. Not one thing in here I wanna forget—not my photographs or my hardwood floors, not that old magnolia out front or the smell o' soot from the fireplace. Yes sir, tonight I got to take it all in and then weave me the finest basket I ever made. I got lots of weaving to do and lots of thinking to do, but first I think I'll take me a bath. I need the warm water to cleanse me so I'll be nice and ready to meet sweet Jesus and see Daddy Jim tomorrow—if'n tonight turns out to be my last night alive.

Chapter 16

TODAY'S MY BIRTHDAY. I'm kinda hoping the Lord decides to bring me on home today, that way my gravestone will say, "Essie Mae Laveau Jenkins, born and died in the very same day." That sure would be something.

I don't have no real fear of death. I know it's gonna be a whole lot better than the way things are down here on Earth. I seen Jim just as plain as day after he was dead, so I know you go on to live with Jesus when you go. Well, if'n you believe in Him, I reckon. Don't much like to think about what happens if you don't.

Most days, I don't fuss too much about what I'm gonna wear, but today is different. I made sure my underwear and brassiere was the nicest ones I got. If I up and die today, ain't nobody gonna find me in holey drawers, no sir. This blue flowered dress with the buttons down the sleeves will do just fine. You know how folks always say, "I wouldn't

be caught dead in that"? Well, you ever stop to think what you
would be caught dead in? It's a funny thing, I tell you.

Preacher Jefferson always tells us we ought to live every day like
it's our last. Now that I'm here, I got to say I believe him. I ain't paid
too much attention to things before, but this morning, my milk and
banana tasted extra good, and I just couldn't wait to set my eyes on
EJ. I hugged him and squeezed him and told him how much I love
him—something I should 'a been doing every day, sure 'nough.

"Today's Friday, Grandmama," EJ says to me. "You look like you're
dressed for church. What's the big occasion?" He winks at me.

"Can't an old lady look nice if she wants to?" I ask him, reaching
up and pinching him on the cheek. Then I start picking at the
calluses on my hands—all them years of basket making sure has
taken its toll.

I ain't talking too much, so EJ says, "You know I'd never forget
your birthday, right?"

"I know. I know it, child." Then I hush up.

"I have to say, you sure are acting sorta weird. Come on,
Grandmama, tell me what's going on."

"I told you, nothin', EJ. Now hush up or I'll find me a hickory
stick." That makes him leave me 'lone, sure enough, and when we
driving to my stand it's real quiet, so I get to thinking hard. Am I
ready to go? Don't I need some sort o' will or something? I know
I ain't got much, but I 'spect I need some piece of paper telling
people who gets what and all that. Then it occurs to me. Only one
I want to leave anything to is EJ.

"EJ, baby," I say when we pulling to the side of the road and he's fixing to get out the car. "Sit here for just a minute, will you?"

"What is it?" He looks real concerned.

"Well now, I don't want you thinkin' this means nothin', 'cause it don't but, well, I—"

"What is it already?" He's getting right impatient with me.

"Baby, I just want you to know that if anythin' ever happens to me, well, that everythin' I got, I want it to go to you."

"Oh, Grandmama, c'mon. Nothing's gonna happen to you." He's looking nervous all a sudden.

"Well now, I ain't sayin' somethin's gonna happen, I'm just sayin', if'n it did, is all."

"I don't want to hear any more talk about this, Grandmama. You're starting to freak me out. C'mon, let's get you set up."

EJ lays my baskets out real nice and hangs 'em up so the little white tags with the prices on 'em is just a-blowing in the wind. I usually don't put the tags on 'em—I just ask for whatever price pops in my head. But today's different.

I love the look of them baskets hanging there—and the smell of 'em. Boy, I sure am gonna miss the smell of sweetgrass. 'Course I 'spect in heaven I'll have all the sweetgrass I want. No, I can't get too attached to the things of this world—have to keep my eyes on the prize and keep my face up to the sky.

EJ comes to me real slow and then reaches down in his pocket. He pulls out a little ol' box with gray velvet on the top. "Happy birthday, Grandmama," he says.

"For me?" I put my hand to my chest.

"Go on, open it up." He's grinning from ear to ear, and when I open that box, my eyes just fill up with tears.

"Heavens, EJ. This is beautiful!" It's a long gold necklace with a tiny gold sweetgrass basket hanging there. He unlatches the clasp and then walks back behind me and lays it 'round my neck. Then he wraps his arms 'round me and squeezes real tight.

"I love you," he whispers in my ear. And those words just echo down in my soul. *I can die a happy woman now,* I think, *hearin' words like that.*

"I love you, too, EJ, baby. I love you too."

"You want some company today?" EJ asks me. "I mean, it *is* your birthday and all."

"I'd love some, baby. Thank you much, but you know Jim's here with me. Don't need to waste your time out here talkin' to me. I'll be fine."

He stoops down and grabs me by the shoulders. "You sure? I'll be happy to stay."

"I know you would, honey. Now go on, shoo!" EJ leans down and hugs me real tight. I hold on to him and breathe him in good. I want to remember his smell forever. I can feel the softness of his shirt on my cheeks and all a sudden, my tears just let loose. Lord have mercy, I get to shaking and carrying on, so he sets me in my chair and gets down on his knees.

"What's wrong?" he asks me. His eyes is welling up. "Are you sick? Tell me the truth."

"No, I ain't sick," I tell him. "I just love you, EJ. I love you like you was my very own. I can't tell you what you mean to me.

A boy your age shouldn't have to take care of his old grandmama, but you do. You always were a good boy, EJ. God blessed me like I didn't deserve when He give me you. Promise me you'll always do your best, baby, hear? I may not be around forever, but I'll always be with you right here."

I reach down and grab his hand and pull it up to his heart. I'm trembling a good bit, and he's crying now. I ain't seen him cry since he was a little ol' thing. We hold on to each other and rock back and forth 'til I realize what I done to him—how I done torn him all up.

"C'mon now, straighten up. You best be goin', boy. I got baskets to sell and you got schoolin' to tend to. I'll be seein' you 'gain when you come 'round to pick me up."

I can tell he don't want to but EJ forces a smile and walks away from me slow-like, not s'pecting it might be the last time he's ever gonna see me alive.

Chapter 17

WEAVING AIN'T NOTHING BUT PUTTING PLAIN THINGS TOGETHER and making 'em prettier than when they was all alone. Sitting here looking back on my life, I guess that's pretty much what the good Lord had in mind when He set me down here in the world. I can picture Him looking down on me right this second. He's a-grinning, just so happy I done it figured all out.

Now, this here basket I been sewing—this one's the prettiest I ever made. Got nice bulrush stripes, and these little pine needle knots 'round the top—we call 'em French buttons. Yes sir, this one sits, oh, 'bout knee high, and be good to hold just about anything, I reckon. But this one's gonna be for EJ, my grandbaby, so he can put in it whatever he likes. I reach down and grab me some more palmetto leaves so I can finish sewing it up. I ain't got much longer, no sir. Soon as I put this little white tag on it what says, "For my sweet baby EJ, Love, Grandmama," the basket's finally gonna be done.

Whooee! I sure am tired 'cause I ain't never put one of these together without stopping before—'less you count that basket I made for Mister Jeffrey and Miss Clarice a while back. But I'm real anxious to get this one finished 'cause this here's my special basket—the one that's gonna put me and my sweet Daddy Jim together once and for all.

See, right down in the bottom, I started me a little starter coaster and then worked my way on up and out. In the middle of that coaster is a palmetto knot holding a hair of mine and a hair of Jim's I been saving all these years. Didn't know I was saving it 'til I found it on a dress shirt of his hanging up in the closet last night. I ain't never washed his clothes after he died, 'cause sometimes I like to go on in there and stick the cloth up to my face just to try and catch a whiff of him. Works too. So, deep down in this basket is these two little hairs of Jim and me—so we gonna be together again in the flesh real soon. Jim's real excited and I am too . . . I . . . Hold on just a second, Miss Nancy's having a fit.

"What's that, Miss Nancy?"

"Car's comin', Essie Mae! Get out the way! Out the waaaaaaaaay!"

Lord have mercy, I don't know what got into that girl, but sure 'nough, Henrietta's pulling over on the side of the road, and she ain't even slowing down none!

"What in tar-nation, child?" I ask when she steps out the car. I'd thought for a second she was my Mack truck coming to take me out o' here. I'm trying to catch my breath, but it just ain't coming fast enough. Girl scared me half to death, what she did, and my chest is starting to feel all tight.

"I'm so sorry, Mama!" she says, running over to me and setting me down in my chair. "Are you okay?"

"I'm fine, but what in the world are you doin'? Drivin' like a crazy woman!"

"Oh, I was on the phone with my boss. He's not happy I'm out here, is all," she tells me, sitting down in Jim's pink chair. She hesitates just a second 'fore she does it, then sits down anyway. Henrietta ain't never believed Jim comes and talks with me every day. Just thinks it's one o' them loose screws I got.

"Well, what you doin' out here?" I ask her. "Shouldn't you be at work, sure 'nough? Oh I know. You come to take me 'way to that Sunnydale Farms."

"No, Mama. That's what I came to talk to you about."

"You can talk all you want, Retta, 'cause I ain't goin'!"

"Mama! Just hear me out." I wrap my arms up tight on my chest and stare off up the highway. "Mama you're seventy-eight years old today and . . . well, I just wanted to wish you a happy birthday."

"Child, you ain't never come to see me on my birthday before. Why you startin' now? Oh, I see. You feelin' guilty 'bout stickin' me in that home, ain't you? Well, you can just forget about that. I don't want your pity. Just go on back to work now."

"Mama, now stop it. I really am here to see you. EJ told me you were acting funny. You feeling okay?"

"Heavens, child. I'm fine. 'Cept for you scarin' me half to death, I'm good as I can be."

"Well, good." Henrietta gets real quiet then reaches down in her purse and hands me a pink envelope.

"What's this? A card? Oh, that's nice," I tell her. A little pain shoots through my heart. Last card I remember getting from Henrietta was one with big colored balloons she'd drawn all over it. She was nine years old and had just come off the school bus grinning from ear to ear. She was 'til she got in the house anyway. She come into the kitchen and pulled the card out her backpack. She was handing it to me real sweet when all a sudden, she noticed I was over at the sink cleaning up blood off my skirt.

"What's that?" she asked me. I didn't know what to tell her. She must 'a seen something was wrong on my face though, 'cause then she jumped up and ran over to the window.

"Where's Scruffy?" she asked me, her breath fogging up the glass. When I didn't answer, she turned 'round real quick with fire in her eyes. "Where's Scruffy? Where is he? Is he all right?"

Scruffy was just like his name, scruffiest dog you ever wanna lay eyes on. Henrietta had found him when she was six years old and begged me every day to bring him indoors. I put my foot down and kept it there, sure 'nough. Ain't no mangy dog setting foot in my nice clean house, no sir.

"Retta, baby, come here a minute," I told her as I come 'round and grabbed her hands. She pulled away from me real quick.

"He's dead, ain't he?" The tears started to roll down her cheeks. "You killed him!"

"I ain't killed that dog, Retta, he just run out in the road, is all. The man what hit him ain't even seen him when he done it. He was real sorry. He sure was."

Henrietta ran off screaming into her bedroom and slammed the door. I looked there on the kitchen table at the birthday card she made me. "Mama, you're the best mama in the whole world. Happy Birthday. Love, Henrietta," it said.

After that day, neither one of us ever talked 'bout Scruffy again. Seems there's lots o' things Henrietta and I don't talk about much.

Well, getting back to that pink envelope I'm holding, Henrietta says, "Just open it, Mama." So I do.

I pull out this big white card with one o' them flowerdy poems on it. You know the ones, where they so impersonal you might as well not get one a'tall?

"That's real nice," I tell her, slipping it back into the envelope it come in.

"No, Mama," she says, grabbing it from my hands. "You need to open it." She pulls it out the pink envelope again and hands it to me. When I open it up, I feel real faint all a sudden, and I can't see real good. I squint my eyes and say, "Retta! Is this . . . you givin' me a check?"

"I am, Mama," she tells me, smiling and sitting back in her chair like she's all satisfied. "Enough to pay for your taxes." She takes my hand in both of hers. "You're not going have to lose your house, Mama."

"I'm not?" My mind's going fuzzy. "I don't understand, Retta. Why? Why you doin' this?"

"Mama, don't ask me why," she says all testy. "I just . . . I don't know if you're doing so well and I . . . putting you in a home with you hating it so much, EJ thinks it'll just kill you. And I certainly don't want that on my conscience, now do I?"

I can tell she's trying to be sweet 'cause it's my birthday. She tries to smile at me, but Lord have mercy, it's just too much. My eyes are welling up and I'm starting to cry. Now I go to lean over to her but somehow I lose my balance and I fall out my chair instead. Henrietta yelps and bends down on the ground to pull me up, but when she turns my face to her, she starts screaming.

"Mama! Mama!" she's hollering real loud now, and Miss Nancy's coming over. "Call an ambulance, quick! Go grab my phone!" Hen-rietta's pointing to her car and Miss Nancy runs fast as her stubby legs can take her, but it's too late, and Henrietta knows it.

"Oh Mama, I'm sorry! I'm so sorry!" Henrietta rocks me in her arms and boo-hoos right there in the dirt. Truth be told, it's the nicest moment I've had with her in years. Too bad I can't make no sounds to tell her so.

Chapter 18

FOR HALF A SECOND, I THINK I'M DEAD. I ain't never been dead before, but I'm pretty sure that's what this is. Not like I can see Jesus or angels or Daddy Jim even, but I don't feel no pain, and it's kinda like I'm watching the goings'on from in the air somewheres— sorta over Henrietta's shoulder. I see my body lying there, not moving. Is that what I look like? Great God in heaven, I *am* right old, sure 'nough.

I'm studying the wrinkles in my face and my chair what's knocked over—that's when I see it—my love basket for Jim and me. It ain't done yet. *It ain't done yet!* No, no, I can't be dying now. My basket ain't even ready. And Henrietta gave me a birthday card. And she loves me. She's crying there, look at her! *Oh, baby. I love you too. Honey, Mama's right here. Don't you cry none. I'm just over here!*

This ain't right. It can't be my time. Jesus, if You're listenin' to me, it ain't my time! She gonna give me the money! My baby gonna help me keep my house! I don't gotta go no nursin' home. Can You send me on back now? I never finished my basket, see? Come on and send me back, Jesus. Can't You see, my sweet baby, Henrietta's waitin' for me. I got to go. It ain't my time. Go on and tell Daddy Jim I'll see him right soon, but I got me some more livin' to do, yes sir. Sweet Jesus, let me live a while longer!

The next thing I know, feels like I got lead in my bones and my chest feels like it might freeze up solid like a wet palmetto leaf on a cold December night. Henrietta squeezes my hand real tight. My eyes ain't even open but I know it's her.

"Oh, Mama. Thank God! Oh, Mama. You're going to be okay. Everything's going to be just fine. Don't worry. Mama, listen to me. Can you hear me? I love you! I'm so sorry. I just can't tell you, I'm so, so sorry!"

I think I'm saying "I love you" and "I'm sorry too" back to her, but none of the sounds come out, I reckon. No matter, I know I'm alive now. I'd know what this old body feels like any day.

I try to put a smile on my lips as we speed away in an ambulance, the siren blaring in my eardrums. And if I ain't smiling on the outside, you can bet like pecan pie on the Fourth of July, I'm a-smiling on the inside. *Thank You, Lord, for keepin' me alive! Sweet Jesus, I reckon I owe You one.*

"She's weak," I hear a man say. There's tingling in my fingers.

"Is she going to be all right?" That's Henrietta's voice. *Hey, baby. Mama's here.*

"We're very optimistic," the man says. "She's quite a fighter, you know."

"Yes," Henrietta walks over and sits down next to me. She grabs my hand and says, "Yes, she is."

I hear beeping. There it is again. Beep, beep. Sweet Jesus, can't they turn that beeping off? I hear someone laughing down the way. Footsteps, wheels rolling. I reckon I'm in the hospital. Hope they brung me to East Cooper and they didn't drive me down to MUSC over that dad-gum skinny bridge. If that don't kill me, I don't know what will.

"Hey, Mama. It's me, Henrietta. I'm here. I've been here all night. Can you hear me?"

Yes I can hear you, I say. *Can't you hear me?*

"Mama? Can you hear the words I'm saying to you? You're in the hospital. Mama, the doctors say you're going to be just fine. You just need to open your eyes now. Can you open your eyes, Mama?"

I try. I push on my eyelids, but they won't listen to me.

"It's okay, you don't have to right now if you don't want to. You just rest now. All right? Just rest. EJ's going to be here soon. Won't that be nice?"

Henrietta leans in close to me. I can feel her breath on my face and smell her faint perfume. Smells like apricots and fresh figs to me. I breathe in good as I can, but there's tubes up, down, and every which-a-way.

"The doctors say you'll be just fine, Mama," she whispers to me. "I know you'll be just fine. And Mama? You don't have to worry a thing about your house anymore, okay? I've taken care of everything. The house is yours for as long as you want it."

Glory hallelujah, baby. Praise God.

Retta stops and sucks back a sob, then she stands and moves away, blowing her nose.

Thank you, baby, I say to her. I don't think she can hear me though. Then she leans in again.

"Mama!" she whispers to me real urgent-like, crying all the while. "I just want you to know, I didn't want to put you in a nursing home—not really. I just—my marriage, Mama." She blows her nose again and leans so close I can feel her breath on my ear.

"I knew this would happen. I was afraid you'd get too sick to be on your own, and—don't get me wrong, Mama, I love you and I'd care for you, and Edward—he's a good man. We just don't need any more stress, that's all. There's just some things you don't understand. I don't know why I'm telling you all this, Mama. Not like you can . . . hear me . . . "

Retta boo-hoos like a lost puppy, and it tears my heart plumb to shreds. The last thing I hear 'fore I disappear again is the sound of my baby girl crying for her mama.

Chapter 19

I don't know what day it is. My joints are stiff. I wiggle my toes to make sure I'm alive. Are they wiggling? Lord have mercy if I know. I still can't open my dad-gum eyes. Are they glued shut?

My mouth is dry. Feels like there's cotton in there. I hear that ol' beeping noise still, so I must be alive. The noise don't bother me so much now. I wonder how long I've been here.

"Miss Jenkins?" asks a syrupy sweet voice.

My name's Essie Mae. Just call me Essie Mae, I say.

"Miss Jenkins? It's Darla. I'll be your nurse this morning. Now, don't mind me, I'll just be coming in every hour or so to check your vitals. You and me, we're becoming fast friends, aren't we? Yes we are. And I just love your family," she says while pinching the dickens out o' my arm.

"Oh yes, I've met your daughter and your grandson . . . he's

111

quite a looker, isn't he? Oh, and I met your son-in-law, I think it was. He's very nice. Quiet. He brought you that big beautiful vase of flowers by the window. Have you seen them yet? Oh, they're just gorgeous. Yellow and white daisies and marigolds, I think. Lots of baby's breath and exotic-looking flowers that I can't even tell you the name of. No, Miss Jenkins, you're just going to have to open up your eyes to see them, all right? Why don't you open your eyes soon? I know everyone would be so happy if you did."

She reaches under my behind and pulls some cords out. Then she straightens my bed sheets and fluffs my pillow. "Oh, and I just can't believe how you weave those baskets! You are so talented! Well, when you get out of here, I'm going to get you to weave me one, okay? Just like the one sitting over there in that chair. A friend of yours brought it down here. I can't remember her name, but she said she weaves with you every day. Macy? Mary was it?"

Nancy? Nancy brought me a basket?

Darla lowers her voice like she has a big secret. "Between you and me, Miss Jenkins, it's against the rules to have all that grass and such in here—cardiac patients and allergies you know—but I let her sneak it in here anyway because I like you so much. She said it's the very one you were working on when you—well, before you came in here. I thought you'd like that."

My basket? Jim and my's basket?

"And guess what? Your daughter's trying to finish that basket for you. Isn't that something? Yep, said she hasn't done it in years, but she wants to do it for you. Isn't that just the sweetest thing you ever heard? Now you go on and get well, Miss Jenkins. How about let's open those eyes up soon so you can see what a good job she's doing, okay?"

Sweet Jesus, no! Please don't let Retta be sewin' my love basket. I'm tryin' to live, baby! Oh Lord, sweet Jesus, have mercy on us all.

Don't know how long I been out but the first thing I see when I open my eyes is my handsome boy, EJ. He's cloudy but I know it's him.

"Grandmama? Can you see me? Oh, I can't believe it, Mama! Come here! She opened her eyes!"

"Mama?" Henrietta grabs my right hand and 'bout squeezes my fingers off. "Great God in heaven." She takes in a deep breath and a tear escapes down her cheek. She's the prettiest thing I've ever seen. Henrietta smiles and then puts her head on my chest and cries.

It's okay, Retta, I say. I wish I could stroke her hair, but my arms is too weak. *I can see you now. You sure are pretty. Hey there, EJ. Don't you cry, too, or you'll get me goin'. Can you hear me? Is my mouth movin' yet?*

"Hey, Grandmama," he says, leaning down to kiss me slow on the cheek. "You had us pretty worried for a while. Can you see me? We missed you, you know."

I missed you too, baby. I blink at him. I can blink. My, how God is good.

"Grandmama, Miss Nancy and Miss Georgia have been selling your baskets for you. They've been making good money, so you're going to be in fine shape when you go home. Isn't that great? And you won't believe it but Mama's been weaving too."

"That's right," Retta says through sniffles. She wipes her nose on her tissue. "Me. *I've* been making baskets, can you believe that? Just like you always wanted. It all came right back—just like I hadn't missed a day."

Why that's the nicest thing you could 'a said to me, Retta. I know you're sorry. I forgive you.

She looks at EJ, and he takes his cue and walks to the window. Henrietta sits on the bed and takes my hand in hers.

"The baskets, Mama. I know how important they are now. I'm beginning to, anyway. You know, I've been sitting there, morning and night sewing little baskets and then bigger ones and all the while, my fingers just move like someone else is moving them. Is that how it is for you? Mercy, it's incredible. If I didn't have that grass in here, I don't know what I'd do. Mama, can you hear what I'm saying? Can you say something?" She looks at me fearful.

My lips won't move. I try to stick my tongue out to lick my lips. I push and I pry and I pray. *Let me talk, Lord. Please. I got to tell her not to weave my basket, okay? I need more time with Retta and EJ, Jesus. Open my mouth for me so I can talk now.*

"Ma." A prehistoric sound escapes from my lips. EJ runs over real quick-like and sits on the other side of me. His eyes show nothing but white.

"Ma," I say again. Shoot. That ain't what I'm trying to say. *Come on now, Essie Mae. Do better than that.*

"Ba," I say, blinking.

"What? What is it, Mama? What are you trying to say?"

"Ba. Ka." I grunt.

114

"What? Say it again, Grandmama." EJ's on the edge of his seat.

"Ba. Ka. Ba. Ket."

"Basket? Basket? Are you saying 'basket'?" Henrietta squeals and hugs EJ over me. "Mama, did you say 'basket'?"

Don't weave my basket, Retta. Don't weave my basket!

"Ba ket."

EJ runs over and grabs my love basket and brings it over excited as a June bug in May.

"Look, Mama," says Henrietta, lifting off the lid. "After I weave just a few more little ones for practice, I thought I'd finish this one for you. Would you like that? What do you think? It's the big beautiful one you were working on. How about it, Mama? Me and you working on the same basket—it'll be mother and daughter weaving together like we did when I was little."

No, Retta!

"Ba ket." Lord have mercy, it's no use. She's grinning like the Cheshire cat, and I'm getting tired. I close my eyes and my babies simmer down.

"Is she going to sleep?" asks EJ. "Is she okay?"

"I think she just needs to rest," says Retta. "She's had a big day. Let's let her sleep. You can go on home, EJ. Here's some money. Take a pizza to your father for me, would you? I'm going to stay here with her for a while and weave." Then she whispers, "Tomorrow, see if you can bring me some more grass, all right? I'd like to get started on her basket as soon as I can. Maybe that will give her something to look forward to."

I hear 'em kiss each other and give a big, long hug. Retta's never been one for hugging, so I'm glad my being in here's bringing them two together. Then EJ clomps on out the room leaving Retta staring at me real quiet-like and me, praying to God I get my voice back before tomorrow comes.

Chapter 20

Jim? That you?

"Yeah, it's me, Mama."

I thought you weren't never coming to the hospital. You ain't been here to see me yet! Where you been?

"I still ain't in the hospital, Mama. I'm just in your head."

In my head? Well, I swanny. Don't that beat all. Aw shucks. I ain't dead, am I Jim?

"No, you ain't dead, Mama. Retta's here with you though. She been weavin' all mornin'. You best now get up and tell her to stop it or you'll be comin' to see me sooner than you want to."

Retta! My eyes pop open like they got strings attached and I see Henrietta weaving that big ol' basket in the corner. Her hair's pulled back away from her face and she got bags under her eyes I ain't never seen before. I can smell the sickly cleanness of alcohol and hear that beeping noise again. I turn my head to the left and see this white machine counting my heartbeats. There's a little red line moving this way and that.

The walls is covered in a pale flowerdy paper and outside my window, the sun's reflecting off a dusty metal roof. I can see real good today, praise Jesus.

"Mama?" Retta puts down her grass and sets the basket gentle in her chair. She walks over to me with hope beaming out her eyes.

"Well hey there," she smiles at me. "I was wondering when you'd wake up. You feeling better today?"

She sits down 'tween me and that beeping machine and rubs my chin. "You look a lot better today. You've got nice color in your face and your eyes are much brighter. The doctors say you're doing just fine. Are you going to talk to us today, Mama?"

I go to try and work my mouth, but Retta turns her head when we hear a knock at the door. All a sudden, my eyes get wide when the biggest bunch o' flowers walks into the room and trailing behind it Mister Jeffrey, Miss Susanne, and her great big ol' mama too.

Henrietta stands to greet 'em. "Well hello," she says, sugar sweet. "How nice of you to come by. My, aren't these just beautiful? What a nice gesture, Jeffrey. You really shouldn't have." Henrietta takes the flowers from him and sets them on a little table nearby.

Jeffrey nods at her and then makes a beeline over to me. He scoots in real tight next to my hips and holds my hand. I can smell fresh-cut greens on him, and his skin is nice and warm.

"Miss Essie Mae," he says, his voice crackling like fire. His eyes well all up and he tries again. "Essie Mae, you doing all right? We've all been

118

so scared we were going to . . ." He sniffles and reaches toward me. He takes my hair in his fingers and smoothes my braids. "It's good to see you."

I blink my eyes at him. I hope he can see me smile.

"Oh, and look who else came to see you. My new best friends are here. I present to you the Misses Maybree." He swoops his hand out toward 'em and Susanne leaves her mama to walk over to my other side. Her features, usually small and crisp, are swollen up like she been sick.

"Jeffrey here is just in love with you, I'm afraid," she says. "He's had me up all night long talking about you. I feel like I know you better than my own mother."

Henrietta fidgets and drops a cup on the floor and leans down to pick it up.

"You try and get well now," Susanne says. "When you get out of here, we'll have to go do some girl things together, okay? I'll have you over for dinner one night. Mother would just love that, wouldn't you?" She waves for her mama who shuffles over on flat cow's feet.

"Oh, she'll be just fine now," says Clarice, waving her arms in my face. "Quit fussing over her so much. Isn't that right, Miss Essie Mae? Why, when I was in the hospital for my hernia operation, everybody was just "boo, boo, boo" over me, too, and after a while, I told them all to just go on and leave me to rest. Isn't that right? But really, we would love to have you over when you get out of here. Now make it *soon*. Okay?"

Lord have mercy, stop talkin', woman.

"Maybe it *is* best if we just let Mama rest a while. She's got a lot of healing to do and the doctors don't want her getting too excited." I hear annoyance in Henrietta's honey voice. She scoops up the flowers in the vase and says, "I'll put these in Mama's big beautiful basket before nightfall. I'm almost done with it, you know."

Clarice squeals over the basket and makes a fool over her for working on it which pleases Retta to no end. Jeffrey looks like the life might get sucked right out from him if he don't breathe in deep enough. A tear streaks down and leaves a spot on his shirt. He wipes at his face and then leans down to me. He kisses me gentle on the lips. Ain't no white man ever kissed me on the lips. His mouth is so supple and small, it's like being smooched by a baby boy.

"You know, when Mama got sick," he says, "I didn't know what I was going to do." I tear up and he wipes at my cheek. "And when she passed away, about the only thing that got me through was knowing that you and Daddy were still in my life."

I blink at him and try to say, "I love you too, Jeffrey. You're a real good boy," but nothing comes out but a breathy sigh. Miss Clarice grabs Jeffrey by the arm and pulls him toward the door like she owns him and gonna take him for a walk. She got her clutches on him all right.

They all promise to come back tomorrow and beg me to get my rest and get well soon. I try to tell 'em I will, but I can't help seeing that big basket in the corner. It's got just two more French buttons and the knob on top 'fore it's done. I try to soak in every detail on Jeffrey's face 'fore he leaves—if'n that basket gets done 'fore he comes back to see me, and if'n it's the last time I ever get to see him.

Soon as everybody leaves, Henrietta gets out that bulrush and her fingers work like lightning in the summer sky. 'Fore I know it, seems an hour or two done passed. I hear her take a deep breath and then she walks on over to me to show me what she done. Stuck in the top o' that basket are all them pretty flowers Jeffrey brung me. Retta sets the lid down on my belly so I can see how fine her work is, then she kisses me on the forehead and says, "Goodnight, Mama. I'll see you in the morning, okay? You just get some rest now." She lingers in front of my face and says something I ain't heard from her in years: "I love you, Mama." Then she brushes her fingertips over my eyelids and closes them for me. Retta squeezes my hand on her way out the door and I listen to her footsteps get lighter and lighter as she walks down the hall.

Good-bye, baby. That's some mighty fine weavin' you done. Retta, Mama loves you more than you'll ever know. You done me right proud, sure 'nough.

When I was a little girl over in Six Mile, I'd stay outside all day tending to the chickens and fiddlin' 'round the yard. Mama was always real sweet to me and let me play with the neighborhood children a while 'fore it got dark. Then she'd call for me—I could hear that call from a mile away and I'd always come a-running. I'd drop whatever or whoever I was playing with and just come on home fast as my legs could bring me.

"Essie Mae? Essie Mae? Essie Maaaaeeee!" She only had to call for me once and I'd be belly up to the table, grabbing a big ol' crumbly piece of cornbread and sopping up the juice in my hot bowl of beans. Mm hmm, them was good ol' days. Times seemed so easy even though I know now they weren't that way a'tall. And soon after that, Mama'd be raising me all on her own after what happened to Daddy in the field one day. He was planting some summer corn when that big mule we had, Bess, done lost her mind and kicked him good. He lost part of his mind and his left eye that day. Yes sir, that was a cryin' shame. Daddy weren't never quite the same after that.

"Essie Mae? Essie Mae?" I can hear Mama calling me. "Essie Maaaaeeee!" Great God in heaven, there it is again.

Mama? Mama, that you? I ask, 'fraid she might answer.

"E da me, baby. I da yo mammy. Oh, sweet Jesus, I miss ya, Essie Mae."

Praise God, Mama, is it really you? It's been so many years! I can't believe it, but . . . Mama?

"Yes baby? What is it?"

Is it my time? Mama, is it time?

"Yes, e time fa go. But ain nuttin' fa worry 'bout. Yo mammy de right yah now. I gwine be wid you all da wey."

I feel pressure on my feet like somebody's holding my socks on. I hear crying and sniffling. EJ gets to wailing and Retta's grabbing my shoulder, shaking me. Then she loosens her grip and falls to the ground. *Baby, you all right? Retta?* I try to open my eyes but I can't. Dad-gum, Henrietta must 'a finished my love basket. *Oh, Retta baby, I'm so sorry I got to go now. I'm so sorry! Can you forgive me? I don't wanna leave you. We's just gettin' friendly again. I can't leave my EJ neither! Oh sweet Jesus, what have I done?*

I squeeze a tear out my eye and all a sudden, a peace like a flying sail o' white comes out from nowhere and lays its blanket right over me.

And all my worry is gone like a dandelion traveling in the breeze. My babies'll be just fine. I know it now. Everything gonna be all right.

"Essie Mae?"

Yes, I hear you, Mama. I'm comin'. Don't worry now, I'm comin' on home.

PART II:

*like everythin' I ever 'magined
and then some*

Chapter 21

I bet the newspaper ain't gonna say a thing 'bout my dying a'tall. Not like nobody important died or nothing. Not like I was a politician or a movie star or somebody people looked up to and would sorely miss. No. I was just an invisible old sweetgrass basket lady. And I'm dead. That just means one more abandoned stand on the side of the road.

My dying sure did sneak up on me, though. Ain't hardly felt a thing, neither, 'cept a little twinge in my chest. Now, that's the way a body wants to go, sure 'nough. I'm lying on that bed with everybody I love all 'round me when my body gets real light. I put my hand out to touch Retta's face, but I start pulling away right fast up into the air. Then I see pretty colors just as bright as they can be, swirling all around me.

Next thing I know—praise Jesus, hallelujah! Here I am standing in what gots to be heaven 'cause it don't look a thing like Mount Pleasant, South Carolina. There's puffy white clouds everywhere and seems like golden grass as far as the eye can see. I turn my head and look at Mama who's holding my hand. She's wearing her nice wide-brim hat I always loved and a pretty brown dress with a dark velvet sash.

"Mama!" I cry and we hug. She's just as beautiful as ever with not a wrinkle on her face. Her waist is tiny and her hips are round. She's a young woman again, glory be.

"Mama? Are we in heaven?" I ask her.

"Us gettin' dey, baby," she says, swinging my arm like a schoolgirl. "Come yah. Us git a lettle wey ta go yet."

Mama and me walk kinda slow, her holding my arm. I feel safe like I ain't felt since I was a little girl in my mama's lap. It's near the best feeling a body can have. We move in silence as I listen to the wind blowing around me. The grass whispers to keep on going.

My eyes seem like I got glasses on what make everything real bright and colorful. I'm seeing hues I never even seen before. I'm caught up in it all, but then I stop.

"Henrietta, Mama. And EJ. They gonna be all right?" I can't stand that I left 'em. "They gonna make it without me?"

"Dey awright, Essie Mae. Come yah." She brings me to a great big oak tree tipped in purple and red. She sits me down in a real nice wood chair at the foot of it and says, "Now ress yonda. I gwine fa show you sumtin'." And she sits herself down next to me.

Well, we're sitting there and Mama's humming. The breeze gets blowing real good, when all a sudden, Mama says, "Dey awfully proud ob ya, Essie Mae."

"Who is? For what?" I ask, not knowing what in the world she's talking about.

"Yo kin, yo ancestah, yo root," she says. "Dey all up yah—mos' ob 'em anyhow."

Mama stands up and swoops her arm out beside her and next thing I know, there's black folks stretched out a mile long down the lane, lined up and waiting to see me. And each one comes up, one by one, like we's greeting at a wedding or some such. They give me a hug and a kiss and tell me "Thank you" and "I sure am proud" and words like that. Some of 'em is speaking Gullah, and some of 'em I can't even understand a'tall 'cause they speaking some African language. Midway though the line, I pull Mama over behind that big oak tree and say, "Mama, what in heaven's name is all this about? What's everybody thankin' me for?"

"Fa what you done, gal," Mama says. "Fa da good mark you lef' back dey. You right yah een hebun now, but da work you lef' 'pon da Earth ain ober, baby." She smiles at me my favorite smile in the whole world and squeezes the backs of my arms. Then she gives me a warm look in my eyes and says, "You ain let yo root die down dey, an' you kepp da spirit alive. You done very well, baby. You gwine see."

We stand back up and finish with our greeting, and when it gets to the end of the line, I grab at my heart when the last person walks up. Lord have mercy, it's my sweet Daddy Jim! Whooee! He looks just as handsome as ever—just like he did when we first got married. Jim's walking over to me, looking like he's gonna give me a big kiss. And now look at me, pretty like I used to be, wearing a white fancy dress with my nice white patent leather shoes.

"Glory, Jim, that didn't take very long a'tall, now did it?"

"No, Mama, not long a'tall." Jim grins at me real big, then leans down to give me a hug. He kisses me flat on the lips, and I don't even have to step up on my toes.

"Yes sir, my love basket's a powerful thing—works every time, don't it, Daddy?" I'm right tickled at myself.

"Sure 'nough, Mama. Works every time."

Mama hugs me tight and then walks off behind the tree. Jim holds my hand as the world 'round me starts changing. There's flowers now and palmetto trees—looks like I found myself right back on home ground. He pulls me to him, and we start walking down this long dirt lane. It's just like the drive up to Boone Hall Plantation near my basket stand in Mount Pleasant—the prettiest place I ever seen. We stop to rest a second at a little swamp with turtles and ducks swimming all in it. Jim puts his arm around me, and I look up to the sky. It's as blue as I ever seen it. He bends down and kisses me real light on the ear, and I'm telling you, I got a feeling down deep inside me I ain't felt in 'bout a hundred years or more. Jim looks down in my face and whispers, "Better keep on walkin', Mama." So we do.

There's great big oak trees bowing down to greet us on either side o' the lane. Pretty Spanish moss is lazy like a hound dog, drooping off the branches, coming down to touch us. The sunshine peeks on through the trees every now and then and lights up my white dress so bright it nearly hurts my eyes. Then we come to the end of the lane, and you won't believe what I see next. Not on the edge of loud ol' Rifle Range

Road, but at the end of this beautiful drive is our little lime-green house just like I remember it when we was first married. And the big ol' magnolia tree out front is in full bloom. I tell you, I'm 'bout to cry at the sight!

I get to running straight for the house, but Jim stops me and then gets down on one knee. Oh, Lord. He takes my hand in his and my stomach gets all to fluttering.

"Essie Mae, I love you. Will you have me forever?" I feel the heat of his hand and it shoots all through me. It's the 'xact same thing he told me when he asked me to marry him.

I pull him up by the scruff o' his neck and say, "James Furlow Jenkins, I'd be mighty happy to."

Jim stands up and dusts off. We're giggling now, and he reaches 'round and picks me up off my feet and carries me into the house. It's in real good shape. Whooee! The floors don't creak none and the stove and fireplace look brand new. In fact, everything looks so clean you could eat right off it.

Jim carries me on to the back room—our bedroom. He sets me down and walks over to the window. His long arms swipe open the curtains and then he lights up a beeswax candle like he knows I love, blows out the match, and sets it in the sill. The smells o' honey and smoke, fresh linens and wood oil mix together and roll on over me just like heaven itself.

Jim walks up to me real slow and I can see his hands trembling. He looks me in my eyes and kisses me real soft as he unbuttons the front of my dress, one button at a time. I feel shivers go up my spine, and my blood is fixing to boil. I 'bout lose my breath when he stoops down and nibbles on my neck. And when he lays me down real gentle on top of the bed, over his shoulder I catch a glimpse of myself in the mirror 'bove the dresser. It's hard to believe my eyes.

My skin is black and smooth, and my breasts is swollen up in a real good way. At first I have a hard time looking, 'cause it feels like spying on somebody else. But it's me, sure 'nough. My body ain't old no more, and neither is Jim's.

I turn my head and watch him sit on the edge of the bed and unbutton his long-sleeve shirt. He smiles at me, and I smile right back, raising up on my knees and leaning over to him to help him slide it off his hands. I grab his white T-shirt down by the waist and pull it on up. Jim's arms is high up over his head, and I watch in the mirror as the muscles in his back ripple up. Good Lord have mercy! I run my fingers along his chest. He's moist and firm, and I just can't stand it no more.

Jim wraps his arms tight 'round my little bitty waist and lays my head down soft up on the pillows. He climbs up on top of me, and I close my eyes, breathing in his sweet musk. Every now and again, I peek through my eyelids to see candlelight flickering off his molasses skin. Laying with Jim is just like the first time we ever done it but with all them memories o' the other times bundled up with it. I got to say, Reverend Jefferson never told us folks did this up in heaven, but it all makes sense to me now. Sweet Jesus, ain't no doubt I'm in heaven now for sure.

Chapter 22

HEAVEN'S LIKE EVERYTHIN' I EVER 'MAGINED AND THEN SOME. Jim and me get to sit here in these nice rockers on our front porch and look on down the lane through the oaks. Mama and Daddy live over yonder past the pecan trees in a real nice house, so I'll be able to see 'em much as I want to, I reckon. Mama's gonna make her okra soup and cornbread tomorrow night and have everybody over. Whooee! I sure have missed Mama's cooking.

It's a funny thing 'bout heaven. You get to see a great big picture now—things start to make sense to you what ain't made sense before. It's a wonder we understand each other a'tall down on Earth, what with us only seeing little snippets of folks every now and again.

Take for instance, I'm feeling sorta silly now, 'cause turns out, I ain't had no magic powers in me a'tall. I found that out when I seen Auntie Leona this morning—yes sir, she's here too, praise God. I was kinda worried about her making it up here, what with the hexes she'd put on people and what not. I sure was glad to see her, though. She's looking better than ever. First thing she done when she seen me was laugh 'bout my love baskets.

"Essie Mae!" She squealed and hugged me hard, almost picked me up off the ground. "I missed you girl! I been watching your goings on with your 'lo-ove baskets.' Ain't you a trip?"

"What you mean, Leona?"

"Your love baskets, baby. You don't really think you was doin' magic, now do you?"

"Well, weren't I?"

"Naw, you weren't, Essie Mae. You was prayin' to Jesus, plain and simple. Jesus got the power, baby. Any power you was feelin' was a-coming straight from Him."

"You mean my love basket for Jim and me ain't what killed me? But Retta finished it, and then I up and died. Ain't that right, Jim? Ain't that what happened?"

Jim just looked at me, shying away and backing up a couple steps. Guilt all over his face.

"James Furlow Jenkins! Why in heaven's name did you tell me to make them love baskets?" He just smiled at me and held my face in his hands real sweet. "It give you somethin' to do, now, didn't it, Mama? You weren't bored, now was you?"

So there you have it. Not one thing I thought I done with my love baskets actually happened 'cause of me. That don't matter, it's all water under the bridge now, what they say. And I get to be here with Jim and sweet Jesus, and who in they right mind would complain about that?

Seems like people I need to be seeing's been dropping by the house all day long. Yes sir, all my loose ends is getting tied up nice. It's a mighty fine feeling, I tell you what. Mama and Daddy just left. They come by to give me some sugar. What they told me 'bout my dying was my heart was ailing me for the longest time. I was a time bomb just a-waiting to go off any second; I just ain't known nothing about it. Ain't that something? Turns out I was gonna die no matter what that day, basket or no basket. The same thing goes for that old man and his dog too. I run into 'em up here, Mister Clayton and Happy, this morning right 'fore I seen Leona. That sure was a good time, seeing both of 'em all young and full and healthy as all get-out. Clayton laughed at me real hard when I told him I sure was sorry for killing 'em both.

I've only been here couple days, but I swanny, just one day in heaven's like a whole lot of 'em on Earth. I can do anything I feel like and never get tired, never having to worry 'bout the sun going down and ruining all the fun..I can even sneak on down to Mount Pleasant like Jim used to do. He showed me how. Nobody knows I'm there, but I can do it just the same.

Watch this—I'm going right now.

I give Jim a kiss (can't seem to get enough o' them kisses), and then I head on down to our old house on Rifle Range Road. Ain't like I got wings or nothing, I just set my mind to it and off I go. I find EJ and Henrietta peeking 'round in there. It's awful quiet with neither one of 'em saying much. "Hey Retta, baby," I say. "Hey there, EJ." It's the strangest thing, them not knowing I'm right here beside 'em.

Funny thing is, I can hear what they thinking. Brings tears to my eyes—both of 'em walking from room to room, remembering things about me. EJ sits down at the kitchen table and looks over at the stove, picturing me making his supper. His eyes well up, and he looks down at the table, thinking 'bout the talks we used to have. He's remembering right now bringing Felicia over to meet me. All a sudden he's worrying 'bout taking her home to his mama.

Henrietta's been a long time in my bedroom, poking through my closet and thinking 'bout laughing and cutting up with me in there. We did that some when she was young, you know. When she weren't off in a bad mood, that is. She thinking 'bout when she was little, trying on my dresses and great big shoes and clomping 'round proud like the queen o' England. She sits down on my bed and runs her hand over my sheets. Remembers crawling up under the covers 'tween me and Daddy Jim on a rainy night. Retta never did like a good storm. Uh oh. Now she fighting back tears. Don't get me started.

"Don't cry, baby. Mama right here," I say.

Henrietta pulls out a nice dress of mine that she give me few years back. It's the color o' fresh cream and has a real nice silky feel to it. "I always did like that dress, Retta. That's a mighty fine choice."

She hugs it tight and then starts boo-hooing. She's thinking 'bout taking me to that Sunndydale Farms couple months ago. She keeps seeing my face looking so sad and pitiful. She knows she done that to me. "Oh, Mama," she says real soft and shaking. "Mama, I'm so sorry. I'm so sorry! You just don't know. I guess you'll never understand."

"Well no, Retta. That's one thing I don't understand yet. Why'd you wanna put your old mama away?"

I s'pose I'll keep on listening and watching her. Maybe one o' these days, I'll understand my little girl.

Chapter 23

YOU AIN'T NEVER SEEN NOTHING 'til you been to a good ol' Lowcountry wake. When a person dies, anybody who ever knew 'em and everybody related in just the littlest way gets together and tells stories and stuff. Right now, there's a wake going on for me. I tell you, my little house ain't never seen so many people in it, 'cept for when my Jim died—there was almost as many people back then. All of 'em was on my mama's side, seeing as I ain't met nobody from my daddy's side 'cept Auntie Leona.

There's aunts and uncles here and cousins and second cousins and kissing cousins and grandbabies—I can't count 'em all.

"Hey Boo, 'membah dat time Essie Mae an' Jim de come over to de house an' git ta dancin' aw night lon'? 'Membah how we laf an' stuff?"

"Lawd have mercy!" That's my second cousin Leroy. "Liked to put a fire out with all that stompin' 'round!" He gets up, hopping and dancing, I reckon making fun of me 'cause he's swishing his hips. It's okay though and right funny. Sure is nice having people all happy, remembering things about me. It's a whole lot easier to take than seeing folks sad.

The young ones, too, they get to laughing and cutting up and talking Gullah just like the old folks. Then they call each other by nicknames, and everybody has a real nice time. Yes sir, I sure am enjoying the wake. Everybody ought to see their own, I recommend. The smell o' mashed potatoes and country ham on sweet buttered biscuits is enough to make this ol' dead lady wanna come on back alive!

Got my body laid out in front the fireplace and I'm wearing that pretty cream dress. Look real nice, too, for a dead person. I got that pretty sweetgrass basket necklace EJ give me 'round my neck and some gold clip-on earrings o' Henrietta's. Oh, now she's remembering the man at the funeral home, when he asked her if she wanted to get me dressed for my big day. She told him no, it was too much for her. Now she's fretting maybe she should 'a done it anyhow. "Don't fret, baby. I reckon it'd be hard for me to do too."

Lord, now she's worrying 'bout my funeral tomorrow. Wondering how she gonna hold up. "It's okay, Retta. You doin' just fine," I say. "And I tell you, if my funeral's anythin' like this here wake you put on, baby you can count me in."

You know, I can still remember to this day going to Gullah funerals way back. They was a lot different then. Gullahs are real respectful of the dead, and they want to make sure they go on to the afterworld and don't come back for haunting. Back in 1939 when my grandmama died, I can remember Mama turning the mirrors in the house backward, facing the wall, so Gran's spirit wouldn't reflect. Somebody banged on a drum to let everybody know she'd passed too. Then we all walked procession-style to the graveyard down by the marsh. We stopped at the gates and asked the ancestors could we come in. They musta said *come on in* for sure 'cause we did just that.

After Gran was buried, everybody danced around, praying and singing. We smashed little cups and saucers and bottles and stuff on top of her grave. That way, she'd have everything she needed to stay good and buried and we'd "break the chain" so that nobody else in the family would have to die. After that we went on back home and made a big ol' meal of grits and greens and possum, and we left a plate on Gran's porch for her spirit to fill up on.

That's when things were different though—tradition was important. Why, I 'spect the only Gullah tradition gonna be at my funeral is that my grave'll face east. Gullahs used to do that so a spirit would know how to make it to the water and back over to Africa—where they come from. But I don't need that, I reckon. I already found my way to the homeland, heaven.

"Sit right here," I tell Jim, finding us a nice couple seats on the front pew next to Retta and Eddie. She's wearing a different black dress from the one she had on for my wake. This one's got black lace on up the sleeves and matches her hat. "Hey there, Retta." She still can't hear me.

Folks is just a-rolling in the church, one after the other. "Jim, look over there. Remember Mister Scott down to the General Store? He'd always hold some peaches for me in the back room, a whole lot better than all the others. Ain't that nice he come to pay his respects? I swanny, is that Vernell? I thought she moved down to Georgia! Did she come all the way back just to see me? Hey, Vernell!"

I watch as everybody I know files into the Mt. Zion AME Church. There's Reverend Jefferson and his wife with that same big ol' black hat she always wears to funerals. I don't think she owns but one. Here come Miss Nancy and her son. "Hey, Nancy!" They walk on up to my body lying in that coffin.

"Don't she look real nice," Nancy says, sticking a flower in next to me.

"Well, thank you, Nancy. But you ought to see me now!" Miss Georgia comes in all by herself and sits down next to 'em. Gracious, she looking mighty old.

"Oh no, Jim. Who invited her?" There's Bertice Brown over in the corner just a-jibber-jabbering to anybody who'll listen. I can hear her now, probably gonna talk Eartha Lee's ears clean off. Talking 'bout "I heard somebody did this to that person" and "ain't it a shame." Girl got a big mouth, I tell you what.

Well now, what's this? All a sudden, Bertice's big ol' bottom lip likes to hit the floor. Everybody's head turns, including mine and Jim's, when pretty little Miss Susanne Maybree and her great big mama, Clarice, come in. But who's that behind 'em?

"Great God in heaven, Jim! Look!" I tell you, holding hands and making a scene is my sweetie, Jeffrey Lowes, and a skinny little

141

man with a mustache and a tight black suit. "Looks like he might be Mexican, what you think, Jim?"

"Mm hmm, reckon so," he tells me. "Seems like they pretty tight to me."

Looks like Jeffrey thought my funeral'd be a good place to come out the closet for whatever reason. Now I know it for sure; ain't no way my love baskets worked. Jeffrey's still just as homo-sexual as they come, Lord have mercy.

Well, that don't change the way I feel about Jeffrey none. No, he's still my sweet boy. Can't understand what would make a man wanna be with another man like that, but I reckon I'll talk to Jesus and see if He can't do nothing 'bout it. I'm just gonna have to get used to Jeffrey being with a man, seeing as I can watch all the goings on down in Mount Pleasant from up in heaven now. But don't think I'll be peeking in his bedroom. Ain't nothing I wanna see in there, no sir.

I can't say as I'm enjoying my funeral much as I always figured I would. When I was alive, I thought I'd like to see who shows up and how sad they is and such, but it ain't much fun a'tall. 'Specially having to see my grandbaby torn plumb to pieces. Look at him. His face all puffy, and he's crying on and off. That just ain't something you wanna see when you love somebody, sure 'nough.

"Look Jim. There she is! Ain't she cute just like I was tellin' you?" Sitting down beside EJ's that sweet little white girlfriend of his, Felicia. Seems she's getting a lot of looks herself, what with EJ choosing my funeral to bring her out of *his* closet too.

Poor Henrietta sure is having a time, though. She's sitting right next to me and keeps burying her head in tissue every few minutes, 'specially when somebody comes up to her and tells her how sorry they are for her loss. I feel bad 'cause she really is suffering, but I ain't sure which is worse to her, me being dead or EJ introducing his white girlfriend for all to see. From the look on her face and the thoughts in her head, I can tell he ain't told her 'bout Felicia 'fore just now. Smart boy, that EJ. Smart boy. Watching Henrietta all torn up, I ain't got no ill feelings toward her. She'll always be my baby, I just wish I could tell her that, is all.

"The Lord giveth and the Lord taketh away," says Reverend Jefferson. "Blessed be the name of the Lord!"

Everybody claps and says, "Amen!"

"Dearly beloved, we never know when death'll come."

"Ain't that the truth! Amen."

"Sister Essie Mae is a-goin' on home. For her, ain't no sufferin' no more."

"Hallelujah."

"Ain't no cryin' no more."

"Hallelujah! Praise Jesus!"

"Ain't nothin' but God's glory for her to look 'pon now!"

Yes sir, Reverend Jefferson's putting on a nice sermon, sure 'nough. Arms are waving and everybody's a-swaying. Then he has everybody sing "Going Up Yonder," just like I would 'a wanted. I sit there, too, in the front pew, singing just as loud as I can. I get to crooning when we start "Amazing Grace"—I tear up too.

Mm hmm, it's a real nice service, far as funerals go. But the nicest thing 'bout it is seeing all them children I used to nanny for. They's all growed up now, and I believe I count all of 'em here—'cept for

143

Lonnie Williams—he's military, over in Asia or some such place. No, everybody's here including Jackson Hemmingway—you know, of the Isle of Palms Hemmingways? Well, his family got all kinds o' money, but they was real nice people to work for. Jackson was a pill back then, if you ask me, but he growed into a nice-enough fella, I reckon. "Hey there, Jackson. You lookin' real good." Boy done me proud, what he done. Got elected as a state representative, I believe, and lives over in Columbia nowadays. I seen him couple years back when he stopped at my stand to buy some baskets. Said they was for "constituents"—that's what he called 'em anyway. Not sure what it means, but I do know they got some mighty fine baskets. Sure is nice to know Jackson cares I'm dead.

They buried me, facing east, just like I figured. Put me next to Jim's grave on one side and Mama and Daddy's on the other. Leona's is there, too, couple spots down. The laying in the ground part was 'bout the roughest thing I seen yet. Jim and me left early 'cause I was right tired of folks crying. I couldn't wait to get on back to heaven and have me a good time with everybody up there.

A funeral sure can tell you a lot about a person, but not everything. Take for instance, most folks put on a certain face when they in front of everybody else. They might be grieving harder on the inside than what they look, or laughing harder, whatever. Looking at my Retta, nobody would ever know what was going on inside her. She come off at my funeral just as proper as she could.

But in the weeks that come after that—after EJ showed up with

Miss Felicia to the funeral and let his mama know she was his girl—they was having a heck of a time with Henrietta, yes sir. She tried to be all nice and proper 'bout it in front of 'em, but deep down she was mad as an egg-bound chicken 'bout them two being together. Pretty soon, she couldn't hide it no more.

"I just cannot believe that boy can't find one black girl in this entire county that's good enough for him to date," she said when I was peeking in on her house. "What, black girls aren't good enough for him?"

"Now, Henrietta," said Eddie, putting his arm on her back. She just pulled away like she always do. "I don't think it's anything like that. EJ's a grown man now. If he finds somebody who's special to him, then by all means, we'd better support him. I think he's pretty serious about this girl."

"Serious? Ha!" She folded her arms up real tight.

"Times have changed, Henrietta," said Eddie. "It's not that big a deal anymore."

"Not that big a deal? We'll see about that," she huffed, and then stormed into the bathroom to pout a spell. I swanny, that child always could throw on a good pout.

Couple hours later, EJ was sitting on the sofa, moping 'bout what to do, talking to his daddy. "She'll come around," Eddie told him. "It's just going to take her a little time to get used to the idea because she's old-fashioned. Don't worry, son. I'll handle your mother."

Seem like a-handling Henrietta ain't something Eddie done too well 'cause next thing I knew, she was threatening to kick EJ out the house if'n he didn't leave Felicia alone.

"You just don't understand the trouble you're going to have in life with a white girl by your side!" Looks like that weren't the smartest thing for her to say, I reckon, 'cause EJ done packed his bags that very night and moved on down to my lime-green house on Rifle Range Road.

It was EJ what talked Henrietta into putting up the money to save my house. That's why it was fitting it go to him when I was gone. I made sure I wrote me a will on a slip of paper and tucked it in my basket 'fore I died. Alls it said was that I left EJ everything I got, including my house if'n the IRS let him keep it. He said he was mighty grateful to have it, but he weren't ready to live there 'cause the memory of me was too fresh. I reckon he got over that right quick when Henrietta pushed him hard enough. He set up house there just a few weeks after laying me to rest and asked that girl, Felicia, to marry him.

Chapter 24

October

THE BEST PART OF BEING IN HEAVEN is getting to be with Jesus. When I was alive, I loved Him, but I ain't never seen Him before. That's where faith comes in. I'd talk to Him all day long and sometimes I felt like He talked right back; but now that I'm here, I get to see Him and talk to Him and really spend time with Him. He's the nicest fella you ever want to meet. Oh and guess what, now? He ain't white, no sir. 'Course, ain't black neither. Got His own color, sure 'nough. Real bright and shiny—I can't put it to you any better than that. "Ain't that right, Jim?"

"That's right, Mama."

And you know how folks might say "to know so-and-so is to love him"? Well, now that I know Jesus better, I love Him even more than I ever done on Earth. He comes over to the house real regular to visit with me and Jim and see how we doing. Never seem like He's in a hurry or nothing, 'though I know He's got plenty to do. And when He's around, I feel like I might just bust with being happy. "Ain't that how you feel, Jim?"

"Mm hmm." Jim feels it too.

Yes sir, we both agree, Jesus is the best thing 'bout being here, sure 'nough.

Up here in heaven's a whole lot more entertaining than being there on Earth too. It's like everything you got down there that's good with none o' the bad stuff. None o' the bad folks neither. Well, I reckon some bad folks is here if'n they accepted sweet Jesus 'fore they died. And they sure ain't bad no more, that's for sure. That's what I'm hoping for Henrietta anyway—praying for her every day 'cause I wanna see her up here with us someday.

Let's see, it's been two months since I been up here in heaven. And EJ and Felicia are getting married today. Ain't that quick? I ain't never heard of folks throwing a wedding together in a little over a month, but they done it. If it's true love, I reckon ain't no time to waste.

It took her a little while, but Henrietta come around to the idea of EJ and Felicia being together 'bout a week or two ago, just in time. Retta thought, white girl or no white girl, this wedding's gonna reflect on her, so she ought to be here, sure 'nough. Not to mention, she ain't got nothing to hold over EJ no more. With him having his own house and being able to live his own life, she figures she'll lose her only baby if'n she don't start acting sweeter to him.

And let me tell you, this is a beautiful wedding, just beautiful. Felicia's mama and daddy, Mister and Miz Lewis, they got us here at this real pretty French Huguenot church in downtown Charleston, and it sure is nice—white peaks up all over the church with a red roof and tall pointy windows to look out of. And blue velvet on the pews with white Calla Lilies tied on the ends.

I got to say, I ain't never been to a white-folk wedding before. Jim ain't neither. We sitting over on the groom side right up in front next to Henrietta and Eddie. Looks like they left two seats empty for us, so we went ahead and took 'em. They got the biggest set o' organ pipes I ever seen in my life down behind the preacher—like to go plumb up to the ceiling! But it ain't nothing next to the sight o' the congregation itself.

"Look at that, Jim," I tell him. "The church is split plumb down the middle—black folk on one side and whites on the other!" The black half got lots o' colored hats and fans and movement and such, and the white side's all muted down, just as proper and boring as it can be. I think so, anyway. We're on the black side, looking 'round at all our old friends again. There's Reverend Jefferson. He ain't the one gonna marry 'em though. No, the one doing that's a white, mostly bald fella with a pretty quiet voice, if you ask me. Gonna be hard to hear a word he says.

"Hey, Retta. It's a fine day, ain't it? I'm so glad I get to be here for this. I sure ain't wanted to miss it," I tell her. She don't hear me though. Just keeps turning and smiling and a-waving to everybody. I think that smile o' hers is on there permanent 'cause she ain't took it off, not once. Her face don't show it, but I can hear it in her head—she's worried 'bout what everybody else is thinking 'bout her.

She forgets all 'bout that soon enough when sweet EJ walks on down to the front o' the room.

"EJ, my baby." She says it to herself, but Eddie hears her. "You're

149

all I got now," she says. Eddie squeezes her arm, and that's when I hear it. Something I ain't never known before 'bout Retta. She's sitting there looking at EJ and thinking o' some other baby I ain't never known about! Only thing is, she ain't never had that baby. Must 'a been the pregnancy gone bad. Lord have mercy! And she's thinking 'bout Daddy Jim too. It must 'a been a awful time for her, 'cause that's when it happened, sure 'nough! I can see it all so clear-like in her head.

"Oh, Retta, why you ain't never told me 'bout losing that baby? Is that why you got even meaner when Daddy died?" But she can't hear me—not a cotton-pickin' word.

For a minute I can't think straight—can't think about EJ or the wedding or nothing. I'm trying to piece my Retta together. "Why in tar-nation you never told me 'bout this? I could 'a helped you, Retta! Lord have mercy, why you ain't let me help you though all that?"

I'm 'bout to get to blubbering on account o' I ain't been as good a mama to her as I thought! What kind of mama can't help her baby through a time like that? Lord have mercy, she ain't trusted her own mama with the truth. And Eddie? I can't for the life of me figure out why he kept quiet too. I reckon Retta's the boss over there anyhow and told him to keep his mouth shut. Lord have mercy.

All a sudden, the organ starts tooting and everybody's head turns. We turn too, and there's Felicia looking just like an angel in white. She flows on down the aisle real slow on her daddy's arm, and when he drops her off with EJ, I know Henrietta sees the same look I do. I swanny, that boy and that girl are so smitten, the only color they seeing, looking at each other, is the golden glory o' Jesus I was talking about.

Chapter 25

January

I'LL TELL YOU A FUNNY THING, FELICIA'S 'BOUT THE BEST THING to ever happen to Henrietta. EJ's only been married 'bout three months, but Henrietta spends more time at my old house than she ever did when I was alive. It took her a good while, but she actually likes being with Felicia, though she won't admit to it outright. Yes sir, now that she knows her better, Henrietta's grown real fond of that girl 'cause she just wants EJ to be happy. 'Course, that don't stop her from worrying none. I listen to her talking to Eddie one night 'fore they turn the lights out.

"Edmund?"

"Yes, honey," he says, rolling over 'cause he was almost asleep.

"You think they're going to have children together?"

"Who?"

"EJ and Felicia," she snaps at him. "Who do you think?"

"Well, of course, they're going to have kids, Henrietta. That's what married people do."

"Well, that doesn't mean they'll be able to have them, now does it? We couldn't have any more after EJ, and Mama and Daddy didn't have any more after me."

Eddie don't say nothing.

"But—if they do have a baby, what's he going to look like? White or black?" she asks.

"Heaven if I know, honey. Just go to sleep."

"Edmund, what I mean is, what's the child going to think he is? White or black? And if you tell me neither one, what in the world will that be like for him? He's not gonna feel like he fits in anywhere."

Eddie stays quiet on that one. Henrietta thinks he gone to sleep, but he ain't. He's just a-laying there, thinking 'bout what she said. After while, their minds go heavy, and both of 'em set to snoring. It's a good thing they getting some sleep this night 'cause I know something they don't know yet. I know Miss Felicia's already carrying EJ's baby.

EJ and Felicia are having Henrietta and Eddie over to the house for Sunday supper. Felicia's made a nice big meal of spaghetti and meatballs and garlic bread just sopping with butter. EJ pours little glasses o' red wine for everybody 'cept Felicia. Nobody's noticed yet she's only drinking water.

Everybody's enjoying the supper, Eddie praising Felicia for what a good cook she is and EJ just a-beaming at her and grabbing her hand 'neath the table. Then everything gets real quiet, and EJ shifts in his seat. Henrietta can tell he's hiding something, so she tells him go on and spit it out.

EJ folds up his napkin real nice, sets it on his plate, and stands up real slow. He's a-grinning from ear to ear and walks 'round to Felicia's chair, leaning down over her shoulders.

"Well, Mom, Dad, we have some good news." You could hear a pin drop. Henrietta and Eddie both know what's coming. "We're expecting a baby. You're going to be grandparents!"

Henrietta grabs at her chest and swallows hard. Eddie stands up real quick and knocks his chair back onto the floor. He comes 'round and hugs EJ real tight, then Felicia, 'course he's a lot more gentle with her.

"Praise God!" I'm shouting. "Hallejujah, we gonna have a baby!" They can't hear me but I don't care. I'm gonna have me a great-grandbaby!

Henrietta's got this funny little smile on her face and's trying to take it all in.

"Well, Mama?" EJ comes 'round and grabs her hands. "What do you think?"

She stands up after a minute and wraps her arm 'round his waist, and then looks at Felicia.

"I think I couldn't be happier," she says, just like that. But that ain't really what she thinking. Having a tough time with it. She done accepted a white girl as her daughter-in-law, but ain't quite wrapped her mind 'round a mixed baby, no sir. Still worried about that, all "what kinda life's a mixed baby gonna have" and so forth. She sucks it up real good though, and I'm proud of her for it. Sticks a big ol' smile on her face. Then Felicia comes on over and hugs her tight.

"Well, we've got a lot of work to do, now don't we?" Felicia asks, grabbing Henrietta by the hand and pulling her down the hallway to go look at where the nursery's gonna be.

We're in Henrietta's old bedroom, and it's all quiet. Retta don't know what to say. Felicia's on her hands and knees, looking through my leftover sweetgrass stuck back in the closet. I can smell that sweetgrass in her hands just as fresh as day. She runs it through her fingers and thinks about me sitting at my stand. She smiles when she remembers how EJ told her Daddy Jim used to sit with me, too, in his pink plastic chair. Then she looks up at the wall 'bove the crib. They painted the walls green but it's bare 'cept for that.

Felicia hands Henrietta some grass to hold and says, "I want to know everything about EJ's family. I know all about my family, but I need to know more about yours. I think it's important."

Well now, that's a smart thing to do, child.

The boys head on outside, and Felicia makes some tea for the girls. The two of 'em sit down at the kitchen table, and I'm right here with 'em, happy as I can be. All a sudden, Henrietta just opens up and tells her word for word the stories I told her growing up. It sure is nice to see she paid attention to something I said, anyway. She tells her about me and Jim getting married. About my mama and daddy and Africa and New Orleans and sweetgrass. That's when Felicia says, "I have the best idea! Will you make me some tiny baskets to hang over the crib?"

Henrietta's quiet, thinking. "Well, I suppose I can . . . I haven't sewed since Mama died, though."

"But you know how. Oh please, you have to, it'll mean so much!"

Henrietta smiles and they walk on back to look at the grass some more. She picks it up and brings it with her into the living room. Over the next few hours, Henrietta weaves tiny baskets while Felicia's all hypnotized, listening to stories 'bout me. I ain't never been able to weave that small 'cause my fingers was always too fat. The palmetto leaves is all dried out, so it's taking her longer than it should 'cause they keep splitting in two.

"Mama used to spend hours and hours making baskets," she tells her. "She'd weave 'til her fingers were raw and then if somebody came to her stand and she decided she liked them for whatever reason, she'd just give it to him—for free! Used to drive me crazy. She was always like that though, giving things away."

"It's a good Christian way, Retta," I say.

"Like this one time," she keeps going, "I think I was a senior in high school. I had this really nice pair of shoes. They were black with little straps that came up around my ankles. Mercy, they were the prettiest shoes I'd ever had. I wore them to the prom, and then when I went back in the closet to get them for a date, they weren't there! Mama had taken my shoes and given them—along with a whole grocery bag of clothes—to this family at our church, the Chisolms, I think. Their house had burned down, and they'd lost everything."

"Wow," says Felicia. "That was pretty sweet of her."

"Yes it was, child," I say.

"Well, I know it was sweet of her now," says Henrietta, "but at the time, I was furious. Yes, Mama and I just rubbed each other the wrong way most of the time."

"Maybe it's because you two were more alike than you thought," says Felicia, with a sly grin on her face.

"Maybe." Henrietta goes back to weaving and keeps her mouth shut for a while. "There. All done," she says, showing off 'bout eight or nine of these cute little baskets.

"I love them, I just love them!" says Felicia, hopping up from the floor. She hangs them tiny baskets from her fingers and hurries on back to the room to hold 'em up against the wall. "These are perfect. Thank you so much, Henrietta."

"Well, don't tell anybody, but I kind of enjoyed it," she says. "Maybe one day I'll teach this new baby to make baskets. Boy, Mama sure would be happy to hear me say that."

"Why yes, I am mighty proud, girl."

"She always did want me to sew, or at least understand why she did." *If only I had done that before she got sick*, she's thinking. *Maybe things would have been different between us.*

"It's okay, baby," I tell her, though she can't hear a word. "Don't fret no more, Retta. I still love you."

Chapter 26

July

CASSANDRA MAE WHITE was born at six thirty this morning, July the fifth. She's as precious as she can be and a real pretty color, like malted milk. She got her mama's eyes and her daddy's mouth and her granddaddy's long legs just a-kicking all around.

They named the baby after Felicia's grandmama on her daddy's side, Cassandra Lewis, and EJ's grandmama, me, Essie Mae. I got to say, it's one o' the happiest times I ever had, even being in heaven and all. Jim and me standing there behind Felicia's shoulders yelling, "Push! Push!" She only has to push two or three times, sure 'nough, and out comes this beautiful little wrinkly baby. Oh, how I wish I was solid and could hold her now, but I'm here with her, and that's good enough for me.

The strangest thing happens when Henrietta and Eddie come in to see this new baby. Retta leans over and peeks in Felicia's arms, yes sir, takes one look at the pretty baby with her reddish-brown hair and just a-boo-hoos right there. She gets up and runs out the room just to keep from slobbering everywhere. Well now, EJ gets a look on his face like, *Mama, what in tar-nation got into you?* Then he runs out after her. Jim and me go too.

EJ finds his mama leaning over by the Coke-cola machine. There's a light flickering over her head flashing *50 cents, 50 cents.* He puts his arm on the back of her shoulders and says real sweet-like, "Mama? You okay? What's wrong?"

She wipes her nose with the back of her hand and looks up at him like a sad little girl. "Nothing's wrong, EJ. I'm just happy for you. I'm real happy." Then she puts her face in her hands and boo-hoos some more.

"You're not crying this way because you're happy, Mama. What is it?"

Retta stays silent for a while. Then she says, "I'm happy, EJ. There's nothing else to it." She leans in and gives him a kiss on the cheek. "Now get in there and be with your new baby. And that sweet wife of yours."

I think EJ can't be no happier if he'd just won a million dollars, but I know Retta ain't really said what she was thinking. She's plumb in shock at how the baby looks so white. *By the grace of God, Retta,* I'm thinking. *Child, get over this and get on with things.*

We follow EJ and he opens up the door real quiet and comes over to his wife and child. He sits down next to 'em on the hospital bed and pulls that little thing into his arms and looks her in the face. That baby's squinting up her eyes and yawning so cute. What a precious girl!

EJ takes off her little cap and runs his fingers over that red hair. Then he sings to her, "Cassandra Mae? I'm your daddy. Yes, I am. And I'm going to love you 'til the day I die and then some. Oh, we're gonna have some good times together. We're gonna play ball and color pictures. We're gonna see the world, you and me. You and me and your mama, that is."

He leans over to Felicia who's watching and gives her a real sweet kiss that seems to go on forever. That's when Jim and me back on up out the room to give 'em all some privacy.

That little baby girl's turning everybody's life upside down. Eddie's proud as a peacock and Henrietta like to turn into a whole new person, a sweet one, with that baby around. And Mister Lewis, Felicia's daddy, he just about the proudest man you ever want to see. He been hugging everybody and even sent boxes of fine cigars to everybody he knew. EJ had him send cigars to all my old men friends, too, including Jeffrey Lowes and his daddy down to the Sunnydale Farms and even Jackson Hemmingway in Columbia and his daddy over to the Isle o' Palms. Well now, turns out Jackson's so tickled I had me a great-grandbaby, he calls up EJ and they get to talking.

"You know, I'm heading back to Charleston for a meeting next week," Jackson tells him. "You think I could stop by and see you for a while? I sure would love to catch up—and see that new baby of yours."

Well, when he pulls on up to my lime-green house, his eyes fill with tears, remembering me, how I loved him and cared over him. Lord knows I raised that child for twelve whole years of his life. He spent plenty of time with me in that old house.

The look on Jackson's face says it all when he walks in the front door and sees Felicia holding that baby and EJ standing right next to her. "EJ, how are you? So good to see you," he says, shaking his hand like he might pull it plumb off. "And you're Felicia." He leans over his big belly to give her a kiss on the cheek. That boy sure did grow into a big fella, I tell you, what with him eating everything in sight when he was little. "I met you at Essie Mae's funeral. I'm Jackson Hemmingway."

Then he goo-goos over the baby and says she's the spittin' image of me. You know, I might have to agree with him on that one. Jackson, EJ, and Felicia sit down and while Cassandra Mae sleeps, they talk 'bout old times—and they talk 'bout me.

"She sure was a fine lady," says Jackson. "I loved her like my own mother." I'm real touched to hear him say that. I ain't never known he cared for me so much.

"I feel the same way 'bout you, baby," I tell him. My voice ain't nothing but the wind to him though.

"You have any more of her baskets?" he asks, looking up at the little crooked one I left sitting up over the fireplace. They say they do back in the closet. "Sure is a shame she's not at her stand anymore. I know she loved it."

"Not like her stand's there anyway," says EJ. "They tore it down right after she died. In fact, Miss Nancy and Miss Georgia aren't there either. Somebody bought the land on both sides of the highway. They're putting up a little strip mall now and some offices on the other side."

"You don't say," says Jackson. "What a shame."

Yes, it is. A crying shame, what it is.

"What's even worse," says Felicia, "there's hardly anywhere for basket ladies to set up anymore."

"Well, it's not like there's much sweetgrass left anyway," says EJ, going over and picking up the baby. She's starting to whine, sweet thing.

Jackson sits there real quiet. His forehead's all furrowed up, and he keeps rubbing his whiskers on the right side of his face. What's a-running through Jackson's mind are some powerful thoughts, sure 'nough, 'cause Jackson is a powerful person. Always was. Powerful personality. Powerful parents. And power begets power. Mm hmm, in them few minutes of quiet, things is beginning to happen, and Mount Pleasant as I once knew it ain't never gonna be the same.

PART III:

ain't no hoodoo goin' on up here

Chapter 27

Two Years Later, April

THAT LITTLE BABY IS GROWING LIKE A WEED. "Cassie" is what they calling her now. She's just shy of two years old, and has everybody wrapped 'round her finger. EJ and Felicia been living in my little house on Rifle Range Road, happy as they can be. Both of 'em done graduated from college, and EJ got himself a job working in a li-berry. It ain't what he wants to do forever, but it pays the bills right now. Felicia's a real good artist and paints full time. She sells her paintings of basket ladies and flowers and stuff over at the Hamlet Gallery in downtown Charleston.

Henrietta ain't working no more at that office. She ain't been real nice to the folks there and after a while, they weren't so nice to her back, so she quit. Problem was, Henrietta ain't the kind o' person to take to sitting around doing nothing. No, that girl got to have something to do. So Retta figured she should be 'round the baby more, and Felicia don't mind none. She's just a-painting fast as she can, and says it's nice to have somebody else in the house to watch after Cassie. Henrietta plays with the baby and when Cassie's napping, she takes to making baskets—so many, they piling up in the corner now.

I'm down here on Rifle Range a good bit these days. Little Cassie's clip-clopping 'round on the hardwood floors in her mama's big red shoes, carrying a sweetgrass basket over her shoulder just like a pocket book. She fills it with little books and toys and brings it on over to her grandmama, Henrietta, sewing by the fireplace.

"Thank you, baby," she says, taking the basket off her arm. "Now here's another one. Go fill it up for me." Cassie scoots off to the back of the house. That's when the phone rings and EJ picks it up. It's Jackson Hemmingway. Now, EJ ain't heard a word from Jackson after he paid a visit a couple years ago. Figured he was just another politician doing his thing. But this morning, he up and calls EJ out the blue.

"You still have an interest in politics?" Jackson asks him.

Looks like EJ's smile gonna eat up his whole face. "Yes sir, I do."

"I've been thinking about your grandmother and about the sweetgrass situation in Mount Pleasant. I know it's taken me a while to get back, but I think we can do something about it. Sound like something you'd be interested in?"

Well, it sure 'nough is. EJ's right beside himself, jumpin' up and hootin' and hollerin' when he hangs up the phone. I sure am excited too; and so's Jim and Mama and everybody else when I tell 'em up in heaven 'bout what's fixing to take place on Earth. Jackson's agreed to help EJ start one of them non-profit organizations to protect the history and culture of sweetgrass basket weavers. All sorts of Gullah traditions in danger of being lost is gonna be protected. Hallelujah!

Soon enough, EJ gets all excited and quits his job at the li-berry. He turns that little green house on Rifle Range into the home base for The Grass Roots Society. Ain't that cute? I thought it was clever of him. Come up with that name all himself.

Now EJ wants to have a meeting with the sweetgrass basket ladies in town to find out how he can help. He looks up Miss Georgia, she's moved over next to the Piggly Wiggly. He finds Miss Nancy over by the Presbyterian church. Her son helped her pick up and move her stand when the developers come. Now, she got a heater in that little back room of hers for when it gets too cold. I tell you the truth now, ain't nobody can weave when their fingers get all numb.

Miss Georgia calls up a bunch o' other basket weavers and pulls 'em together for EJ to talk to—brings everybody over to the house on a Saturday afternoon. I figure I'm one, too, so I show up for the meeting to give my two cents.

Now, here's the thing 'bout weavers. Don't many like giving interviews much. Lot of 'em ain't friendly like me neither. But they all know EJ's my grandbaby, and everybody's right excited that somebody's gonna stand up for 'em now. I tell you, one by one them ladies walk on up to the porch dressed in all their Sunday finest—blue, red, green, purple—you'd think it's a hat party or something with all them pretty hats perched up on their heads. I reckon somebody told 'em they'd be getting pictures taken, too, maybe for the newspaper. But ain't nobody from *The Post and*

Courier here. Ain't no *Moultrie News* neither. EJ just wants to get to know 'em and find out what they need.

"What we need is more sweetgrass," says Nancy after taking a sip of her sweet iced tea. "My son can't keep goin' out the state to bring me mine. He got his own job and family he's tendin' to now."

"Ain't that the truth," says Eartha Lee. "But I got to have me a place to set my stand. Man come by yesterday said, 'Find another place.' Lord have mercy, I'm too old. I ain't got time for this."

"This is good," says EJ. "Keep your ideas coming." Felicia's over there, taking notes real quiet-like. Her hand's just a-scribbling every word these ladies say.

Georgia's over there in the corner, nodding her head so hard I think it might jiggle off. In her low grumble she says, "Don't wanna pay no sales tax neither. I been readin' 'bout it in the paper these days. Lord help us if they make us pay. Gonna be even harder to make a livin' on baskets." Miss Georgia do sell a lot of hers, so I reckon she'll be giving a good chunk of money away.

"How 'bout let's get us some good tourist traffic all year long, not just in the spring, summer, and fall," says Charletta Jones, taking off her pink hat and scratching her head. She sits over there by Hamlin Road. She been there ever since I known her.

"I got one, I got one!" I yell, raising my hand. "I wish folks would understand how hard it is to make a basket—how long it takes, too, so they know why the baskets cost so dad-gum much. I used to get tired having to haggle 'bout my prices. I'd just soon send 'em on up the road. Can I get a 'amen'?" I throw my hands up in the air.

Shucks, ain't nobody heard me. It's a good point, though.

EJ and Felicia's just as pleased as they can be and the basket ladies too. For the first time I seen 'em excited 'bout something. Feel like some things actually gonna happen for 'em. It's a good feeling I tell you, having something to look forward to. Before we leave, EJ makes all us ladies honorary free members of The Grass Roots Society. Then I go on back up to heaven and make Mama a member too.

May

EJ got to working real hard, talking to Jackson on the phone every now and again for advice and putting his plan together. He'd sit there at the kitchen table with papers stacked up all 'round him, so him and Felicia and Cassie had to start taking their meals over by the fireplace instead. After while, it was pretty clear EJ couldn't do it all himself no more. No sir, that boy was gonna need some help.

Turns out, Henrietta couldn't stay unemployed for long. She was there in the house with all that Grass Roots Society work going on, so she dug her hands in and got to helping. She's a real hard worker, too, but EJ found out quick why she weren't liked so much at that office she'd been in. Yes sir, after 'bout the fifth time o' her snapping at him and coming over and correcting something he's working on, EJ has 'bout has all he can take.

"Mama," he says, clenching his fists together. "You have got to stop or this isn't going to work."

"Oh, I see." She cuts her eyes at him. "You think you're all better than me now, don't you. Yessa boss. Anythin' you say, boss."

"Mama, this house is too small for both of us to be in it, and since it *is* my house, how about you go on back home and work from there?"

Well, wouldn't you know, Henrietta's big bottom lip gets to shaking and her eyes all moist. She sure is sensitive nowadays since the baby been born. "Fine," she huffs, standing up real quick and grabbing her purse. "I know when I'm not wanted."

She looks down at Cassie who's reaching up to hand her a book. "Book. Book. Boooook!" she says, trying to get her attention. Henrietta wants so bad to hold her but just busts out crying and runs on out the door.

Lord have mercy, Felicia flat tore up EJ's hide when Henrietta left like that. "Look at what you did to your mama," and "How can you kick your own flesh and blood out of the house?" After while, EJ don't know which one is worse, working with Henrietta or having Felicia mad at him. Well, I reckon I know which one was worse—he called up his mama and asked her to come back.

Chapter 28

August

LAST COUPLE MONTHS, EJ and Henrietta been working real hard together, trying to be real sweet to each other too. They started lobbying for changes in the local government—met with developers and town council people in Mount Pleasant and with Jackson Hemmingway's help, you just won't believe what they done. It took a little while, but Henrietta found a developer to donate land to The Grass Roots Society. They gonna use it to grow sweetgrass. That's it. Just to grow sweetgrass and nothing else. Don't that just beat all? There's a nice piece o' land down by the Cooper River Bridge they gonna turn into a regular sweetgrass farm. It's taking lots of doing, seeing as special farming folks got to be brought in to figure out how to grow it there.

Next thing Henrietta done was talk property owners on 17 to lease the town of Mount Pleasant that little strip o' land that sets right up 'gainst the highway. Yes sir, ain't nobody got to fear losing their stand no more. Hallelujah, Jim and me can't believe what we seeing. I ain't never been so proud of Henrietta in my whole life. And she's happy too. Working close with EJ like that's made her happier than I ever seen her. She sure is working hard to make him proud of her.

And EJ? I'm real proud o' him too. He's running the business part of The Society and getting to be real respected, sure 'nough. He visits all sorts of organizations and school groups, talking 'bout Gullah culture and how important it is to keep it alive.

And Felicia ain't about to be left out neither. She got up with her artsy friends and's working on putting together a festival. If the first one comes off good, there's gonna be one every year right smack dab in the middle of winter to try and get more tourists to come 'round. She talked with the mayors of Charleston and Mount Pleasant and the South Carolina Department for Tourists or something, and they helped her work out a plan. She's pulling together storytellers and artists and singers, poets and chefs and of course, sweetgrass basket ladies. Yes sir, the whole works. And she been calling on all sorts of businesses, too, to get 'em to donate money and be sponsors. And you'll never believe who she called on one morning.

"May I speak with Jeffrey Lowes, please? Hi, Mr. Lowes, this is Felicia White with The Grass Roots Society. I'm EJ's wife—you know, Essie Mae's grandson?" She went on to tell him 'bout the project and asked him would La Belle Fleur be interested in becoming a member and sponsoring the festival this year. He said yes and he was so honored to be asked, so he come on over to meet with her.

Now after my funeral, Jeffrey's kinda kept to himself. He'd come out the closet, and people ain't talked to him much that day, what with nobody knowing what to say to a man holding another man's hand. Plus, he was grieving 'cause I was dead. Miss Nancy'd offered to sell him some baskets every month, same as I done, and he's been pickin 'em up reg'lar, sure 'nough. And EJ's had lunch with him couple times just to see how he's holding up. But this was before The Grass Roots Society got started. Jeffrey ain't known a thing 'bout that.

I'm waiting for Jeffrey when he pulls on up in the driveway. He has to sit still for a second when he sees that big Grass Roots Society sign stuck up 'gainst my fresh-painted lime-green house.

"Sweet Essie Mae," Jeffrey says on his breath as he walks up. Little Cassie runs out the front door when he comes in, and Henrietta runs out after her, threatening to pop her little fanny if she don't come back inside. Felicia greets Jeffrey at the door. "Hey there! Come on in, I'll get you some iced tea. How've you been?"

"Good. Real good, thanks. Boy, I know this house so well," Jeffrey says, "and I love what you've done with it."

Felicia stops and looks around at the walls. "Well, there's a lot more to do, but we've painted and fixed the yard some. We're happy here."

EJ's sitting at the kitchen table, yapping on the telephone. He's shuffling the papers all stacked up next to him. When he gets off he comes over and shakes Jeffrey's hand. "Jeffrey Lowes. You've probably spent as much time here as I have. Nice to see you again."

"Good to see you too, EJ," he says, smiling and running his hand over the back of my sofa.

"Have you met my daughter?" EJ asks him.

"Not yet, but I'm pretty sure she skimmed me on the way in."

"Mama, come here! Jeffrey, this here is Essie Mae's great-granddaughter, Cassie Mae," he says when Henrietta carries her kicking and wiggling in the door. That child is just a-giggling.

"Hi, Miss Henrietta. What a beautiful granddaughter you have. Hey there, Miss Cassie Mae. She's beautiful. Truly," says Jeffrey.

"Uh-huh," Retta says, nodding in his direction. Seems pretty rude, tell the truth.

"Well Jeffrey, how's the flower business these days?" asks Felicia, filling in Henrietta's quiet space.

"Can't complain," he says. "I've been doing a lot of weddings lately. Just did a fabulous one down at the William-Aiken House for the governor's daughter. It was unbelievable with roses and orchids . . . we even had wrought-iron chandeliers hanging from the live oaks."

"And Victor?" asks EJ. "How's he doing? Still enjoying that new job?"

"Just fine, thanks for asking," says Jeffrey, looking a little uncomfortable talking about his boyfriend.

"Good grief," Henrietta says real low. She's over in the corner, trying to weave a basket and eavesdrop at the same time. Her nose keeps a-twitching, and I know that ain't good. Whenever that girl gets to twitching, better look out, 'cause there's a storm a-brewing, sure 'nough.

"Tell him we said hello," says Felicia. "I don't think I've seen Victor since the funeral. Hey, we ought to have you two over some time."

EJ looks over and sees his mama's face. He remembers his daddy calling her "old-fashioned" so he says real quick-like, "Uh, I know Essie Mae would be happy you're here. She'd be real happy you're thinking of helping us out."

"I am so thrilled you've started this group, EJ. It's so, soooo important. And I'll tell you a secret," he says, leaning in to EJ real close. Henrietta's ears perk and her back shoots up so straight she 'bout falls out her chair. "I know some people in this town. A lot of powerful people. You just say the word and let me know what you need. I can find a way to get it done."

EJ ain't sure what to say to that. Has to let it sink in on him a second or two. "I'll keep that in mind," he says, putting out his hand for him to shake it. "Like I said, we just appreciate anything you can do to help."

"My pleasure. Well, it's been so nice to see you all and to see Essie Mae's house again. I miss her so much. EJ?" He nods at him and EJ nods back. "Henrietta? Nice to see you again." Jeffrey backs up toward the door and sticks his fingers up next to his head like he's talking on a telephone. "I'll talk to you soon, Felicia. Call me and let me know when and where you need me."

After Jeffrey shuts the door, a big ol' green monster swells inside Henrietta, and she pipes up. "I always knew that guy was a fruitcake," she says, scowling up her face. "Don't know why Mama loved him so much. He just gets on my last nerve. Oh, and he just lo-oved Mama. Well, why wouldn't he? She doted on him like he was her very own or something."

Well, there it is. I never knew Henrietta was jealous of Jeffrey. Not in a million years would I 'a guessed that! It might sound real naïve, but I swear it's the truth. She was the most independent child I ever seen and didn't seem to need me much a'tall. Pretty much handled her own affairs. Is it possible Henrietta's been jealous of all them children I watched over the years? There were a lot of 'em too. Great God in heaven, I just keep learning new stuff 'bout that girl.

Chapter 29

September

EARLY ONE MORNING, EJ AND FELICIA GO RUN DOWNTOWN to talk with a restaurant owner, so Henrietta comes by to watch little Miss Cassie. She's sitting at the kitchen table trying to finish up on some paperwork when Cassie comes a-running by like the speed o' lightning. That child's buck naked as a jaybird and got her clothes thrown out all over the floor.

"Cassandra Mae White, you come here and put your clothes back on this minute!" Henrietta don't hear nothing back. Me neither. It's real, real quiet, and that ain't what you wanna hear when a baby's naked in the back of the house. "Cassie? Cassie, come back here!"

Henrietta gets up to look for her. She walks on in to Cassie's room and peeks 'round the closet door. Then she looks over in her mama and daddy's room, but the girl ain't nowhere. Then she sees the bathroom door—it's shut tight. Retta smiles and walks up real slow, trying not to let the floorboards creak. Then she grabs on the doorknob and turns it real quick.

"Boo!" Henrietta yells, pushing it open. Cassie squeals, jumping 'bout a foot in the air. Then Retta notices there's the hole in the ground next to the commode. And over by the tub is a big white loose floor tile. Cassie looks just like the cat what ate the canary sitting there naked next to it and holding a little black book marked *Leona*.

"Whatcha got there, honey?" Retta asks her. The baby smiles and hands it over, hoping she won't get no spanking.

"Well, my goodness," she says, opening up the pages and flipping through 'em. "Looks like you found your great-great-auntie's diary." That's when my stomach sinks. Lord, I remember it now.

Back in the early 1940s, there was this real bad outbreak o' flu bug to hit Charleston. Lots of folks was dying from it, sure 'nough. There was plenty o' root doctors coming out the woodwork, too, 'cause when people is dying, folks call on every power they got. There was something they used back then called "Life Everlasting." I guess it was called that 'cause when you used it, you'd get life everlasting one way or the other, either down on Earth or up here in heaven.

Well, Auntie Leona, she got the flu real bad and was awful sick—terrible sick, so she found a way to get hold of some of that root medicine. Well, what she thought was pure juice, turned out to be chest rub instead, made with Life Everlasting plus whiskey, lemons, and turpentine. She drank lots of it so it'd work faster on her, but in two days, poor Leona was dead.

Well, after Auntie died, Mama and I was cleaning out her belongings, and I come 'cross this little book o' hers. Had all sorts of potions and chants and instructions on doing her New Orleans voodoo. It told her secrets 'bout the magic she done, even 'bout putting Mama and Daddy together. So I tucked it up under my shirt and carried it on home. I ain't never wanted that thing to fall into the wrong hands, so I pulled up a loose floor tile in the bathroom and buried it there. I tell you the truth, I forgot about it all them years 'til now. And the one person I 'spect I'd never wanted to find that book done found it now, sure 'nough. Henrietta don't know it yet, but she's the most powerful person in Charleston and Mount Pleasant, hands down.

Chapter 30

MAMA USED TO TELL ME that a body could be controlled by bad spirits taking over—that's what the Gullahs believed anyway. So Mama'd keep little bits of wadded-up newspaper in our shoes thinking the spirits would have to read each and every word 'fore messing with us. Shucks. When Henrietta found that ol' book of Leona's, I'd 'a given my right arm to have some newspaper wadded up in her shoes. Now Henrietta's got that book in her hands, it's like the devil himself done crawled up in her to roost. Since she ain't good friends with Jesus, I reckon that's pretty much what happened to her.

Henrietta's drinking some coffee and reading the Sunday newspaper one morning when all a sudden she gets to cursing real bad. "Diggity-dang gay man!" Well, that ain't really what she says, but her words are just too awful to repeat. Yes sir, Retta's just a-spittin' her coffee 'cross the table. In all my years on Earth I never heard her talk that way.

"What in the world?" says Eddie, standing up real quick and grabbing for his napkin. "What is wrong with you?"

"You see this?" She stabs the paper with her finger. Eddie looks down at the front page and sees a real nice picture of EJ and Mister Jeffrey Lowes shaking hands. The headline reads, "Local Florist to Head Society Fundraising Efforts."

"What is he thinking?" she yells, standing up and pacing the kitchen in her robe. "Your son just put a [gay man] in charge of raising money for The Grass Roots Society, Edmund! Who the [boopity-boop] is going to give money for African-Americans to a white [gay man]?!"

"Henrietta! That's enough! Here, let me see it." Retta's words are so bad, Eddie grabs the newspaper out of her hands. "It says here Jeffrey's been doing a great job of finding new members, Henrietta. Big ones too. Look here, the Rothschilds, the Fairbanks, wow!" Eddie closes his lips and his eyes moves back and forth over the words. He flips to the next page and keeps on reading.

Henrietta walks over to the counter and picks up tiny little crumbs with her fingernails. Then she crushes 'em up good and flicks the dust off into the air. I can hear what she's thinking, and let's just say you're glad you can't hear it. The evil thoughts to come into that girl's head are so ugly, I'm ashamed to be her mama. She's torn up bad over *her* boy, EJ, taking kindly to somebody else. "Didn't I do a real good job for him?" and "What in the world would make EJ pick Jeffrey over me?" And there it is. I see it now. Henrietta feels just like she did as a little girl with me doting on Jeffrey. Oh, how I wish I had known 'bout that back then. I sure 'nough would 'a done something 'bout it.

Henrietta's been studying that little black book of Leona's every night—memorizing every last word. Can't wait to try something out. She read all about Leona bringing Mama and Daddy together and a lot of other good things she done with her magic. But that ain't what interests Henrietta. No, Retta wants to know everything she can 'bout the bad stuff. I was thinking she'd turned over a new leaf after I died, but sure 'nough, the Henrietta I always knew just can't help but showing herself. And with the devil all roosted up in her, I reckon there ain't much she can do 'bout that, anyway.

Toward the middle of the book, if I remember it right, Leona wrote of the time she made poor ol' Martha Sewell's teeth fall out. Martha was Mama's cousin twice removed and was married to a man named Wilbur Sewell. Now Mister Wilbur was a fine-looking man. Had a farm up the way in Seven Mile and worked in it every day so his skin was dark like burnt toast, and his body was bulky in all the right places.

Now Auntie, she didn't go with men much, mostly 'cause they was scared of her. But not ol' Wilbur Sewell. He was always just as nice as he could be to her. Didn't mean nothing by it, though, seeing as he was married and all. But his wife, Martha, ain't known that, and she thought she seen Leona making eyes at him in the feed n' seed when he was picking up some hog slop. Well, Miss Martha started bad-mouthing Auntie and calling her real bad names for a woman back then, so when Auntie Leona caught wind of it, she gone and whooped up some hoodoo on her.

See, folks was getting together for a fish fry at our house. Yes sir, I remember it like yesterday. Mama had a big spread on the table with red rice and corn on the cob, and the first time Cousin Martha bit down on it, every last tooth in her head falled out—every last one. Poor ol' Martha ain't never said another word 'bout Auntie Leona after that. Auntie was mighty proud of what she done too—ain't even felt the smallest twinge of guilt neither.

Looks like Retta's got some Leona in her, I tell you what.

Monday morning, Henrietta come storming in EJ's house just mad as a hornet 'cause she'd had some time to sit and stew. She found EJ in his bedroom not even finished with tucking his shirt in.

"Edmund James White, have you got marbles in your head?"

The baby and Felicia hear the fire in her voice, so they stay hiding in the nursery with the door shut.

"Mama," EJ says, spinning 'round to see her in the doorway. "What's wrong? Something wrong?"

"I'll say there's something wrong," she says, coming inches from his face. "Are you crazy? You made Jeffrey Lowes the head of fundraising? Why didn't you speak to me about this first? Do you *know* what this is going to do to the Society?"

"Mama, calm down," EJ says, passing her and walking up the hall to the kitchen. "Jeffrey's a great resource for us. He's brought us so many sponsors already, I'm just amazed. And he knows lots of people in town—he's a florist, for Pete's sake—does all the big-wigs' events."

Henrietta stays right on his heels and sits down at the table, breathing in real deep.

"He's perfect for the job, Mama, and you ought to be thankful he's helping us so much. Now what has gotten into you?"

Henrietta's still. She watches him pour himself a nice cup of black coffee and then sit down. "EJ, he's gay," she says, real slow and in a real low voice.

"So?"

"So? Are you kidding?" Henrietta pushes up her sleeves. "Do you want to destroy everything we've worked for in one fell swoop?"

"Oh, come on, now. Don't you think you're being just a little overdramatic?"

Henrietta bites her lip hard and holds her fists under the table. "I am not overreacting, EJ. I'm being practical, and thank God, because it looks like I'm the only one here using her head."

"Okay, Mama. So he's gay. What do you think that means exactly? You think he's going to hit on all the sponsors? Is that it? He's going to have orgies and seduce the mayor and the governor and anybody else who comes in his path?"

"No, EJ," she says, taking a deep breath and trying to calm down. "It's not that. He's . . . he's . . ."

"What is he, Mother? White?" EJ's getting mad now. "Is that what this is about? Oh, I don't even believe it! I thought you were all past that mess . . ."

"No, no, no, it's not that he's *white*," Henrietta's backpedaling real quick. "It's just that, well, I don't know that *he's* the right person to represent the Society is all. I mean, wouldn't it make more sense to have a black person who actually knows something about African-Americans to be the one soliciting money for them?"

"Mother, so far, neither you or me—African-Americans mind you—have done as good a job attracting sponsors as Jeffrey."

"Hmmph. Well, I can see this conversation is going nowhere. You sure do have a hard head, EJ," she's wagging her finger in his face, "and you just better hope Jeffrey Lowes doesn't mess things up, 'cause when he does—and I say *when* he does—don't come running to me to help you fix things."

Henrietta flies out the front door and slams it hard enough to shake the house. When she gets home, she picks up that book of Leona's and goes to studying. Lord have mercy, she gonna make darn sure poor Jeffrey Lowes is gonna screw things up.

Chapter 31

JIM AND ME ARE OVER AT THE FISH POND near our house in heaven, just a-setting here with our rods, when a dust storm kicks on up the lane. When it gets closer, we see it ain't just dust, but Auntie Leona running faster than a buck in hunting season.

"Essie Mae! Essie Mae! She shouts at me, trying to catch her breath. The beads 'round her neck jump up and down, smacking her in the nose. "I'm so sorry, I just found out. I feel just awful!"

"Awful 'bout what?" I ask her.

"Your mama just told me 'bout Henrietta finding my diary. I came here just as fast as I could."

Yes sir, Mama and Daddy know all about Leona's meddling in their love life by now, but they get a real kick out of it, sure 'nough. I ain't rightly sure why Leona's all a-fearing and having a fit, though. This is heaven, and folks just don't get riled up like they used to.

"I feel like it's my fault," she says. "I can only imagine what that girl's gonna do—got a temper just like I did. Lord 'a-mercy."

"Leona, now calm down. It's just as much my fault as yours," I tell her, getting up from my seat. "Why, if I'd burned that book 'stead of buryin' it under the bathroom floor, she wouldn't have it in her hands today."

"Well, I s'pose," she says. "I just wish there was somethin' I could do."

Daddy Jim sits there real quiet just a-watching the two of us and scratching his chin. Then it comes to me.

"Daddy," I say, turning to him. "How is it you sat and talked with me for all them years on Earth? You reckon one of us could do that—go and talk with Henrietta?"

Jim shakes his head. "Sorry, Mama. You can go down there and all, but she ain't gonna hear you or see you 'less she asks to."

"Is that right?" I ask.

"That's right."

"So there ain't a thing we can do to keep Henrietta from puttin' the hoodoo on anybody who crosses her?"

" 'Fraid not," says Jim.

"Well, I just can't sit by and do nothin'," says Auntie Leona, wringing her hands. "I'm goin' down there and see what I can do."

"Suit yourself," says Jim, throwing back a brim and then casting his rod out again. I go on back to the house to sit in my rocker and look down on Earth to watch the fireworks fixing to start.

Auntie Leona always was a powerful presence. She's a real intense lady, so much you can feel her just a-being in the room with you. I think it used to tickle her, knowing that. Must be driving her crazy being down there now with Henrietta, trying to get her attention and Retta not having a clue she's there.

"Henrietta! Woo-hoo, look at me!" Leona's yelling, waving her arms in Retta's face. "Can't you see me? I'm right here!"

Henrietta slumps up against the headboard on her fluffy bed and pulls a pilla up under her knees. "Auntie Leona, you devil," she says, flipping to the next page. She can't see Leona hovering right over her head and acting like a fool. Leona bounces from one side of the room to the next, trying to knock over the lamp or a stack of magazines. Nothing. She pounds her fists on her chest and screams and hollers just as loud as she can, but Henrietta just keeps on reading.

"Mr. Lowes, Mr. Lowes," says Henrietta, smiling and sitting up straight. "You sure are in love with your sweetie pie, now aren't you? It would be a terrible shame if all of a sudden he went straight." Henrietta cackles and slams the book shut. Her mind is racing now that she has a plan. And let me tell you it ain't a nice one neither. Poor ol' Jeffrey. Not that I approve of him having a lover, but he sure is 'bout to hit some heartache.

Henrietta gets up out the bed and tucks that little book in her pocket. Auntie ain't about to give up, so she stands there 'gainst the wall just a-pushing and pushing on that little light switch, hoping if the lights go out, it'll give her a good scare. I wonder if it would 'a worked too, 'cause 'fore she has a chance to do it, Henrietta comes on over and flips it herself. Then she walks on out the room humming "When the Saints Go Marching In" and leaves Auntie Leona in the dark.

⌣

Jeffrey Lowes is real fond of Miss Susanne Maybree. Since she's got her own marketing business, he decided to use her to market the big fundraising event he's planning for The Grass Roots Society in two weeks' time. She designed a cute little logo with a basket on it and put ads in the paper and all for what he named the "Sweetgrass Soiree." It's gonna be a fine party, sure enough, with music and dancing and a live auction too. I ain't never seen one of them, so I'm getting right excited 'bout going.

Well, Miss Susanne come on over one day to show Jeffrey an ad she's fixing to put in the paper.

"What's this?" she asks, pointing to his front door covered in dirt and ashes. Jeffrey don't know, but cleans it up real quick. Looks like Henrietta's already been there.

After while, Mister Victor comes home early from work. He's a butcher at that nice shop in the center of Mount Pleasant, and he'd been having a nice day 'til all a sudden he'd gone to feeling queasy. Looking at all that raw meat and blood just weren't sitting right with him none, so he cleaned up and come on home.

"Hey, Vic. This is a surprise," Jeffrey says, standing up from the sofa. "What are you doing home so early?" Jeffrey comes over and tries to give Victor a kiss on the cheek, but he turns away.

"No get too close," he says. "I no want you get sick."

"Oh, are you feeling bad? Here, come sit down," says Jeffrey, feeling his forehead then walking him over to the sofa. "Susanne and I were just looking at an ad for the Soiree."

"Hola, Susanne." Victor gives a tired wave.

"You want some hot tea? It might make you feel better," says Jeffrey, rubbing his hands together. "Susanne? You want some?"

"That sounds nice," she says, crossing her legs in her short red skirt.

Jeffrey walks on back to the kitchen and Victor closes his eyes and takes in a deep breath. "Sorry I such a bad host," he says. "Do you mind I put my head back?"

"No, not at all. In fact, here," she says, pulling a pillow out from behind her back and walking it over to him. "I don't need this, but you look like you could use it."

"Gracias."

Susanne puts her hand behind Victor's head and lifts it up. Her perfume drifts up his nose, and when she tucks that little pillow back behind him, he opens his eyes just in time to see her bosoms bouncing up and down 'neath her blouse.

Lord have mercy.

It don't take too long, a week maybe, 'fore Victor's coming home late and sleeping on the couch. Jeffrey don't know what's wrong with him neither.

"Are you feeling okay?" he asks him. "Did I do something wrong? Talk to me, for Pete's sake." Victor just keeps quiet and brushes him off. How's he ever gonna tell him he's falling for a woman—and not just any, but Jeffrey's best girl?

"I guess them bosoms' what done it, 'cause poor ol' Victor ain't known what hit him. Sure looks like he got the hoodoo whooped on him," I'm telling Leona. "I reckon it's the beginning of a lot of heartache for my sweet Jeffrey. And don't you just know Henrietta's behind it all—every last bit."

"I tried to stop her, Essie Mae. I really did," says Leona, letting me pour her a fresh cup of lemonade. We both can see what's a-happening in Victor's head. "I just don't know what else I could 'a done. Well, it's all over now. The ball's in motion." She just sits there on the sofa, staring 'cross the floor and clucking her tongue.

"And you're sure it was Henrietta what got to Mister Victor?" I ask, sitting down next to her.

"Oh, I'm sure. I was there when she drove over and put the hex on him. Not a dad-gum thing I could do about it neither."

"Well then, what's done is done," I say. "Maybe that's all she's gonna do."

"Are you kiddin'? Oh, no, trust me. Once she sees him straightenin' up just a little bit, that girl's gonna be drunk with power. Lord have mercy, I know what it feels like too." Leona's eyes cross a little bit and she rolls her head back.

"Well, can't you work some counter-magic on her, Leona? You know, to reverse what she done?" I think it's a real smart question if you ask me.

"I wish I could, Essie Mae. I sure do. But we're up here in heaven, girl. Ain't no hoodoo goin' on up here. No ma'am."

"Hmm. I guess you're right."

Me and Auntie Leona are just a-sitting here sipping our lemonade and staring at our glasses. With not a-one good idea 'tween the two of us, we ain't quite sure what to do 'cept to sit back a-watching and waiting.

Chapter 32

November

IT'S ALMOST TIME FOR THE SWEETGRASS SOIREE. They're getting the Hibernian Hall on Meeting Street set up real nice and pretty. Jeffrey's minding every last detail from the flowers to the food and the music. He got the Amen Singers to sing old-time gospels and then the Beachin' Groove is gonna come in and finish out the night. Two fancy chefs from Charleston gonna serve up real good Lowcountry fixings too.

Yes sir, folks is starting to sign up left and right, and the guest list is reading like a Who's Who and a Who Ain't Nobody A'tall. The mayors of Charleston, Mount Pleasant, and Summerville signed up, plus lots of them state politicians too, including Jackson Hemmingway. The governor and his wife are gonna be there—Jeffrey's real excited 'bout that. And there's even talk that a senator or two might come along. Well now, mix that up with a whole bunch of old sweetgrass basket ladies in big ol' hats and what you got is a fine time waiting to happen, I tell you what.

Miss Susanne's been coming 'round to Jeffrey's house just 'bout every day 'fore the party. She shows him banners she's had printed up and asks him questions o' where he wants the signs and all, then they pull out clothes they're thinking of wearing for the big event.

"Oh now, that's to die for, Susanne! You just *have* to wear that one. You look like a regular vixen, mee-ooow."

"What, this old thing? I could never wear it," she says. "I won't look half as nice as you. How about this one?"

"Oh, now maybe that would work too. Go put it on." And back and forth they go.

It's two days 'fore the party now, and they finally got it right, so they decided to get their outfits cleaned. Mister Victor said he'd drop 'em off along with his tux. Well, on his way, he stops at a Burger King parking lot and Lord have mercy, he's pulls out Miss Susanne's dress. He slips it under his nose and tries to inhale every last bit o' her smell. Oh, now, that boy's got it bad, sure 'nough.

Over on Rifle Range Road, EJ and Felicia tuck Cassie in her crib. She's wearing a cute pair of pajamas with ladybugs all over 'em, and her hair's still damp 'cause she's just out of the bathtub. There's a little puddle of water settling on the floor tile covering the hole where Leona's diary used to be. "Now I lay me down to sleep," they say, thanking God for all sorts of things. "Bless Mama and Daddy and Granddaddy and Grandmama . . ."

And over in West Ashley, in a nice brick house with the bedroom light on, Henrietta's holding her black sequined dress up in front of the mirror. She smiles at herself and puts out her hand. "Well, how do you do, Mr. Mayor? So pleased to meet you." She gives a big toothy grin. "I hope you're having a fine time. Will you be spending a lot of money tonight? I bet you will. That's wonderful. Oh, the party? No, no, that was Jeffrey Lowes. He put all this together."

The smile slips off Henrietta's face and she hangs her dress back up in the closet. Then she walks over to the bed, looks 'round to see if Eddie's coming, and when he ain't she pulls out that little black book o' Leona's and carries it with her to the bathroom. She latches the door and then turns the water on in the tub. It's a real big tub, too, so the water can run a while without Eddie wondering why she's been in there so long.

Henrietta pulls the lid down soft and then sits on the commode. She flips through the pages then stops way in the back on a page what starts, *These are things I never tried, but I know they work, because I've seen what happened . . .*

Eddie is downstairs making a late-night sandwich and listening to the water rushing upstairs. He walks 'round to the sofa, takes a bite of roast beef, and flips on the TV, figuring he has 'bout half an hour 'til Henrietta's ready for bed.

Up here in heaven, Auntie flies in the front door, comes a-running to me, and 'bout knocks me over. I'm at the kitchen sink washing up after supper, and the dish I'm holding falls out my hand and breaks. "Auntie Leona, what is it? What is it now?" I ask her.

"It's worse than I thought," she says, panting and grabbing her chest. "Henrietta's in a bad way. She's plannin' some stuff I ain't never even tried myself!"

"Well, that might not be so bad, right?"

"Oh, no," she says, shaking her head 'til the bobby pins pop

193

out her hair. "It's bad. All of it, I promise. Henrietta's got some evil intentions, girl. And with my powerful voodoo, what in the dickens gonna happen at that sweetgrass party? I just can't even watch."

"Well, you're *gonna* watch," I tell her. "'Cause we're goin'. Right Jim?"

Daddy Jim perks his head up. He's been sitting at the table listening the whole time but acting like he ain't. He looks up at me and shakes his head.

"Oh, Mama," he says, putting his face in his hand.

"That's right. You, me, Leona, Mama, and Daddy—we're all gonna be there, and anybody else who wants to come too."

"But that ain't gonna help, Essie Mae," says Leona. "You seen me tryin' to get to Henrietta. A breeze was more powerful than me." Leona sits down and starts pulling her beads through her fingers. I'm just sitting here, scratching my chin and staring out the window.

"Might be somethin' we can do," says Jim, all a sudden. I straighten up real quick.

"Really? What is it?" asks Leona.

"Well, I ain't never got too good at it myself, but well," he looks like he's struggling, "Essie Mae, you 'member that one summer when all them baskets kept endin' up on the dirt? And you was just a-cussin' and fumin'? Well, it weren't the wind what knocked 'em down like I told you. I was just kinda bored and got to tryin' to make things move—worked, I reckon."

"Oh, Jim, really?" Auntie Leona comes up behind Jim, hugs him 'round the neck and keeps kissing him on the cheek. "Can you show us how?"

"You little booger, Daddy. Yeah, show us how," I say, grabbing his hand.

"Well, I reckon it can't hurt," he says, pushing us off and getting up from the table. He turns to us and says, "Well, come on now. Go get everybody together. Time's a-wasting."

Leona and me are excited as two cats on a fishing boat, and we run like lightning through the pecan trees over to Mama and Daddy's house.

Chapter 33

IN THE LOWCOUNTRY, when we would have family reunions, we'd pull everybody together and have a big ol' oyster roast with lots of drawn butter and fried shrimp caught fresh that day. Folks I ain't never seen before from all over would come out the woodwork. "Oh, so you're my mama's second cousin twice removed? I see. Nice to meet ya," or, "Why, ain't you a spittin' image of your granddaddy on your daddy's side." Well now, take that and multiply it by a hundred. That's how crazy it is here in heaven. Auntie Leona and me done pulled every relative and ancestor of ours together to learn how to make things move on Earth again.

Now that the visiting has quieted down, all you can hear is the birds singing in the trees. We're in this big field o' wildflowers overlooking Mama and Daddy's pecan trees. Sure is pretty here. Think of the prettiest place on Earth you ever seen. Well, this is nicer, I tell you what.

Jim's strolling from person to person giving everybody a lesson. I love watching him talk with our African ancestors. Each one of 'em sure is beautiful to me with cloth wrapped around 'em in nice bright colors. Their hair and skin is real natural. Just beautiful people, I tell you. And the accents! Lord have mercy, I thought Gullah was pretty. I ain't heard nothing 'til I listened to my great-great-great-grandmama talk. Sound make me wanna fall in a trance.

Now, I got to hand it to Daddy Jim, 'cause I know this is hard for him. He ain't never been one to talk much, 'specially not to bunches of people at a time.

"Mama, Daddy, Leona," I say. "C'mon now. Let's go and help Jim. He taught us what he knows—ain't no reason we can't go on out and teach this stuff too. Time's a-wastin', you know. Sweetgrass party'll be here 'fore we know it."

Mama and Daddy head off down by the river, and Leona takes off in the other direction toward the trees. I'd say there's a few hundred people here, but ain't all of 'em going to the party. No sir, that'd be too many. Most folks here are just looking to make things move again, is all.

I walk on over to this fella dressed in a colored skirt up to his knees. He's tall as the dickens and got lots of colored beads hanging loose 'round his neck. I'm guessing he's from Africa.

"I'm Essie Mae. You on my mama's side or my daddy's side?" I ask him.

He nods.

"Okay then." I start miming the lesson with my hands and

body. I'm moving my arms this way and that-a-way, and he seems real intent on me. Studying me real hard, sure 'nough. He picks up quick on what I'm doing and follows along.

"That's good," I tell him. "Real good. You just keep workin' on it, you hear? I'm gonna go on over to this next fella, and in a little bit, we gonna go down on Earth and try it out. All right?"

He nods and waves at me, and I walk on. I do the same thing with the next fella and the next and the next. It's a good thing I'm married to Jim, I tell myself, 'cause these men sure are pretty! Whooee! What a treat.

It's been a few hours now and Jim's coming over to me.

"I think we done as good as we can up here, Mama. What you say we go on down and practice on Earth?"

"Hot dog, Jim, I can't wait!"

"Now, we can't all go at one time," my daddy chimes in, wrapping his arm 'round Mama's waist.

"No, we can't rightly do that, can we?" says Jim. "Listen here. Split everybody into five groups and pick a nice big place. Whoever you taught, take 'em with you. Spend some time down there gettin' it right and then we'll meet back here in a couple hours. Sound good?"

"Sounds good," everybody says. I'm tickled to death 'cause I get to go down there with all them beautiful men. Oh, don't worry, my Jim's the only one what really does it for me. But it's fun keeping company, I won't lie.

"Leona," Jim says. "Where you takin' your group?"

"N'awlins," Leona's eyes light up. "I ain't been there in ages! Gonna take everybody down to the French Quarter and see what we can do."

Mama and Daddy say they heading down to the beaches on Isle o' Palms and Sullivan's Island.

"Well, I'm a-gonna go down to Boone Hall Plantation, over by the water," says Jim. "We'll have plenty room over there. Mama? Where you takin' your group?"

Well, I don't know. But all a sudden I get me a real nice idea. "Jim, I ain't never been nowhere but South Carolina and heaven, so my group's going somewhere real nice in Africa. Yes sir!" Jim smiles at me like "why ain't I thought o' that," and then we round everybody up.

"Anybody know a good place to practice movin' stuff down in Africa? Should be a real nice open space," I say. "Can anybody speak English to me?" Nobody says nothing. Then a little old lady in a gold and purple batik steps forward and says she knows a real good place.

"Abene," she says. "Abene. Abene is home."

"You speak English!"

"Little," she says, holding her thumb and finger 'bout an inch apart.

"Bintu," she says, pointing to her chest. "Bintu."

"Ah, Bean-too," I say. "My name is Essie Mae. Nice to meet you, Bean-too."

"Esi," she says, pointing back at me. "Esi mean 'born Sunday.'"

"Born on Sunday, is that right? I always thought I was born on a Wednesday."

She smiles, and I smile. "Well, let's go then," I say, and we head on down for Africa.

Mama always told me stories 'bout Africa, 'bout the lions and elephants and zebras and such—so I know a little bit about it. But nothing could 'a prepared me for actually being here. We're in this little fishing village, Ah-bean, in a place called Senegal on the west side of Africa. The grass is real lush green and there's palm trees all around a lot taller than the palmettos we got us back in Mount Pleasant. It's hot, but there's a real nice breeze coming off the 'Lantic Ocean, and wild horses and cows is lapping up water in little puddles down behind the dunes.

Bean-too walks us down the beach a ways 'til we come to the dad-gum biggest tree I ever seen in my whole life. It's wide as a house and gnarled up and knotted like an old man's knuckles. Bean-too points at it and says, "Banta Woro. Tree is sacred. Silk cotton."

"Is that so?" I ask her. Folks form a circle 'round that tree and get to hopping up and down and chanting and such. I ain't got a clue what's going on, but I get to hopping myself. Turns out, that tree is over seven hundred years old. Wanna know something even better than that? Bean-too, here, says her family's the ones what planted it seven hundred years ago. Don't that just beat all? Heaven sure is a wonderful place. Where else do you get the chance to meet people cross all times and places?

Well, we leave the big sacred tree and walk on closer to the water. A handful of folks gets down on their knees, and they get to crying and wailing and carrying on. Bean-too says the slave ship what took 'em to Charleston left not too far from here. I stand here and watch 'em cry. I look out over the water toward Charleston, and I'm quiet. We all are.

We get to walking again and pass some grass on the dunes dancing in the wind. I'm itching to go and pull me some—sure would be pretty in a basket—but then we come up on five horses swatting tails and chewing on grass. All a sudden them horses look up at us and get to neighing and carrying on. "What in heaven's name?" I say. "Can they see us?" Sure 'nough. The horses turn and run over the dunes 'long the water rolling up on the sand. I hear 'em clip-clopping in the distance now, moving just like the wind. I sure do wish Jim was here with me. Pelicans start circling above us. I'm pretty sure they see us too. It sure is something being 'round animals here on Earth. Makes me feel like I ain't even dead no more.

Well, we walk 'long the beach a ways and find some real pretty pink sea shells. I stop everybody and tell 'em to pick one and work on making it move. I'm having a heck of a time with mine, when all a sudden this man in a skirt gets to jumping up and down and hollering. He's just a-laughing and carrying on. Then I hear it all around me. One by one, everybody's moving them little sea shells, but darn if I can't get this one to move.

"Well, hallelujah!" I shout, when my shell gets to moving. Then I pipe down again, 'cause I done picked me out a hermit crab, sure 'nough. That little ol' booger just gets up and walks away all by himself. I work at it and work at it some more on a shell I'm sure ain't alive. Boy howdy, what a feeling I got me when it flies up through the air.

"Whooee!" I'm screaming and hugging folks around me. I'm pretty sure everybody done made something move, and the critters 'round us is acting all sorts of funny now. I can see some village folks coming 'cross the way to see what all the ruckus is about.

"Come on, everybody," I say, waving my hands in the air. "Time to go on home."

Bean-too takes a short walk over to that giant tree and lays her hands on it. Then she takes one last look around and heads on over to us.

"Don't worry," I tell her. "You can come back."

I'm coming back, myself, I say, 'cept not out loud. And next time, I'm bringing Daddy Jim.

Chapter 34

TODAY'S FRIDAY. The Sweetgrass Soiree is tonight. It's been a busy day already for folks up here in heaven. Everybody's excited and getting ready. We ain't exactly sure if we can stop Henrietta's hoodoo, but it sure sounds like it might be fun anyway. Not a-one of us been to a party like this before with powerful people like mayors and senators, no sir. And none of us been guests to a fancy place like Hibernian Hall neither.

Auntie Leona's making a big fuss over what she's gonna wear. She says it'll be like some kind o' Mardy Graw party she used to go to back in New Orleans. Well, I don't know much about that, but I'll just bet she's getting too dressed up.

"Auntie, what in tar-nation is that?" I ask her. She got red feathers sticking up out the top of her head and a bright red shiny gown to go right along with it. "We got names for a woman what looks like that, Leona," I say, smiling at her. She wiggles her hips and winks at me.

"Oh, now, you're just jealous," she says. "But don't worry, I got one for you too, baby."

"Ain't like nobody's gonna see us anyway, Leona," I say. "We're dead, 'member?"

"I know, I know, but can't a body have fun?"

"I reckon." She puts me in a little yella and black striped dress with no sleeves a'tall. When she zips it up my back, my bosoms try and pop out the top. "Leona," I say, "I look just like a big ol' bumble bee. And a pretty loose one, at that."

"You look just like a sexy tigress, Essie Mae. Jim's gonna love it, mark my words. Here. Put this on too." She hands me little mask made of yella feathers that straps 'round my head and covers my face up. It has two little holes for my eyes. I put it on to be a good sport and peek at myself in the mirror. I tell you this, I can't even recognize myself. This can't be me. Not only is my body like a teenager, I'm all covered in feathers and shiny stuff. Lord have mercy on us all.

"I s'pose this is fine," I tell her, as she crosses her arms and looks me up and down. She makes a long whistling noise. "That's enough, Leona. I'll be goin' on home now."

I wear my dress back to the house and when Jim sees me, I think his eyes might pop out his head. "Essie Mae? That you?" he asks me, coming up real slow. He pulls the feather mask off my eyes and smoothes down my hair.

"You know it's me, Jim. Now don't make fun."

"Oh, I ain't makin' fun, Essie Mae. You look real nice."

"You think?"

"I think," he says, taking my hand and pulling me down the hallway. "But I bet you look even better out of it."

I wonder how come I never knew big ol' fat bumblebees have so much fun.

It's been a couple hours. Daddy Jim and I showered, and we're sitting on the front porch in our rocking chairs. We're drinking coffee—mine's black, and his has sugar and cream just like always—and we're looking down on Earth to Charleston. Things down there's busy today too. This is what we seen so far.

Henrietta come on over to EJ's house and Cassie was still in the crib, so she went on back and asked Felicia if she could get her up for the day. She said that'd be all right.

Henrietta walked into the nursery real slow and heard some humming. Cassie was a-laying there, kicking her feet and looked up at her, smiling.

"Hey baby," said Henrietta, throwing her arms out. "Your grandmama's here."

Cassie stood up real quick and pulled her pink blanket 'round her shoulders like a shawl. "Jacket," she tried to say from behind her pacifier. In my day, we never used them things.

Cassie's hair was standing up this way and that so Henrietta walked her on into the bathroom and grabbed a comb. She tried to work it through a couple times before the baby had a fit. Then she set Cassie down and took the comb to her own hair, staring at herself in the mirror. She studied the lines 'round her eyes, but thought she looked pretty good anyway and blew herself a kiss. She sure was in a good mood, but I ain't sure that was such a good thing, knowing she got hoodoo up her sleeves.

"Felicia," said Henrietta. "You got somebody to watch the baby tonight?"

"Yes, I do. Mrs. Simmons next door's going to watch her. Cassie just adores her."

"That's good. You know what you're going to wear?"

"Yep. It's not much, but I think it'll do. You all ready, Henrietta? You excited about tonight? There's gonna be tons of people there—everybody in town practically. Oooh, I can't wait."

"It sure will be something." Henrietta followed Cassie into the kitchen and put back the papers she took off the table. "EJ, you need me to take care of anything for the party tonight?" she asked him real sweet.

"No, Mama. I think Jeffrey's got everything under control."

"We'll just see about that," she whispered under her breath. "All right then, I'm going back home. I have some things I need to do. See you two later!"

She turned 'round, started humming, and flitted out the front door like a butterfly dancing on a honeysuckle vine. Lord have mercy, we gonna have our work cut out for us tonight. Leona's promised to stay real close on her, so at least she can't pull nothing we don't know about.

Things ain't so happy over at the Lowes' household today. Jeffrey woke up to an empty bed again. He got up to call for Victor, thinking he was on the couch, but he weren't even home. He finally rolled on in 'bout six thirty. Jeffrey was waiting for him in the living room, setting right next to that pretty love basket I made for him. I reckon it's pretty if nothing else.

"Well, good morning," he said. His arms and legs was crossed, and that right foot o' his just kept a-jiggling and shaking up and down. "Well?"

Victor didn't answer him. He just walked on past him to the bathroom like he weren't even there. Jeffrey up and followed him, but the door shut right 'fore he could get there.

"Victor! Tell me what's going on. It's somebody else, isn't it? I wasn't born yesterday, you know. You're seeing somebody, now who is it?" Jeffrey pounded his fists on the door, and when he heard the shower come on he slid down it, quiet and still.

"Victor, why?" he whispered to nobody. "Why are you doing this? Today was going to be such a big day . . ." Jeffrey stayed there on the floor, propped up against the bathroom door and when it finally opened twenty minutes later, he fell back.

"I sorry," Victor said, real quiet. He leaned down to touch his shoulder, but Jeffrey got up without a word and walked on out the front door.

Over at Susanne Maybree's house, things was kinda strange too.

"Susanne, who was over here this morning?" Clarice Maybree was sitting at the breakfast table and peeked out from behind the newspaper.

"Nobody, Mother."

"Susanne? I'm not stupid. My bedroom's right next to yours,

you know. Come on, tell your old mama. At least one of us is having some fun. Is he somebody special?"

"Mother, it's none of your business. And nothing happened. Trust me. Come on, let's just have breakfast. You want cheese on your eggs?"

Clarice just sat there saying nothing. She watched Susanne cooking in her white fuzzy robe and pink feather slippers.

"Is it somebody I know?" asked Clarice, shifting in her seat and grabbing her juice glass.

"If I tell you, will you leave it alone already?"

"I promise."

"Yes, Mother. It's somebody you know."

"Oh, goodie! Is he going to be at the party tonight?"

"Mother! You promised."

"I know, I know. I just want you to meet somebody nice. That's all."

"Ugh! All right, Mother. Yes. Yes, he'll be there tonight. But no, I'm not interested in him. Now here, eat your eggs, I've got to start getting ready. I have to be over there real early to get set up."

Clarice watched her walk down the hallway and out o' sight, then stabbed into her eggs and stared on out the window, chewing like a chipmunk. She finished her eggs and then went a million miles away, 'membering Susanne's daddy who run off on her when Susanne was twelve years old.

"Daddy, go on and get the door, would you?" I'm a little nervous and excited 'bout tonight, so I figured I'd weave a little. I'm sitting over here in front o' the fireplace and making a real cute basket. Just a little one, though, 'cause my fingers ain't fat no more and I can sew just as small and tight as I want these days.

"Well now, look who it is. Hey, Mama. Hey, Daddy."

"Bonjour, *ma petite fille*," says Daddy.

"Bonjour, Daddy. Boy, ain't you bein' fancy today."

"Oh, 'e so 'cited. Been talkin' French at me aw day long—but I ain complainin' none." Mama winks at me, then smiles over toward Daddy. It's a real strange thing seeing your mama and daddy the same age you is. They's all young again, too, just like when they was first married. They still act like Mama and Daddy though. They was always real sweet to each other and frisky too, sometimes.

"I ain know what ta do wid yo faddah while us bidin' time, so I figguh I bring'm on ober yah."

"Well, come sit down here with me, Mama. Let's weave a little. Jim, can't you boys go on outside and do some manly stuff—fishin' or huntin' or whatever it is you men folk do?" I wink at him, and they wave as they leave.

"Here, Mama. Take this nail bone. I'll get me another one." I walk in the kitchen and head for my stash o' spoon handles—a never-ending supply just in case I need 'em. Then I go back and sit down on the sofa. "You got you some grass already, Mama?"

"Yes, baby."

We been weaving for a while, just a-humming and not saying too much when Mama pipes up. "You talk ta Jedus 'bout Henrietta?"

"No, not really, Mama."

"Well, why not? Ain you t'ink us need aw de hep us can git t'night? Jedus wanna hear 'bout eb'ryt'ing."

"Oh, Mama. You know it just like I do. Jesus already knows what we're up to. He knows we're gonna need His help."

"But did you ax Him, Essie Mae? 'E may know eb'ryt'ing, but 'E want you ta ax Him anyhow."

Mama's been up here a whole lot longer than I have. She knows Jesus better than I do, I reckon.

"I'll talk to Him, Mama. You're right—as usual." I smile at her, and we get back to weaving. After while, somebody 'bout bangs the front door down.

"Essie Mae! Open up, it's me!"

I open the door and see Auntie Leona's face. It's a nasty shade o' green.

"Oh, Lord have mercy, she's conjurin' up loas!" She runs 'round the room with her arms waving up in the air. "Oh, Lord Jesus, help us, she's conjurin' up spirits."

"Whoa, slow down, Leona," says Mama, patting the seat next to her on the sofa. "Calm down an' sit down, Leona. Us cain't figguh a word you sayin'."

Leona sits down and draws in a deep breath.

"I was just down there with Henrietta. She's gonna do everythin' in her power to ruin that sweetgrass party and make Mister Jeffrey look bad as she can. She's tryin' to ruin his good name 'cause she's all eat-up with bein' jealous. Lord have mercy, she gonna wreck everythin' EJ's been workin' so hard for! And what's worse, she's plannin' on callin' up spirits—voodoo spirits that walk on the Earth."

Mama and I just look at each other with blank faces.

"See, I used to call on 'em back in N'awlins for help—'specially if I was plannin' somethin' bad." She looks up at the ceiling. "Forgive me, Jesus."

"Da's a long time ago, Leona," says Mama. "Now go on."

"See, these spirits or loas, they sure do got minds of their own. You never quite know what they gonna pull."

"Well, do you know who she's conjurin' up?" I ask her, putting my hand on her arm.

"Oh, yeah. Do I ever. There's two of 'em. Let's see, the spirit of beauty's gonna be there. I reckon Henrietta's hopin' to get a lot of attention 'stead of Jeffrey. Anyway, her name is Erzulie, and she's pretty as they come, and powerful. Got all the charms of a woman too—likes to flirt and carry on."

"Well now, she don't sound so bad, Leona," I say. "We can handle the likes o' her, I reckon."

"Oh, you think so?" says Leona. "Better hold on to your men folk if you know what's good for you. I sure have seen her cause some trouble in my day."

My stomach sinks a little, and Mama looks like hers is sinking too. Gonna have to have me a talk with Jim, I reckon, 'though I've never had no trouble with him before.

"Okay, well you know 'bout Erzulie but here's the worst one. Not sure what to do about him—he's a loose cannon, he is. His name is Ogoun, and he's the spirit of fire."

"Ah-goon, the spirit of fire," I say under my breath.

"He drinks a lot so he's pretty unpredictable—likes to set things on fire just for fun. Oh, he's dangerous, that one."

Mama stands up and walks over to the window. After a minute

of quiet she says, "Gals, us got da work cut out fa us t'night. Leona, go on out an' tell eb'ry'body ta keep dey eyes open fa dey spirits us gwine see t'night. Essie Mae, you 'membah what us talk about? Us need Him mo' den eber now. Go run out an' find Jedus. Make sho 'E gwine be wid us dey t'night."

"We best be gettin' ready then." I set down my basket and smooth out my skirt. My stomach jumps a little when I think about slipping on my bumble bee dress again. "Go get Daddy and y'all hurry on home. We'll meet out in the field again in an hour, hear?"

Mama and Leona scurry on out. Jim comes back in smelling like dead fish.

"Been fishin', Jim? Go on and get your shower now." When he walks on by me, he tries to plant a kiss on me but I squeal. "Come on Jim, not now! Time's a-wastin', sugar, and you smell just like a skunk!"

"Maybe I need somebody to give me a good cleanin', Mama."

"You sly ol' dog, Jim. I got to get ready. Now go on, shoo!"

I can hear the water running now, thank goodness, 'cause I need to slip my dress on and then go find Jesus right quick.

Chapter 35

"WELL, WHAT DO YOU THINK?" asks Auntie Leona, throwing her arms up in the air like she's on *The Price Is Right*. She's standing in her sequined red gown with them plumb-awful red feathers sticking up out her head. I s'pose I can't talk none, seeing as I'm in this sexy bumblebee outfit.

Jesus said He'll be there to help us out tonight, so we're all in the middle of this field here in heaven, just a-waiting for the word to go on down to Charleston. Auntie Leona's in charge tonight, seeing as she knows the most 'bout the hoodoo going on.

I twirl and look all around me. There's Mama and Daddy looking real spiffy. Daddy's in a nice white suit and tie and Mama's wearing a tight-fitting green dress with a fur stole 'round her neck. She always did like that thing. I think it looks just like what it is though—a dead fox.

I'd say there's maybe thirty folks here—most of 'em lived in Charleston at one time or 'nother. But there's a handful of Africans that wanna come too. Like Bean-too, here. She's wearing a real pretty purple batik wrapped 'round her. And I recognize some o' them fellas from our Africa trip yesterday. Looks like they decided not to wear no shirts again. Lord have mercy!

"Well, we ready to go? Ready to go everybody?" Leona yells and waves her hand. We're all hooting and hollering. "Well, come on!" I grab on to Daddy Jim's arm, close my eyes and off we go.

So here's our first surprise o' the night. We was aiming for Hibernian Hall on Meeting Street, but we landed here on Chalmers Street. We ain't too far away, but now we got us a group of fellas banging their hands and heads on the ground, crying and carrying on. Looks like the same folks who done it in Africa yesterday on the beach.

"They say, slave here," says Bean-too. "Slave. Sold here."

I look up and sure 'nough we landed right smack in front of the Old Slave Market. "Good heavens, Jim," I say. "Should we 'a put Leona in charge?"

"Oh, let her be," says Jim, pulling up one of the Africans from off the ground. "Could 'a happened to any one of us."

I reckon so.

We finally get to walking and take a left onto Church Street. Over there's the French Huguenot church where EJ and Felicia got married and St. Phillips in front o' that.

"Uh, Leona?" I ask her, hurrying up to catch her arm. It ain't easy running in heels. "Ain't you takin' us the wrong way? I thought Meetin' Street was that-a-way."

Leona gets a sly look on her face and says, "Yeah, it's that way, but I thought we could take a short stroll this way—take the scenic route. I always did love these churches. And the Dock Street Theatre! Just look at that green ironwork, Essie Mae. Makes me feel like I'm right back in N'awlins."

I open my mouth and Jim gives me a dirty look, so I button my lip. It is pretty here, I reckon. "I just don't wanna miss anythin' important, is all. Henrietta and them voodoo spirits is already there; I just know it."

The air here in Charleston is heavy even in November. I might be in spirit form, but I can still feel the salty humid air just as plain as day. It presses in 'round me, making me feel solid.

We take a left on Queen Street and walk down 'bout a block, then turn left again onto Meeting Street where we see the Hibernian Hall standing there just as grand as it can be. It's big and white and got them great big columns out front what make it look like a Greek temple. When we get closer, we pass a tour group riding in a buggy and pulled by a big black horse. It just clip-clops down the street but then gets to neighing and stomping its feet when it sees us. I reckon seeing thirty dead folks dressed in sequins and feathers would be 'nough to make anybody jump.

We head on in the big front doors and I watch Bean-too and the Africans looking all around as we climb up the spiral staircases. I know they ain't never seen nothing like this. There's a grand staircase on either side o' the foyer that circles clear on up to the second floor. That's where the party is. It's already started. I can hear the Amen Singers already singing, "Over by the river, Lord, down by the river . . ." Sure sounds pretty.

When we first walk in there's this little lane of sweetgrass basket ladies weaving on either side of us. There's a couple o' roadside stands too. Ain't that cute? "Look Daddy, there's Miss Georgia! Don't she look pretty?" Georgia's in a real nice dress and Nancy too. Miss Nancy come with her son, looks like. He's standing behind her mighty handsome in a nice black tuxedo.

"You reckon they gonna make Nancy and Georgia work all night?"

"No, Mama," says Jim. "It's just for show."

There's sweetgrass baskets stacked up everywhere. Great big ones and little tiny ones lined up on a table by the door. They're filled with benne wafers, so they must be party favors or something. And folks is dressed up just like Leona said they would be, sure 'nough. There's Susanne Maybree with Clarice sticking real close by her side. And there's Mister Victor. He's trying to make eyes at Susanne but having a heck of a time not catching her big ol' mama's eyes instead.

Oh, there's Mister Jeffrey, sweet thing. "Woo-hoo, Jeffrey!" I wave my hands at him, but he don't hear me or see me. Sure is strange being dead. Oh, there's Bertice Brown. "Reckon that's the governor she's talking to, Daddy?" He's a real nice-looking fella—kinda younger than I'd pictured him.

"Reckon it is, Mama," says Jim, moving me on through the crowd. The room in here is just beautiful. The floor is real shiny black-and-white checkers, and there's great big long windows on either side o' the room with long purple curtains that go right down and sweep the floor. There's a bandstand down at the far end with them Amen Singers up on it.

And you ought to smell what I'm smelling, praise Jesus! "Let's go on over near the food table, Leona. It's a shame we can't eat earthly food no more, but I got to see me some good Lowcountry fixin's." Our whole group moves on over. There's fried flounder and hushpuppies in real nice silver dishes to keep 'em warm. And big piles o' cheese grits, hoppin' John, and tiny pecan pies to boot! Behind us, big round tables is covered in white tablecloths with napkins and real fine silver and dishes.

Next to the food table there's a man in an apron pouring champagne into skinny tall glasses. And in front of him there's all sorts of liquor—whiskey, rum, and things I ain't never seen before.

"Leona, who's that, you reckon?" I point to a mighty-fine-looking tall black man in front of the liquor table. He's handsome as the dickens and dressed in a red suit with red shirt and tie to boot. He's got this stinky ol' cigar sending swirls of nasty smoke in the air. There's a white man sipping champagne next to him who don't even seem to notice.

"Lord 'a-mercy," says Leona. Her jaw drops. "There he is. It's Ogoun."

"Ah-goon," I say, mesmerized. Jim elbows me in the ribs.

Ah-goon grabs a big bottle o' rum and just turns it up to his mouth. He takes a swig then pulls a cigar up to his lips, blowing fire clear up a foot or two in the air. There's a shiny sword hanging over his shoulder.

"You don't wanna mess with him," says Leona.

"Don't worry," I tell her. "I won't."

"No need to whisper, ladies," says the man in a smooth sultry voice, "'cause I can see you plain as day. Long time no see, Leona." He tips his red hat at her. "You sure are lookin' gorgeous as ever—good enough to eat, I'd say." He licks his lips and looks her up and down. "I see you brought a whole group with you. What y'all down here for? I thought you was up in heaven by now."

"I am," she says, looking right annoyed. "We're here on business."

"You're here for Henrietta, ain't you? Mighty fine lady," he says, smiling. Leona stays quiet and looks uncomfortable. "Ain't gonna do you no good, you know. She brought more than me here. Look over there." Ah-goon pulls out his sword and swings it 'bove his head in the air.

We look around, and I see Leona fix her eyes on a real pretty lady. She's wearing a fancy blue dress down to the floor with gold and pearl necklaces swinging 'round her neck when she sways to the music. She's real elegant and looks mighty wealthy. There's rings and bracelets all up and down her ebony arms, and her bosoms is poking out the top o' her dress like two melons in the sunshine.

"Erzulie," says Leona over her breath, "the spirit of beauty. Watch out for her, Essie Mae." I look up at Jim and squeeze his arm with a warning.

"Don't you be worryin' 'bout me, Mama," he says. "I can handle myself. She ain't all *that*, anyway."

We watch Erzulie come over and get to flirting up a storm with Ah-goon. Them voodoo spirits is just a-chit-chatting and laughing. Erzulie swishes her hips to the music and grabs Ah-goon's hand, pulling a swig o' his rum. Then she looks on over at me and winks at Daddy Jim. Can you believe that? Hussy. I push Jim away 'fore he gets a chance to stare back.

The mayor of Mount Pleasant and his wife walk in the front doors. Real sweet people. I met 'em once when they stopped at my stand few years back. Reverend Jefferson and his wife, Ethel, come on in too. She's in a big red hat the size o' China.

Jim and me are standing here just watching the folks pour in when Henrietta walks right up to us with Eddie at her side. "Retta," I say, putting my hand out to her.

"She can't hear you, Essie Mae. Leave her 'lone." I can feel the tears welling up in my eyes.

"Mama, Dad, I'm so glad you made it." I turn around and see my sweet grandbaby, EJ, with Felicia by his side. They're right off the cover of one o' them magazines, I tell you. EJ's filled out some since I seen him last and Felicia's pretty as a doll in a pale pink frilly dress. "You look beautiful," EJ says, leaning in to kiss Henrietta on the cheek. And she does look beautiful in her long black gown with her hair swooped up real nice. Must 'a gone to the beauty shop, I reckon, for that hairdo.

Eddie shakes EJ's hand. "Son, we're proud of you. You're doing a real good thing here." It's a right touching moment, but then Eddie looks around for Henrietta. Sweet Jesus, she's already disappeared.

"Get on her, Leona," I say, pushing her away from me. Leona hurries off into the crowd to see if she can find Retta. There's hundreds of people in here now, and all us from heaven just standing in a daze.

"Don' you t'ink us should split up?" Mama asks me.

"Jim?"

"Yeah, Mama. Let's split up." He sends a group of Africans to stand at the front door. Mama and Daddy go over by the sweetgrass baskets, and Bean-too sticks close to the food and liquor tables.

"Everybody else, just keep your eyes wide open," he says, shooing 'em off. "Mama, you go on toward the stage and I'll keep a watch over here." He walks on over to the left side of the room by the windows. As I head to the bandstand I pass that lady spirit, Erzulie, making a beeline over to Jim. Of all the nerve! It's all I can do not to run and keep watch over him, but I know he's all right. He can withstand the wiles o' her, I reckon.

He better, anyway.

Oh, listen to that, would you? Music to my ears.

Swing low, sweet chariot
Comin' for to carry me home
Swing low, sweet chariot
Comin' for to carry me home

The Amen Singers finish up singing and Jackson Hemmingway hops up on stage. He's looking real handsome tonight even with that big belly, and he grabs the microphone and taps it a few times.

"Ahem, uh, welcome everyone, to the first annual Sweetgrass Soiree!"

The room erupts, clapping and hollering, then quiets down again.

"It's my special privilege to introduce you to a young man I've grown quite fond of this year. He's a man of great character no doubt passed on to him by generations of strong Gullah and African-American people, my personal favorite being his grandmother, Essie Mae Jenkins."

More clapping and hollering. I feel my face blush and I look out into the crowd to see Miss Georgia and Nancy tearing up and patting their eyes with tissues.

"Thank you, Mr. Hemmingway," EJ says, moving behind the microphone and shaking Jackson's hand. "If my grandmother was alive today, she'd say, 'Baby, I sure am proud.' There's one person who knew my grandmother and loved her as I do, and he's done a terrific job pulling everything together for tonight. Jeffrey Lowes? The Grass Roots Society thanks you. Now come on up here."

Everybody claps and lifts their hands in the air when Jeffrey walks up the steps, bowing as he goes. There's Victor watching him with a sad look on his face. Miss Susanne's next to him, the skin of her arm barely brushing the sleeve of his tux. And Henrietta's behind 'em both, clutching her little black sequined purse like her life depends on it. She's frowning to beat the band.

"Thank you," says Jeffrey, holding his hands out for folks to simmer down. "I want to thank everyone who worked so hard to make tonight a success. And thank you to *The Post and Courier*, for agreeing to cover this event. I look forward to reading about all of you in tomorrow's paper. Especially you, EJ."

He grins and everybody laughs.

"My old friend Essie Mae left her mark on many of us here tonight. She's the reason The Grass Roots Society exists, and it is my sincere wish that her memory and the memory of those who came before her will never be forgotten."

I look around at our group scattered around the room. Everyone is paying attention, even the ones who don't speak English.

Jeffrey goes on. "It's because of support from people like you that these men and women continuing on in Gullah traditions will have a bright and glorious future to look forward to. Now go on, dance, eat, and have a great time. Oh, and I hope you didn't forget your checkbooks, because we've got lots of treats for you on auction in just a little while. Enjoy."

Jeffrey holds up his champagne glass to toast the crowd. The Beachin' Groove starts playing "I Love Beach Music" right on the tail of his speech, and folks get to moving their feet. I got to say, I ain't never felt this way. I swanny, it sure is something to look around and think that little ol' me had something to do with making all this good stuff happen. I'm thinking maybe tonight ain't gonna be so bad after all.

Chapter 36

THE DANCE FLOOR OF HIBERNIAN HALL is just a-filling up with white folks shagging and black folks boogying. It sure is a funny thing to see, I tell you what—black arms swinging this way and white legs kicking that-a-way. Lord have mercy, can't tell nobody apart from here. But I got to keep my mind focused. Got to keep my eye out for Henrietta and them voodoo spirits. Don't know what they gonna try to do.

There's Henrietta over there behind Mister Victor. That can't be good. Now Jeffrey's coming on over to ask him to dance. Looks like this is what Retta's been waiting for, sure 'nough. I can see the excitement on her face. When she reaches in her purse, I try to run over, but it's too late. She pulls out a handful of what looks like sugar or powder and blows it soft on the back of Victor's head. She done hoodoo'd him, sure 'nough.

Lord have mercy, Victor takes one look at Miss Susanne walking by and he grabs her hard, bending her down in a kiss I only seen on the movie screen. Miss Susanne's squirming like a turkey on Thanksgiving Day, trying to get out from under that man.

That reporter lady is standing here, watching all of it, and Henrietta's just a-feeling her oats. She backs away real slow-like so that reporter can get a good look at Jeffrey who's plumb all torn up now. He's glaring at Victor and Miss Susanne, looks like he might light on fire, and he storms on out the room.

"Wait! Jeffrey!" When Susanne does break free, she hauls off and slaps Victor in the face and then tears off after Jeffrey. Looks like she don't want none o' Mister Victor, no sir.

That reporter lady ain't sure what to make of it all, but the mayor of Summerville pulls her away just in time to chew her ear a while. So Henrietta ducks on through the crowd and disappears again, no doubt to go cause more trouble. Lord have mercy, and I'm already tired.

"Auntie Leona!" I yell when I catch her grooving on the dance floor. "What in tar-nation are you doin'? Henrietta's at it already, and you s'posed to be on her like glue!"

"Sorry, Essie Mae. It's just been so long since I seen a good party. I'll get on her, don't worry."

I hurry off to find Jim and tell him what happened but when I find him, he's grinning like a dad-gum drunk over in the corner. Hair's all messed up and his tie's all crooked, and there's that spirit, Erzulie, wiggling her hips in front of him and singing along to the music.

"James Furlow Jenkins, what in the dickens are you doin'?" I grab him by the ear and pull him away, giving Erzulie a look like, *Back off, missy.*

"I ain't done nothin', Mama," he says, talking to his shoes.

"No, he ain't done nothin', Mama, have you sugar?" Erzulie reaches over and runs her fingers 'long Jim's tie. Now, I ain't never been one for getting physical, but I haul off and push that lady spirit clear back to the window pane. I don't even say nothing, just give her a good look and then haul Jim off with me.

"You better not 'a done nothin', Jim. I could just wring your neck." I can't never 'member being so mad at him.

I'm fussing at him good when all a sudden, Jim's eyes get big as saucers. He's looking past my shoulders, and I turn around just in time to see that fire spirit in red, Ah-goon, take a big ol' swig 'o rum. Lord have mercy, he opens his mouth and shoots fire on Miss Georgia's stand! The flames are down at the bottom, and they's getting ready to light up a whole heap of sweetgrass. Great God Almighty, Miss Georgia's weaving and watching people dance, and she don't even know 'bout it yet!

Ah-goon is belly laughing and just a-slapping his knee. He takes another big swig and then heads off into the crowd over to that beauty spirit, Erzulie.

"Jim! What we gonna do?!" I say.

Jim pulls me and we run over to help. There's four Africans and Mama and Daddy trying to push over this great big flower vase sitting at the front door. We push and we push, but the flames is starting to grow! All a sudden, the vase gives—thank You, Jesus— and water and flowers pour all over Miss Georgia and her stand.

Poor thing squeals and jumps up quicker than I ever seen her move. And the rest of the room ain't even heard a thing on account of the music's playing so loud.

"Look, Jim," I say. "It's a shame, what it is." We watch Miss Nancy and her son picking gerber daisies and baby's breath out Miss Georgia's hair. Then they lead her out the room to clean up. Praise God. Somebody bring in a mop.

Well, we're in a real tizzy now. The good thing is, we was able to move that big flower vase and save the whole place from going up in flames. The bad thing is, Henrietta's still here with hoodoo and who-knows-what-all up her sleeves.

I double-dared Jim to set foot near that pretty spirit, Erzulie, again. "You're staying with me now. I ain't losing sight o' you again, no sir." He just hangs his head low. Can't say nothing.

Jeffrey done pulled himself back together real good, and he walks up on stage after a song is over with his head held high. That's good to see. He makes sure not to look over at Victor though.

"Excuse me. Ladies and gentlemen—now for what we've all been waiting for—it's time for our live auction." The room erupts. Folks been drinking a while now, so it's harder to quiet 'em down.

"Now, if you'll look back at the front doors, you can see people bringing in some fabulous items you're going to have the chance to bid on. We have several paintings donated by local artists including our very own Felicia White. We have baskets made by local members of the

Society, of course, and we have some gorgeous flower arrangements made by a little ol' flower shop called La Belle Fleur."

Somebody whistles from the dance floor.

"Thank you, thank you. Ahem, and now, everyone please take a few minutes to get up close and personal with the delicious items we have for you. And come bidding time, remember to reach down deep in your pockets because every glorious cent is going to support Charleston's Gullah roots."

A crowd forms over by the sweetgrass baskets. Felicia's paintings is propped up on brass stands. And they're right nice, too, with big bright colors and shapes showing basket ladies and black farmers hoeing in the field. The other paintings show Charleston buildings and water scenes and stuff. Right next to 'em are more big vases lined up with flowers sticking up taller than Jim.

Folks is oohing and aahing over everything, and Retta watches as they goo-goo all over Jeffrey. She's a-hating every second of it.

"What a fine job you've done, Mr. Lowes," says Jackson. Looks like he brung his rich Mama and Daddy Hemmingway too. They sure are looking nice, older though. It's been a real long time since I seen 'em.

Mama Hemmingway grabs her husband's arm and points to a real big basket set up right out front in a nice wrought-iron stand. It's about two and a half foot tall and shaped like a big ol' egg. It's got a stripe o' bulrush running all the way up and a lid with a great big handle on top. I used to do some like it in my day.

We walk on over to the crowd in front of the baskets and watch as Henrietta's lips start to moving. She's saying something over and over and all a sudden Erzulie sways right on up to her. She scoots in next to me and lays her hands on Henrietta's shoulders, and then that hussy blows right over her ear straight into the faces o' Jackson and Daddy Hemmingway!

"Do something, Jim!"

"I can't, Mama! She already done it!"

All a sudden, them two men look up at Retta and I can see the stars in their eyes. "Why, Miss Henrietta, you sure do look nice tonight," says Jackson. "I see you've grown up real nice, haven't you?"

"Real nice," says Daddy Hemmingway moving in closer to her. "Why, I can remember when you were just a little girl."

"Well now, can I get you a drink?" asks Jackson, fixing to drool.

"Why, yes, that'd be nice," says Henrietta, smiling and batting her eyelashes.

"Don't bother. I'll get it, son," says Daddy Hemmingway.

"No, I'll get it," says Jackson. And back and forth they go 'til Mama Hemmingway's had 'bout all she can handle. She pinches her husband's ear, and when he don't do a thing, she storms off in a huff.

Well, wouldn't you know it, Henrietta runs 'round that room with Erzulie blowing kisses on the men folk, and the lady folks is just a-sulking off left and right. I ain't never seen so many angry women in all my life. But everything changes once they get to Reverend Jefferson and his Misses. They're just a-talking to each other having a nice ol' time when Erzulie blows over Henrietta's shoulder at the reverend. All a sudden, he gets to acting like a fool, giggling and such and tripping all over himself.

"Why Henrietta," he says with eyes big and round. "Is that a new dress you got on? My, my, my, you sure are looking fine." Well, while he's clucking his tongue, Ethel Jefferson decides she ain't having none o' that and she stomps down hard with her high heel on the reverend's foot.

"Ow!" He yelps and jumps 'round on the other foot, then he sees his wife's face and knows he's in big trouble. Real quick-like, he straightens up, clears his throat, and puts his hand right up in front o' Henrietta's face and says, "Get thee away from me Satan!" Lord in heaven, I reckon he *is* a man o' God, sure 'nough. Well, Henrietta likes to die when he does that, and she runs off into the crowd with men folk, black, white, and the other, just a-falling all over her. Guess she's getting the attention she wanted, all right.

"Praise God, hallelujah!" says Reverend Jefferson, smiling real sweet at his wife. "The devil, he was a-tempting me," he says real serious-like, raising his finger up in the air, "but I was saved from his fiery clutches. Praise Jesus, Gawd in heaven, the evil done let us be!"

"Praise God!" says his wife, closing her eyes and lifting her hands up in the air. "Thank You, Jesus."

Well, a group o' basket ladies including Miss Nancy and a wet Miss Georgia see the reverend and his wife just a-praying and carrying on, and then a crowd erupts in worship and laughing. The Amen Singers jump back up on the stage singing, "Nobody Knows the Trouble I See."

The partiers is happier than ever 'cause of the worship going on, plus all the liquor they drunk up. Jeffrey jumps back on the stage after the music stops and gets the auction going. That auctioneer gets to talking so fast, I can't even tell what he's saying. Everybody's holding up these little white fans, and the auctioneer's pointing all this way and that.

Felicia's paintings go for thousands of dollars apiece, and she's just as tickled as she can be, nuzzling into EJ's arms. And would you believe that big ol' egg basket raises the most money of all? None other than Mama Hemmingway herself keeps waving that little white fan 'til she done spent twenty thousand dollars of her husband's money. Praise Jesus! Everybody's cheering and patting Jeffrey on the shoulders, telling him what a fine party it is. He done a real good job, I tell you what. I sure am proud.

The *Post and Courier* reporter comes and sits down 'cross from Retta who's pouting up a storm and giving Jeffrey the evil eye from 'cross the room. I'm watching her, and so is EJ right next to me. That reporter's facing the wrong way, so I can't hear what she asks, but what I do hear from Retta makes me want to crawl right in a hole.

"The party? Oh yes, it's very nice. But really, don't you think this is the *whitest* African-American event you've ever seen?"

"The whitest?" says EJ, showing himself. *Oh Lord, EJ done heard her too.* "I'm sorry, did you say the *whitest*? What, exactly, does that mean, Mama?" Felicia scoots up next to him and tries to calm him down.

"No, it's not like that," says Henrietta, caught off guard and backpedaling quick. "That's not what I meant, it's just that . . . well, Jeffrey organized all this and . . . well, it's sweetgrass, African-American heritage, you know . . ."

That reporter lady is scribbling down every dad-gum word.

"And Jeffrey's white. Isn't that what all this is about? Isn't it what it's always been about?" EJ shakes Felicia loose and calls for his daddy to come over.

His face grows hard as a nail. That ol' boy stands straighter than I ever seen him, and his eyes bore into his mama. He looks like he's gonna fall over or cry, one. "Go on home now, Mama. I can't handle this tonight. In fact, I don't want to handle it tomorrow either. I thought we were past all this mess, but apparently"—he takes in a deep breath and lets it out—"you're nothing but a racist."

"But EJ, honey, you can't be serious! That's not what I meant! I just meant that—"

EJ holds up his hand all mad and sad and backs away from her. Retta looks scared and can't say nothing. She ain't never seen this look on his face and I got to say, I ain't neither.

"Please excuse my mother," he says to the reporter. "And I'd appreciate it if none of this makes it into the paper tomorrow." EJ holds the lady's gaze 'til she gives him a nod and sets her pen down. Then leaning over and grabbing Retta's arm he says, "Dad, please take her home now. Y'all just go on. Please?"

Henrietta makes a funny little peepin' sound and looks like she done ate the canary, leaving yella feathers dangling out her mouth. Them feathers keep her mouth shut at least—thank You, Jesus—until Eddie can haul her on out the door.

Watching them go and seeing the look on EJ's face, my heart is 'bout as still as I ever remember. I know she hurt him bad, and she's awful ornery, but my girl ain't really a racist. She just meant—well, shucks, I don't know—but I fly after EJ anyway, fussing. "EJ, sweetie, what's got into you? You can't treat your mama that way. Two wrongs don't make no right. What I told ya? EJ? EJ, listen to me!"

But he don't hear a thing. He just stops, straightens himself up, and slips a phony smile on his face just for show. It's a crying shame what just happened with Henrietta and EJ. And me and Daddy Jim never felt so helpless. No sir, we just watched our family fall flat apart, and there weren't a thing in the world we could do 'bout it neither.

Now that Henrietta's gone and the party's starting to quiet down, Jim and I look around at the voodoo spirits still walking 'round kinda aimless-like. I wonder what they done to make it so they never quit walking the Earth. Leona says spirit battles like we had down here tonight go on every day, just nobody knows 'cause they can't see 'em. I just praise sweet Jesus looks like we done won this one. The only shame is, after all we done to save Henrietta and Jeffrey tonight and this dad-gum party, with just one slip of the tongue she done more damage than either o' them spirits ever could.

We watch 'em walk by—the spirit o' beauty and the spirit o' fire. But I reckon we done all we come to do, so us spirits o' sweetgrass is heading on back home to Jesus.

PART IV:

home is somethin' you feel deep in your bones

Chapter 37

January

DEEP DOWN IN THE SOCIETY SECTION, *The Post and Courier* the next day read, "Grass Roots Society Event Proves to be Eventful." You can say that again.

Overall, the article was real kind, I'd say. All them bigwigs was quoted as having a great time. "I can't wait for next year's Soiree," said Misses Governor. "Count me in." There was no mention of Susanne slapping Mister Victor and nothing 'bout the fire what broke out neither. Nothing was mentioned 'bout the men folk goo-gooing over Henrietta or all them angry women—and the best part about it, there was no talk of the words "Henrietta White" or "white" a'tall.

EJ's mighty relieved to see his mama ain't tarnished the image of The Grass Roots Society. I'm mighty glad for that too. There's only one problem though: two months gone by and EJ still ain't forgiven Retta for what she said at the Soiree. And what's worse, he told her not to set foot near Felicia and the baby.

I reckon some good come from that night though. Quick as she could, Retta stuck that old voodoo book of Leona's way back in her closet and then buried it under some boxes. She knew it ain't done her no good. I still worry 'bout her though, I surely do.

And you know how the Bible says, "All things work together for good to them that love God"? I believe it. Jesus tells me not to worry 'bout Jeffrey cause He's been talking to him lately. Says Jeffrey's gonna be just fine. He was praised for the party, and his flower business took off even better than before. Victor moved out and then moved on back to where he was from down in Mexico. I reckon everything just ain't worked out for him here. Come to find out, Miss Susanne ain't done a cotton-pickin thing with that man, thank You Jesus. He just kept a-banging down her door and sneaking up on her and such. She told him ain't nothing gonna come between her and her friend Jeffrey. Fact, she's the one who helped Jeffrey get over Victor and sent him on packing. I always knew she was a sweet girl. Smart one too. Maybe there's hope for them two after all.

EJ and Felicia's happy as clams with little Miss Cassie. She's a handful and talking up a storm. And The Grass Roots Society's doing real good too. Membership is up and they's working with the U-nited States government on some kinda protection law for the Gullah coast from South Carolina clear on down to Georgia.

But after while, Daddy and me decided to take a break from Mount Pleasant. All it was doing was causing heartbreak, you know. It's hard to be happy for anything when your own flesh and blood ain't right.

But then one evening up here in heaven I was minding my own

business and frying up some pork chops. I had the edges turning crispy brown in butter and the house smelling so good that Daddy Jim just run on in with his mouth watering. It's a good thing he was there, 'cause that's when I dropped my frying pan mid-air. Somebody on Earth done called for me to be there, and sure enough, away I went.

I found myself back in Mount Pleasant over at the cemetery where they buried my casket. There was my sweet EJ, setting on the ground with his face on his knees. He was talking to my headstone.

"Grandmama? Are you there? I really need to talk to you." Then a tear streaked down his cheek. "It's just I . . . well, I wish you were here. I need you to tell me what to do, Grandmama. I want to be a good father. I want that more than anything in the world. I'm just scared of making a mistake, is all."

"Ain't nothin' gonna stop you from making mistakes, boy," I said. And the most amazing thing happened. EJ heard me! Glory, hallelujah, that boy moved faster than a horse at the track! He looked all around him like flies was attacking. "Grandmama? Is that you?"

"Praise Jesus, it's me, baby! You can hear me?"

"I can hear you! Oh, have mercy! Grandmama!" Then EJ rolled over on his elbows and knees and cried like the heavens done opened up. I put my hand on his head, but he ain't felt it none. And when he stopped crying, I could tell he was wondering if he had some screws loose—if he'd heard me a'tall or if'n I was all in his head.

"I'm still here," I said. "Right over here."

"Where? Grandmama? Jesus in heaven, is it really you?"

"I'm right here, next to you. Look, I'm right here." And would you know it? EJ turned and looked at me. "It's you! Oh, Grandmama!" He tried to put his fingers up to my face, but they went right through.

"Lord, hallelujah, EJ! I missed you so much, baby. But I'm here, see? Just like Jim was there for me. Now you got me, boy. Ain't that just wonderful?"

I got to say, that was one of the finest moments I've had. Being able to be there with my EJ again and have him see me and hear me. Since that day, I show up for him right regular. Sometimes it's in my old house on Rifle Range but other times I go to that same old cemetery when we talk. Don't matter to me none. I'd sit in an outhouse and talk to my EJ if I had to.

EJ's been plumb tore up after the sweetgrass party over not talking to his mama. He says it's worse on his daddy though, 'cause he lets Eddie see little Cassie. He just won't let Retta near her.

"Son, this has gone on too long now, don't you think?" Eddie asked him one day when he come for a visit. "You're going to have to speak to your mother soon. You're tearing her apart."

"Dad, I have a family to look after now. I'm the man of this house, and I can't let Cassie or Felicia be around a woman who we know deep down is a racist. It's just not going to happen."

"She's not that way, son. She's a good woman. She's your mother, for crying out loud. She didn't do you any harm, did she? You cannot keep her from her own grandchild."

"Oh no? Just watch me," said EJ, and I 'bout fell out my chair. That didn't sound like the grandbaby I always knew, and I sure ain't known what was getting into him.

It was a mistake, what he said, 'cause turns out Eddie's a finer man than I thought he was. Now he says he ain't coming 'round EJ's family either. "If she can't come, then I won't either. She's my wife, and she's a good woman."

Well now, don't that beat all? EJ's trying to protect his little ol' family, but all he's doing is cutting it up like a great big ham on Christmas Day. They spent this last one apart, you know. First Christmas EJ and Retta ever been apart. It's a shame—plumb tore me up.

"EJ, what you doin' ain't right. You got to talk to her. Ask her what she meant. Clear the air up 'tween you two," I tell him. Over and over again. But he don't listen. He's so scared of messing things up for that baby of his—he's trying so hard to protect her from the weeds of racism—he gone and dug up the only living African-American roots that baby got and thrown 'em plumb in the ditch.

I still go down and visit with Henrietta some too. Only difference is, she can't hear me or see me. I know it's 'cause she ain't never asked for me like EJ did. That's okay, though. I still get to be near my baby. She's been hurting something awful though. She ain't got a job no more, and she ain't got her family. Fact is, she ain't got nothing good to do with her time a'tall. She just cries when she's alone and don't let nobody else see her do it but me.

Chapter 38

WHEN I GOT TO HEAVEN, I WAS YOUNG AGAIN and getting younger every day. Ain't that something? Jim was too. Every day we'd say, "Boy howdy, ain't you looking fine today!" Lines and bulges disappeared right 'fore our very eyes. Mm hmm, every morning we'd just jump right out the bed and see how pretty we was getting.

I kept weaving too. I love the joy I feel weaving. Ain't nothing like it to take your mind off the things that bother you. And lately, the situation with Henrietta and EJ's been worrying me a lot. Jim and me never knew you could worry so much up in heaven but we do, anyhow. And it's almost like the age is just sliding right back under our skin. It seems like we each put on a few pounds and gotten more tired ever since the Sweetgrass Soiree.

This morning, Jim and me's over at the fishpond near our house, just a-setting there with our rods. Daddy Jim turns and looks at me funny. Says two new wrinkles done cropped up on my face, and he's rubbing his sore elbow that hurts every time he cast his rod out.

We's sure the fish are 'bout to bite when out the blue, Auntie Leona comes a-calling again.

"Essie Mae! Essie Mae! You got to take a look at this!" She's pointing to the top of her head. "You see this?"

I look at Leona, a voluptuous woman with all them curves a man likes. Then I do see something strange. I lean in real close and stare at her widow's peak at the top of her forehead. "Leona? You always had these gray hairs right up here? Seem like I'm just now noticing 'em."

"Gray hairs—I knew it! No, Essie Mae, I ain't been gray for years! I've been young for long as I can remember!" She grabs at her head and runs her fingers down her curves. Then she turns to us, pale as the ghost she is.

"What in tar-nation?" she says, mostly to herself. Leona walks 'round the pond, and I follow her.

"Leona. Tell me 'bout this turnin' young again. Does it happen for everybody?"

"Well, I reckon it does, Essie Mae. Most everybody I seen in heaven turns young after while—some quicker than others. Your mama and daddy did. You did. I did. Let's see. There is this one real old fella, Avery, you met him over at your mama's house. Remember? He's old as the hills, and he been here longer than me even. Come to think of it, he's always complainin' 'bout his rheumatism and such, but I never thought much about it. Poor thing, he's got a grandson in New Jersey stuck in jail for killin' a man."

"You reckon he worries about him?" I ask her, an idea forming in my head.

"I reckon he does." Leona looks at me concerned, and I take in a deep breath. I can tell she's thinking the same thing I am. We're both trying to figure out what in the world's going on. I walk back around and sit down next to Jim who's reeling in a pretty good size brim.

"Leona, somethin' funny's happenin'. Daddy and I was gettin' younger every day. Now all a sudden since the Soiree and after EJ won't let Retta come 'round no more, we're startin' to age again. That sound right to you?"

"Great God in heaven," says Leona, plopping down on a log across from me. "Same thing's happenin' to me. Is it possible that worryin' 'bout your family's got us aging? 'Cause I can't be gettin' old again, Essie Mae. I just can't!" She swipes at her pretty face and her nice plump lips and whimpers like a puppy left out in the rain.

Leona was always known for her good looks—well, her voodoo for sure—but she always was a looker too. She even died pretty. No, Leona never looked poorly a day in her life, and I reckon she ain't ready to start looking poorly in heaven neither.

Next day, we's all at a pig pickin' over at the big magnolia 'hind Mama and Daddy's house.

"Essie Mae, what wrong wid you?" Mama says. "You ain look good." Mama's frowning at me and Jim and at Leona too. "Ain none ob you look good."

We stare at her right back and say the same thing to her. Seems there's a pocket of flab what's grown up and 'tached itself to her middle section. She's rubbing it and confused as all get-out. That's when we all stop in our tracks. We hear a yelp and see that old man, Mister Avery, collapse nearly dead in his frogmore stew.

Some men-folk haul him off home, and we all turn and stare wide-eyed at each other, worry lines growing by the second. That's when Mama tells us 'bout a conversation she 'members having with Jesus once 'bout aging in heaven.

"'E say us all connected," Mama whispers like she's telling a secret. "Eb'ry las' one ub us—on Earth, up in heaven, pas', presen', future . . . Us aw jus' wound up an' tangled tightuh den you can 'magine."

"What you mean?" asks Leona. "What happens down there on Earth affects us even up here in heaven? But that ain't right. That can't be."

"So that old man ain't never gonna get young?" I cut in, starting to get heated. "Lord have mercy, I can't believe it! Ain't there somethin' we can do? Lord, ain't there somethin' *Jesus* can do? We're in heaven for God's sake. Sweet Jesus, forgive me for takin' your name in vain," I say, getting right frenzied up. I got to lean up 'gainst that big ol' tree to keep from falling. I'm sure of it now; we's all getting older 'cause of my dad-gum offspring.

"Well, we could all stop a-worryin'," pipes up Daddy Jim. He's stooping over, rubbing his lower back.

"Now Jim, that's 'bout the most worthless thing you ever said. There ain't no way I can just let my babies stay torn apart," I say, annoyed as all get-out.

"I ain't finished, Mama," says Jim. "I meant to say, either we can stop a-worryin' 'bout 'em, or EJ and Retta can start actin' right. One or th'other."

"Ain dat de truth," Mama says, seeing I'm 'bout to cry and wrapping her arms around me. "Lawd, ain dat the truth."

That's when I know what I got to do. Looks like the only thing I can do for everybody's sake is to keep a-praying for my young'uns and keep a-chattering in EJ's ear. And seeing as Jesus ain't intervened yet and EJ ain't listened to a word I got to say, neither one's gotten me nowhere so far.

Chapter 39

March

THERE'S A PLACE UP HERE IN HEAVEN, down by the marsh grass. I like to go there every day and weave by myself. I'm feeling older, so I like to take it real easy nowadays. I sit down on a nice tree trunk carved out to fit like a chair, and I weave with grass that's dried just right. The palms never split on me, and the baskets go up higher and bigger and prettier than the ones I made in Mount Pleasant any day.

I'm midway though a nice one, has bulrush stripes moving on up, when I hear some rustling in the leaves behind me.

"Jim?" I call out. But no one says nothing. So I go back to weaving, thinking it was a raccoon or a deer or some such. Then I hear it again. This time, I turn around and see something I ain't expected to see. Barefoot and wearing a white smock tied in the back like a baby doll is a little girl no bigger than a minute. Her hair's the color of autumn leaves and pulled back behind her ears. Her eyes are green, a piercing green that takes me aback, seeing as her skin's dark and milky brown. She stands there with her hands in front of her chest, just watching me.

"Well, hello there, missy. What you doing 'round these parts? I ain't never seen you here before." I smile at her and sit up straighter. "My name's Essie Mae. What's your name?"

The girl don't say a word. She just shifts her bare feet in the dirt. I wonder if she got a voice to talk with.

"You live 'round here?" I ask her. She looks around all uncomfortable-like, and I stay quiet and still. Finally, I put down my weaving, and she opens her mouth.

"Don't stop," she says, holding her hand out. I can tell she ain't meant to say nothing but the words just slipped right on out.

"So you *can* talk," I say, smiling and sucking my top teeth. "Why don't you have a seat over yonder. You can watch me if you like."

So I weave. And she watches me. She sits there, white dress on the green grass with the water flowing back behind her and egrets soaring over her head. She fiddles with her fingers and chews on her nails. I sit here, too, studying her face when she's watching my hands. She's right pretty, most likely eleven or twelve years old.

"I've been weaving since before I was your age," I tell her. She glances those green eyes my way, and I get shivers up my spine. "Yes sir, my mama taught me how to weave under an old pecan tree we had back in Mount Pleasant, South Carolina. You ever been to Mount Pleasant?" I ask her. She just shakes her head.

"Well now, does your mama and daddy know you're over this way? When you s'posed to be home for supper?"

"I ain't got a mama or daddy," she tells me. My mouth falls open big enough for flies to come in, and I rest my hands on my lap. I don't know what to say.

"No parents? Well, who you livin' with, then?"

She looks off over the water.

"Ain't living with nobody neither. I live in a little house over 'cross the river." She points real matter-o'-fact.

Now I just can't believe it, so I ask her 'gain, "By yourself?"

"Uh huh," she answers like it ain't no big deal.

Well I swanny, I can't believe what I'm hearing. Here's this cute little ol' thing in her tattered dress and no shoes. This is heaven, for goodness sake! How come a little girl ain't got no parents?

"You want to learn how to weave?" I ask her for lack of something smarter to say. The girl swallows and looks down at her feet.

"That'd be good," she says real soft.

"Well then, I'd be happy to show you how. But first," I hold up my finger, and she looks a-feared. "First, I need to have me some supper. All this weavin' is making me plumb hungry. You like cornbread and chicken-fried steak?" That little thing's eyes turn round and big as I ever seen, and I think she even licks her lips, but then she gets shy all a sudden.

"Ain't you hungry? Come on up and have some fixin's with Daddy Jim and me. Jim sure would like to meet you."

The girl smiles from ear to ear, and I see she got little cornrow teeth, like a baby still.

"You sure ain't nobody gonna miss you comin' home for supper?"

"No, nobody," she says.

"Well now, here I am 'bout to have you over to the house, and·you ain't even told me your name yet."

"Ain't got no name," she says, just like that. That's when I got to say, "Lord Jesus, this child ain't got no name?! Well, what do folks call you?"

"Nothing much. Sometimes they call me 'girl' and other times, 'honey' or 'sugar.'"

"Well, every child's got to have a proper name, now. This just won't do." So now, this little girl and me pick up my grass and the basket I was working on, and we head on back toward the house. We don't say much the whole way, what with me wondering about this young'un. How can this little thing make it alone? How'd she get here? She got to come from somewhere. So I think about that sort of thing as we shuffle on back through the tall green grass. And she looks up at me every now and again and smiles a smile so big that my heart begins to melt just like butter a-bubblin' on the stove.

"Y'ain't got no name?" asks Jim, taken aback. We's sitting at the table just a-looking at each other, thinking it's mighty strange to have a young girl with us for supper. It's almost like having Retta back when she was a little girl. Even looks like her a little. "What kinda folks don't give a child a name?"

I shush him, hoping he won't make no big fuss. "She lives by herself over 'cross the river, Jim, now pass me some cornbread."

Jim hands me a sweetgrass basket filled up with cornbread squares. I grab me one and another for the girl. I set it on her plate and pass her the butter, and she slabs it on like there ain't no tomorrow. Then I ladle some meat and gravy on her plate too. That sweet thing gobbles like she ain't had a bite in weeks.

I can hear Jim chewing a mouthful and then he stops. I look up at him 'cause I can hear the wheels turning in his head. He's watching her. "Well, what you want your name to be?" he asks. "I reckon you can have any one you want."

The girl puts her napkin up to her mouth and looks at Jim and then back at me. Her eyes turn glitter like Christmas morning. It's hard for me to believe nobody ever offered her a name before. After a second or two she says, "Well, how 'bout Henrietta?"

That's when you could 'a knocked Jim and me on the floor with a nickel.

"Henrietta? Well, I'll be," says Jim. "Mama, this girl wants to be called Henrietta, don't that beat all?" Then he turns to her and says, "Well, I think that's a mighty fine name, but it's gonna get confusin' on us, I reckon. How about Eliza or Martha instead? See, our daughter's name is Henrietta too. I'm tellin' you the truth. She lives over back in Mount Pleasant where we's from."

"I like Eliza. I can be Eliza," she says, sounding out every syllable real slow. "E-li-za. I s'pose it could get confusin' anyway. My mama's name is Henrietta too."

Now that's just a coincidence I can't ignore. She smacks her lips and grins at us, her mouth full as it can be of chicken-fried steak.

"I thought you said you don't have no mama or daddy," I say real low, a pit settling down in my belly.

"Well, I don't," she says, matter-o'-fact-like. "Mama and Daddy ain't in heaven yet. They still down in Mount Pleasant."

Well, you could 'a kicked me in the head and it wouldn't feel no different. Jim and me stop dead as two deer in headlights. He looks at me funny, and I start choking on my iced tea. It gone down the wrong way. In the middle of my coughing fit, my face starts getting all hot and flushed. My mind's racing as all get-out. Mount Pleasant? *Mount Pleasant!* I 'member back to EJ and Felicia's wedding; I'd heard Retta thinking about a baby she ain't never had. My knees start to buckle, and I'm scared of what I might hear, but I got to ask anyway. "Your daddy's name ain't . . . Eddie, child, is it?"

That girl baby squinches her eyes up and says, "Naw. My daddy's name ain't Eddie. It's Ray." Then she grabs a hunk of cornbread and sticks it in her pretty little mouth.

Well you could cut the air with a knife 'cause Jim and me's so tense. And when we find out our Retta ain't this girl's mama, we just giggle and get to belly laughing so hard that Jim rolls right on out his chair.

But our peace and laughing don't last too long, no sir. 'Cause soon as we get up and I'm clearing the dishes, I hear Jim say to Eliza from the living room, "Look here. This is a picture of our Henrietta. This is our sweet daughter. Ain't she pretty?" Then I hear a *thump* from Jim falling flat on the floor.

When I come to see what all the ruckus is all about, Eliza's setting there, cradling that picture in her arms. "That's my mama," she says, looking confused. "Why you got a picture of my mama in here?"

Chapter 40

WELL, IT'S HARD TO GET OVER, sure 'nough. Jim and me's so upset our Retta's been with some man other than Eddie. Eddie always treated her right—better even than she should be treated sometimes by the way she acts.

We decided not to say nothing more 'bout it to Eliza last night, but made her sleep over in the spare bedroom. It's fixed up real nice just the way Henrietta's was when she was a girl. There's even a little teddy bear; Eliza slept like a baby, hugging that bear. Jim and me just sat up fretting 'til the sun come back up.

I make Liza some eggs and grits and buttered toast for breakfast. She even eats oatmeal after that and two glasses of orange juice. Sure is a hungry little thing.

The weight of it all makes me stagger like an old mule. She's our grandbaby. Just like EJ. It's hard for us to take in but we got to know more, so we asked if we could walk with her back to her house.

Liza skips a few paces ahead of us, hopping on rocks and picking flowers 'long the way. I hold on to Jim's arm. He's moving right slow this morning—got a look on his face like the whole world's just ironing him to the ground.

"There it is," says Liza, pointing and turning to us. I see what looks like an oversized tree house. It's painted baby blue with a crooked porch on the front and flowers growing out of every which-a-way, in the crevices around the door and in the floorboards.

She holds my hand and pulls us inside. We's in a little living space with two chairs covered in worn stripes and a fireplace with no wood in it. The walls is painted a bright red, and it makes it hard to relax when we so anxious already. She has us sit in them two little chairs, and we feel like giants.

"I'll get us some milk," she says and disappears into the lime-green kitchen. We hear dishes rattling in the other room and Jim pushes himself out the chair to go stare at the wall. There's pictures of people all over it. Most are little people, girls and boys with happy faces and bows and such. Then he sighs when he sees the picture of Henrietta. I move on over to him to get a good look myself.

My throat knots up. There's no doubt about it. It's my Retta, all right. I hold on to my chest and tears come to my eyes. That sweet thing in the other room is our granddaughter, sure 'nough! I think I might bust from being so happy and sad all at the same time.

We move over a little and my weary eyes rest on a wood frame with a man in the middle. I wipe my face and grab Jim's arm tight when I see it. Lord have mercy, I recognize that face.

It's a white man 'bout forty years old. Got balding red hair and a little pointed nose and his lips are just two straight lines. But the thing that does it is the eyes. They's deep emerald green. I remember them eyes. How could I forget? It's all starting to make sense to me now.

I met him one time, back when I was still driving. I'd gone over to the office to meet Retta for something. Must have been dropping off—food?—baskets? I can't remember what right now. But he gave me a real happy hello. I can 'member thinking, *Why that sure is a nice man.*

I turn around and walk back to my chair, and Jim follows me, helping lower me down.

"You all right, Mama?" he asks me. I can't answer him, though. I just keep a-staring at that photograph.

Finally, I find my tongue and say real weak-like, "That man, Daddy. I know him."

"You know him? Who is he, then?" Jim stands next to me, holding my hand and watching that picture like it might move if we don't keep an eye on it.

"That's Ray Fines, Jim."

He looks at me quiet.

"Ray Fines, Jim," I whisper again. "Retta's old boss."

Jim's face goes pale, and he looks like he might stumble. I start to help him sit in his chair but Eliza's back now. She sets three glasses of tall cold milk on a little table then walks him to his seat. Sweet thing serves us one by one, careful not to spill a drop.

Eliza's grinning like a little angel. "I always wanted real family," she says. "They give me these pictures but it ain't the same. I can't believe I got me a grandmama *and* a granddaddy now. But here we all are, ain't we? Ain't that somethin'? Is your milk good? Should I get you some cookies? I got lots o' cookies, you know."

I grab her hand when she's pointing back to the kitchen and say, "No, baby. Just come sit here with us." I look around for another place to sit, but she just plops down Indian style on the wood floor in front of the fireplace.

We stare at that girl for the longest time. I'm just taking in that pretty face. Her eyes are like Retta's if'n they weren't green. And it's hard for me not to feel pain when I look in 'em, knowing my baby done been with her boss man. My mind fumbles on so. I keep thinking, *What could 'a happened? Did he force her to lay with him? Did he take advantage of my sweet Retta? Or worse, did she go with him on her own will? Did she plan on running 'round on poor Eddie?*

Liza looks down at her feet and then out the window when we's so quiet. Finally, I say, "Come here, Liza, baby." And she rises up and walks to me, her hands dangling down her sides.

"I'm just so happy to finally know you," I say, tears streaming down my cheeks. She looks at me funny and then leans in and wraps her arms around me. She hugs me so tight, I think the breath might leave me and never come back. And the smell of her, the sweet innocence of her just a-washes over me. I hope she never lets me go.

"I'll love you forever, little Miss Liza," I say. She pulls back from me, and I see there's tears in her eyes too.

"Well now, don't forget about your old granddaddy," says Jim, and Liza flies on over to him to kiss his forehead.

"You 'bout ready to start weavin', baby?" I ask her after she lets him go, and she squeals with pleasure and runs to the door. Then we walk on out by the water again and have us our first weaving lesson, grandmama and granddaughter—just like it ought to be.

Chapter 41

April

THAT LITTLE LIZA, SHE'S A FAST LEARNER. Sure is. Nowadays, she's almost a better weaver than me, and it's only been about a month in Mount Pleasant time.

I've been weaving a lot with Eliza; it's the most fun being with her. She wants to know all about her family. Mama and Daddy and Leona met her. They're just as smitten as Jim and me. She wants to hear 'bout her mama and family back in Mount Pleasant too. Since she ain't never been to Earth and don't know the way, I told her when the time's right I might take her down myself.

So I tell Liza much as I know 'bout her earthly family. And I don't keep nothing from her neither. I tell her all about her brother—that I love him much as I love her, but that he's being mighty pig-headed right now. That seems to tear Liza up, thinking he's being mean to Retta. The only thing I ain't 'splained to her yet is how her daddy, Ray, weren't married to Retta. That's just something I don't like to bring up.

Last time I seen him, I told EJ I was plumb tired of how he was acting toward Retta, and I was gonna stay away for a bit, hoping that would make him come to his senses. Daddy Jim's been keeping his eye on things in Mount Pleasant, though. Things still ain't right with EJ and his mama. "Felicia's been chewing on EJ," he tells me, "wanting him to call up Henrietta. Says she got her a racist grandmama, sure 'nough, and she knows one when she sees it. And Retta ain't one."

"You think he's gonna call her?" I ask, hoping and praying.

"Don't rightly know," he says.

We sit quiet for a while, me weaving on the porch and him chewing that pipe and whittling a walking stick. Then Liza comes on up wearing a pretty blue dress I sewed her and nice leather shoes.

"Hey, baby!" I wave at her. "Come on up here, sugar. I got something for you."

She pops up the steps and stands there waiting for her treat. A couple times, she don't know what to do with her excitement and sticks her hands out to me. Then, she thinks better and puts 'em round her back.

"What is it? What you got me?" She can't stand it. Jim looks over at me, too, 'cause he don't know what I got neither.

I hold out my hand, fist closed and face down. Then I roll my wrist over and open my fingers real slow.

"What is it?" she asks me. She leans down real close to my hand and looks hard. "You got me some thread, Grandmama? You gonna teach me how to sew?"

"That ain't thread, Liza. Look close. Them is two hairs—one from your mama and one from your brother, EJ." Well, that little ol' thing looks real interested then. Jim do too. Liza reaches out and touches 'em and goes to grab 'em up when I pull my hand back and say, "Careful, baby. These're all I got."

"What we gonna do with 'em?"

"Yeah, what you gonna do with 'em?" Jim asks me, catching on now and smiling like a sly fox.

I grab Eliza's hand and turn it over. Then I undo my hand into hers and leave them two hairs setting in it like gold. She closes her fingers tight on her treasure.

"Now don't you lose 'em," I warn. "You hear? Baby, we gonna weave the finest basket you ever did see with them hairs, and we gonna bring your mama and your brother back together 'gain for good."

Well with that, Liza smiles so big I think her gums might pop out. She holds that one fist closed up so tight I think the circ'lation's gonna cut plumb off. Then she runs down the steps and hollers for me to come on.

"Them ain't hairs, are they, Mama?" asks Jim. "You can't have Retta and EJ's hairs up here. I just know you can't."

"What she don't know ain't gonna hurt her, Daddy. Long as she believes this basket's gonna fix her mama's pain, that's all that matters, don't you think?"

"I reckon so," he says and sucks that pipe. Then I haul up all my grass and pine needles and we leave Jim a-grinning at us while we walk on down the lane toward our favorite weaving spot near the water and marsh grass.

258

Chapter 42

May

NOW THIS BASKET THAT ELIZA WEAVED, it's better than any I ever done in my whole life. She's a natural if I ever seen one. It's almost big as her, sweet thing, and it has real dainty stripes of bulrush going all the way up and French buttons too. There's two real nice handles on the side for carrying and a great big, flat, and steady base where she put them two threads I give her.

"It's done, Grandmama! It's done. I did it!"

"Whooee! Eliza? That is the prettiest basket I ever did see. Ain't no doubt, your love basket's gonna work. Yes it is."

"What we do with it now?"

"Well now, we got to sit and wait a while. I ain't rightly sure what to do next, but I'm prayin' I'll know soon enough."

Well, don't you know? Soon enough comes right soon.

I decide to make a visit with EJ. He don't know I'm coming, but he's easy enough to find—out back behind the house on Rifle

Range Road. He's cleaning up the yard and filling up a bag full o' cut grass.

"EJ, baby?"

He wheels around and looks for me, dropping his rake.

"Grandmama? You there?"

"I'm here, baby, right by the big oak." He looks over and sees me, and a smile spreads 'cross his lips what could melt the North Pole, I reckon.

"Glad you finally decided to talk to me," he says, a little snooty.

"Well, I didn't want to, but I figured I weren't actin' no better than you are. You talked to your mama yet?"

"No. I'm not planning on it either."

I want to fuss at him so hard right now, but I bite my lip and try to take a deep breath instead. "You know there's nothin' more important than family, EJ? Not one thing in this whole world."

"I understand that more than you know. That's why I'm protecting my family from her. Is that all you came to talk about?"

I hold my words while little Cassie comes wandering 'round back. She's just a little bitty thing, wearing a green T-shirt what says Grass Roots Society on it. She's carrying a tiny doll in one hand and waddles over to her daddy and then falls in the grass, rolling around laughing. Lord, I've missed that child! EJ looks at me sad-like and then lifts her off the ground. He holds her tight and smells her hair. I swanny, she looks a lot like Miss Eliza.

"I need to speak to your mama," I tell him, breaking my silence. He sits Cassie down, and she scoots on off toward Felicia who's pruning shrubs across the yard.

"You'll have to go talk to her then," he says, picking up his rake and shuffling some acorns around.

"I can't. She hasn't asked to talk to me."

"Well then, I suppose you'll have to wait until that happens."

"Now listen hear, child. Don't you mouth off to me. I am still your grandmama, and you ain't being nothin' but a dad-gum fool right now."

He looks at me, scared to death.

"You heard me. I'm ashamed of how you're actin'."

"But what about her? What about what she said? What she thinks? For all I know, she thinks my daughter is too white, for Christ's sake!"

I want to tell him, *Don't you dare take the Lord's name in vain,* but I let it go for now.

"Baby, you don't know why she do what she do and thinks what she thinks. I ain't 'xactly sure neither. That's why I got to talk to her." He looks at me like he's 'bout to give in, then his face hardens and he goes to raking faster. I can almost see steam coming from his ears.

"There's someone your mama needs to meet," I tell him, and he stops. He stares at the rake. "She's someone you need to meet too."

"Who is it?"

"You find out soon enough when you meet her," I say, hoping he won't call my bluff. EJ looks at me like the little boy I always knew and loved, and his nose twitches. Then he leans down on that rake handle and cries.

"There, there, baby," I tell him. "Everythin's gonna be all right. You'll see. The mountains in heaven and Earth might move from here to there, but mark my words, this family's gonna be just fine." I hope so anyway. I'm already older than I was when I died, and I just don't think me or Jim can stand no more aging.

EJ rubs his nose on the back of his sleeve, and I can see a mountain done moved off his shoulders, sure 'nough. I see my chance there, so I take it.

"So you'll ask your mama to speak with me? Will you do that, baby?"

After a minute or so, EJ answers real quiet. "Yeah. I'll do it."

When he says those words, I'm pretty sure I hear angels singing. And when I go on back up to heaven, sure 'nough, there they are, serenading Jim in his rocking chair. He's covered in a throw, rocking up a storm, and got the biggest ol' smile on his face I think I ever seen.

Chapter 43

On Sunday, EJ goes to the Lord's house. He puts Cassie in the nursery and sits next to Felicia at the Mt. Zion AME Church. Reverend Jefferson's talking 'bout the benefits of a giving heart and how we should all be servants like Jesus, but EJ ain't listening. He's thinking 'bout his mama. But I believe the good Lord's talking to him anyway. 'Cause once the service is over with, EJ drives his family on home, and while Felicia puts the baby down for a nap, EJ gets on the telephone and sure 'nough, calls up Retta's house.

The phone rings when Henrietta's taking off her earrings. She's undressing after going to that church in West Ashley, and Eddie's down in the kitchen making a sandwich.

"Can you get the phone?" she hollers down to him. He's just a-chomping into some crunchy bacon and all he can hear is the sound inside his head.

After a few rings, Henrietta huffs and runs down the hall to a little table set below a mirror. She picks up the telephone annoyed like, *Who in the world's bothering me on a Sunday afternoon?* And when she hears it's EJ's voice, she almost falls flat. I'm there with her, looking at the pretty curve of her neck. Her hand trembles holding the telephone and after he tells her he wants to come and talk to her, she hangs it up and puts her head against the wall, feeling the coolness of it. She closes her eyes and squeezes out one single tear. Then she smiles and hurries off to her bedroom to get herself fixed up again.

"Maybe he'll bring the baby!" says Retta, dancing 'round the living room. "We need to baby-proof this place. Look at all this stuff! There's danger everywhere. Oh no, we don't have any outlet thingies. She'll get electrocuted! Edmund, what if she sticks her finger in a socket!"

Eddie goes in front of her and grabs her shoulders. "Re-lax, Henrietta. Everything will be just fine. And don't get your hopes up, okay? He might not even bring the baby. Did EJ tell you what he wanted to talk about?"

"Well, no, but I'm sure he wants to work things out. I mean, he could just stay away, right? This is good, Edmund. I just know it is!"

Eddie's eyebrows are stitched together, hoping EJ's coming is good news. You can see in his eyes he's tired, and he don't want his wife to suffer no more.

"Let's just have some tea and wait for him, okay? Why don't you go make some tea?" Retta jumps at the chance to give her hands something to do, and she runs off into the kitchen.

Eddie walks on over to the window and watches the road for EJ. When he sees him, he slips out the front door quiet as he can and meets him when he's stepping out the car. EJ's driving a brand-new one now. My old station wagon's just gathering dust in the lot 'side his house. This here new car's big enough for a family and got a baby seat tied in the back.

"Son," Eddie breathes, grabbing EJ and hugging him hard. He pats him on the back twice and then pushes him away, looking over at the windows. "You don't know how excited your mother is that you're coming over here." EJ stares at the windows too. "Why are you here, son? Are you planning on making things right with your mother? Because if you're not, I'm going to have to ask you to leave."

Well, EJ looks like somebody done shot him in the foot. "I just need to talk to her."

"About what?"

"Dad, I need to talk to my mother. All right? I promise you, I'm not trying to make things worse."

Eddie gives him a stern look and then lightens up. "All right then," he says. "Come on in."

Eddie puts his arms around EJ and tries to usher him to the door, but EJ stops short. "I sort of need to talk to her alone." Eddie's thinking on this, and I'm thinking he's 'bout to tell him to go on home or go to Hades, but he don't do neither.

"All right, then. I'll go." He grabs EJ's arm and says, "But I'm trusting you not to break your mother's heart any more than you already have. She was hoping Cassie was coming over, you know. She's been fretting for an hour that we don't have baby-proofed electrical outlets."

At that, I think I see a hint of a smile come into EJ's eyes, and he turns toward the door.

"Thanks, Dad," EJ says when Eddie picks up a walking stick and heads on down the road for a good long stroll 'round the neighborhood.

I hold my breath when Henrietta opens the door. The tension's so thick, I can see it like a purple cloud hovering over 'em. EJ's all a-jumbled inside and Henrietta's scared to death, not knowing whether to reach out to him or not. She looks back behind him to see if Cassie's there—and then decides to just smile at him and move to the side so he can come on in.

"Would you like some tea?" she asks him, showing her pearly whites.

"I don't know how long I'll be staying, so I guess not." EJ leaves Retta's gaze and walks to the wall of photographs in the living room. He looks at my picture and seems to be working up the gumption to say what he come to say.

"It's been a while, hasn't it?" Retta asks. EJ stays real quiet. "How's The Grass Roots Society?"

"It's fine," he says. "We're making good progress."

"That's good," says Retta. "And the baby? How's Cassie?"

EJ sucks in his breath and thinks about what to say but before he can speak, she says, "I'm just so glad you're here, EJ. I can't tell you how much it means."

"Mom, don't." EJ holds up his hand. "Let me just say what I need to, okay?"

"Okay," she says, lowering into a high-back chair and crossing her legs real proper. Her back's so straight you could flip a flapjack on it.

"I know this is going to sound crazy," he begins, "but, I don't know, you'll just have to take it for what it is, I guess." EJ looks a-pained and puts his face in his hands.

"Grandmama," he says, and his face squinches up. He's trying to hold back tears. "Grandmama . . . *talks* to me, Mom."

Retta's eyes narrow. "She does?"

He looks at her. "Yes, but that's not the point, I guess. Listen. I know this is weird, but . . . well, she told me she needs to talk to you. That's why I'm here. She made me promise."

"She did, did she?" Henrietta stands up from her chair and goes to look out the window. I reckon she's looking for Eddie down the road.

"Listen, Mom, I don't know what she wants. And I know it sounds crazy, but she comes to me. Just like Granddaddy used to come and sit with her. Mom, I swear to you, I was talking to her one day at the cemetery and the next thing I knew, I could see her, and she was talking right back."

With that, Retta looks alarmed like she's halfway believing him. She opens her mouth to speak but nothing comes out.

"So what does she say to you?" she asks finally.

"Well, mostly, she tries to get me to bury the hatchet with you."

Henrietta's eyes fill with tears, and she walks to my photograph and touches my face.

"She says she sees you all the time, but you can't see her because you've never asked to."

"What?" Retta's struggling. Her eyes dart back and forth and she puts her hands on her mouth. Then she says, "EJ, honey, don't get me wrong, but this is all just a little too much . . ."

"I'm telling you the *truth*, Mother. Trust me, I did not want to come here, but I promised her I'd tell you what she said."

"And what's that?" she says, getting huffy. "That I'm a racist? That I'm unfit to be a grandmother?" Retta turns away from him and holds back a sob.

"No, Mama." EJ sits down on the sofa and says real quiet, "She said you need to meet somebody."

Retta gets real still. "Who?"

"I don't know. She wouldn't tell me. She said you have to ask to see her first."

Retta smooths her pants out and straightens her face. She looks like she's 'bout to say something, but then she scurries out the room real quick. EJ just sits there, not moving.

When she comes back a few minutes later, her face is puffy and she's carrying two tall iced tea glasses. She don't say a word, but walks right over to EJ and hands him one. He takes it and looks her in the eyes.

Retta sits down across from him and says real formal-like, "So I'm just supposed to ask Mama to come to me and she will? EJ, Mama's dead. It's taken me a long time to put her to rest. And now I'm supposed to believe she's with me all the time?"

"Just . . . ask to see her, Mom. Just do it. Please?"

Retta jerks her head a little and sets her glass down on a coaster.

"All right then," she says, folding her hands in her lap. "Mother, it's Henrietta," she says persnickety-like. "If you're here, please let me see you."

Some time goes by with EJ and Retta looking around. Nothing happens.

"I don't see her, EJ. She didn't *appear*." Retta stands and walks a few steps. "I think I've heard just about enough. If you didn't come here to try and work things out with me, maybe it's just best that you go now."

EJ huffs and stands up. That's when I know I got to do something.

"EJ?"

He turns around, eyes wide.

"EJ, baby, it's me. Grandmama."

Chapter 44

"GRANDMAMA!" yells EJ. "It's you! Mom, there she is. See? I told you she'd be here."

Retta looks at EJ and then searches over by the door where he's staring. She looks right through me and don't see a thing. Retta looks back at EJ, terrified.

"Honey? Do you see Mama right now?"

"Yes! She's right there. Hey," he sings, smiling and giving a tiny wave.

Retta bites her lip. She ain't sure what to say.

"I don't think she sees me, baby," I tell him.

"What?" He turns to her. "Mom. Can you see her? She's right there. Can't you see her?"

She breathes in real deep and tears well up in her eyes. "No, I can't." Then she walks out the room fast as lightning. I ain't sure if she's upset 'cause only EJ can see me or if it's 'cause she thinks he's crazy. Either one's bad enough, I reckon.

"Mom!" EJ yells after her.

"Just wait here a second," I say. "Give her a minute."

"But why can't she see you?"

"Don't know, baby. Maybe 'cause she don't really believe she can?"

"Well this is just great. Now I look like a dad-gum fool. Why'd I even come here?"

"Hold on, baby. Let me think." Just then, I get an idea. "EJ, run tell your mama that . . . tell her I know all about her baby."·

"What? What baby?"

"Just mind me and run on and tell her that."

So he does.

"What?" Retta says, a strange look coming over her face.

"I don't know, Mama. That's just what she told me to say. Just come on back in here, please?"

"Fine. But son, I have to say, I'm beginning to worry about you now."

Henrietta comes back in the living room and EJ follows her.

"Tell her to go on and sit down," I say.

"She said she wants you to sit down."

Henrietta glares at him and then sits in an overstuffed chair.

"Now tell her again, I know all about her baby—the one she ain't never had."

EJ looks at me hard. He's digesting my words. His forehead gets lines all 'cross it, and he sits real quiet, looking down at the rug. "Mama, Grandmama says . . . she knows all about the baby you never had." He looks up at her then.

Retta pales. She puts her hands up to her cheeks and looks over toward me, her eyes all wet.

"Mom, is this true?" he asks.

"How could you know this?" Retta hisses at him. "Nobody knows! Nobody!"

"So it *is* true?"

"EJ, baby," I interrupt. "Tell your mama to ask to see me again. Tell her to do it now."

"Mom, she wants you to ask to see her again. Ask her just one more time, all right?"

This time Retta really starts crying and it takes her a few minutes to straighten up. When she does, she gets herself all prepared, shoulders squared and knees firmed. Then she says real slow, "Mama? Are you there? It's me, Henrietta. Oh, Mama, if you're there, *please* let me see you."

Glory in heaven, by the look in them pretty brown eyes, I know she seen me at last.

"Mama? Mama?! Have mercy. I can't believe it! Is this real? Oh sh—"

"Watch your mouth, Retta."

"Oh, Mama, it *is* you!" And she laughs and then boo-hoos and runs over and hugs EJ, scaring him half to death. She buries her head in his neck and just lets loose. A tear or two slides down EJ's face, and he closes his eyes and pats her on the back. Finally, them two's together. I'm so touched, I get to crying too.

When Retta finally picks her head back up, she wipes at her eyes and then stands. She moves over to me on padded feet and looks me in the eyes. I can't tell you what it feels like, seeing my baby in the face again. Knowing the barrier between us—between life and death—is gone for good.

"Hey, Mama," she says, quietly. Henrietta smiles a real sweet smile. She puts her fingers up to my face, but she can't feel me. "So it's true. All those years you really did see Daddy."

"All those years," I say.

Retta sucks in a breath real quick and her eyes go big. "Mama? Can I see Daddy too?"

"I reckon so," I say, just when Jim shows up next to me.

"Retta, baby. My sweet girl," he tells her. He's standing here wearing his finest wool hat.

"Oh, Daddy!" She falls down on her knees and starts boo-hooing again.

"It's all right, honey. I'm right here," says Jim. "Daddy's always been right here."

Well, it's all just too much for Retta to take in. EJ finally comes over and gets down on his knees next to her and grabs her tight. She clings to him like there's no tomorrow. Daddy Jim and EJ share a knowing look. I can tell he's so glad to finally see his granddaddy, but there's plenty of time for them to talk later.

After a few minutes, Retta tries to pull herself together. She can't decide whether she should be crying or laughing, so she does both. Jim and me hold hands and we're the happiest we been in a long time.

All a sudden, EJ leaves his mama's side and goes out the room. When he comes back in, he's carrying a big box of tissues and hands one to Retta.

"This is amazing," she says. "I just can't believe it. I *can't* believe it!"

"Retta, baby?" I say real sweet. "Listen honey. There's somebody else wants to come see you."

273

"Really?" Retta sits up on her knees like a little girl and pats her hair down.

"Yes. It's your baby, honey. She's just the sweetest thing. Jim and me, we just love her to pieces."

Henrietta scrunches her face up. She sucks back tears and breathes in and out and then she says, "And she wants to see me? Really? Have mercy. No."

"No? Baby you don't want to see her?" Jim asks, getting upset.

"No! I mean, yes! Of course, I do! I just can't believe this is happening, is all." Retta leaves us then and looks like she gone far off in another world from us. Her eyes glaze over and a pain comes through her face so deep, it hurts me to see it. Eliza's calling to me, wanting to come down seeing as I already done showed her how.

"Retta? You wanna see your baby? We named her Eliza. You like that? You wanna see her now? She's ready for you."

"Oh God. Oh God, forgive me," says Retta under her breath. "Yes," she answers. "I would love nothing more than to see my baby."

"All right, sugar," I say to Liza. "Come on down here quick. Come and meet your mama."

Next thing we know, Liza shows up holding that great big basket what's almost big as her. She looks a little scared, and when her mama sees her, looks like Retta gonna up and die. We think she might, too, 'cause she falls plumb over on her side and cries on the floor like a little baby herself.

"Mama? Mama, don't cry. Here I am. It's just me," Liza says, holding her hand out.

Henrietta's wailing now, 'bout to scare poor EJ to death. He got a terrible look on his face like the world might be ending right here and now.

"Mama? Are you all right?" He picks her up and cradles her shoulders. Retta wipes her nose with the tissue and grabs for another one.

"Oh, sweet child! Oh, have mercy. Oh, baby! My baby, my baby, my baby . . ." Retta reaches her arms out to touch her, but course she can't. I'm watching EJ's face. Henrietta catches mine and then remembers he's here, and her eyes grow big. "EJ!"

"Mama, do you see somebody?" he asks, looking confused. "I can't see her. Why can't I see her?"

Retta looks helpless at me and Jim and we just shrug. "I don't know," I say. "Maybe she's just for you, Retta."

Henrietta grabs at her chest and looks back at Liza.

"Oh, baby. Is it really you?" she cries. "Look at you, honey. You're so pretty. Oh God have mercy, I am so, so sorry! You'll never know. *Have mercy, God have mercy!* I'm so sorry, baby!" Retta clenches her fists and holds 'em up, shaking in the air. Her whole body's shaking now.

"Don't cry, Mama," says Liza, looking scared and starting to get worked up. "Don't cry. It's okay. I love you, Mama. See? I brought you something. Grandmama's been teaching me to weave, and I'm getting pretty good at it. See this? I made this here basket for you, Mama. Here it is. Ain't it pretty? Mama? Do you like it? Do you like it, Mama? Ain't it pretty?"

Chapter 45

"MAMA? DO YOU LIKE IT? Can you see this, Mama? I made it just for you."

All a sudden, my body falls down and hits the ground hard. It feels like a ton of bricks just fell all over me. My body aches with a pain I just can't believe, and my head feels fuzzy and thick. My ears hurt with a plumb-awful sound like rushing waters flooding my brain. Then I hear this funny beeping noise and turn my head to see it. I push and push and all a sudden, my eyes open up. Good Lord have mercy, I can't believe what I see.

Liza ain't here no more. Neither is Jim. But EJ and Retta are there looking down over me, and there's that great big basket Liza weaved, cradled in Retta's arms.

"Mama? Mama! Come quick, EJ! Mama!" Henrietta drops that basket on the floor and leans down on me, hugging me tight. And I feel it. Dad-gum, I feel her warm body up against mine. I feel the wetness of her tears as she kisses my face. I smell the perfume in her hair, and I'd like to bust right outta my skin. I know where I am, but I just can't believe it.

"Grandmama?" says EJ, leaning in and sitting next to me. He puts his hand up on my forehead and runs his fingers over my braids. Then he leans down and kisses me on the cheeks and the eyes and the forehead and everywhere else he can find to kiss. I'm alive. I ain't dead no more, and it's the strangest thing, but I'm confused, and I don't know how to feel about it all.

June

I was gone right near eight months, what they tell me. Which is strange, 'cause in heaven, 'bout four years passed. I reckon heaven time and Earth time ain't the same thing a'tall. Don't matter though. In the past couple months, I've learned how to talk again. I can sit up and visit with my EJ. He comes to see me every day, and every other time he brings Felicia—sure 'nough, they got married while I was away. I just ain't told 'em I was at the wedding too. Felicia's expecting, but Miss Cassie ain't been born yet.

Yes sir, everything seems all fine and good, but I'm getting right tired of being in this hospital bed, and I can't wait to get on outta here.

Jeffrey comes to see me lots and even little Miss Susanne Maybree. They brought flowers and cookies and everything I needed. I got magazines and books and my very own big-print Bible what has my name in it, Essie Mae Laveau Jenkins. I been doing a lot of reading and talking to Jesus who brought me on back for more living to do.

The doctors say they ain't never seen nothing quite like it. I was in a coma for a long while, and they was saying I'd never wake up. But Retta wouldn't listen to 'em none. She never gave up on me. In fact, Retta's been here with me in the hospital room almost every second. She'd long quit her job at that office, and Eddie don't mind none. He lets her come as often as she wants. He's a good man, that Eddie. I'll always love him for that.

Retta would sit there with me, praying and weaving 'til the wee hours of the night. I got baskets growing up all around me. The nurses say that's what brought me back—said it was all them prayers and sweetgrass weaving me back to life.

It took me a long while to get used to the fact that I'm back in Mount Pleasant and not in heaven no more. Don't get me wrong now, Mount Pleasant's a nice-enough place, but it ain't heaven. No sir. My body's fat and heavy and painful. And my Jim don't come to see me no more. I'm still grieving over that. I miss him so much. And I miss Mama and Daddy and Auntie Leona too. Seems like I done lost 'em all over again. But the hardest thing for me to deal with, if I'm telling the truth, is not seeing my Liza. That little ol' thing had grown closer to me than a freckle, and her not being here leaves me feeling real empty inside.

I hope you don't think I'm awful for saying this. I love being back with EJ and Henrietta. But it all takes some getting used to, I reckon. Just like it took a little getting used to being up in heaven.

Now in all this time I been back, I never mentioned to Retta that I knew about Eliza. It never seemed like the right time to me. But today

I'm leaving the hospital to go back to my house on Rifle Range Road, and I got a strange feeling down deep inside me—sure 'nough, it feels like the time has come.

We have a little going-away party for me. All the nurses and staff are there and EJ and Retta, Eddie and Clarice, Miss Maybree and Jeffrey Lowes. Even Miss Nancy and Miss Georgia come over. All the people who love me are there, and it's a real fine party with a sheet cake and party hats. Everybody raises their cups and say real nice words about me. I couldn't ask for anything nicer. And when all my belongings are packed up and EJ's buckled me into Retta's car, he goes on back to his car—still driving my old station wagon. Then Retta gets in beside me, and it's just the two of us at last.

It's a quiet ride, me watching the side of the road, looking at buildings I remember and such. It's nice to see the trees again. I did so miss the trees.

Henrietta sits there, driving, staring ahead like she should. Every once in a while, she looks over at me and we smile. Finally, when we get on that dad-blasted Cooper River Bridge, my mouth starts running so I won't have to think 'bout being so high up in the air.

"Retta?" I say.

"What, Mama?"

"It's mighty good to be back."

"It's good to have you back, Mama. We missed you. I can't tell you how much."

"Retta?"

"What is it, Mama?"

"I was in heaven all that time."

Retta stays quiet. All I can hear is the *wibble, wibble, wibble* of the tires going 'cross the bridge. I can tell she's most likely thinking I had me one long dream, lying there in that hospital bed. But I know the difference. It ain't just a dream.

See, Mama used to tell me 'bout the dream she had when she turned a Christian. She was a young girl 'bout fifteen years old. Back then the Gullah had their own ways o' doing things left over from Africa days. Mama was seeking Jesus so the elders had her go out in the wilderness and look for Him there. She had to wait nearly two days in the dark and scary, all the while praying for the presence of God to meet her. Out there in the woods, Mama had a vision—I can't remember the details now—but that seeker dream was told to a spiritual mother in the Gullah community who knew 'bout those things. She told Mama, yes indeed, she'd met the Lord in the wilderness. Mama was happy as all get-out and a Christian ever after.

So I know what's a dream and what ain't. And I know when my body was lying there in that hospital bed, my spirit was in heaven for real. The good Lord met me there just as plain as you and me.

"I really was, Retta," I tell her when we come off that bridge and get on good ground again. "I was in heaven. I was with Daddy and Mama and Jim and Leona too."

She still don't say a word, but flashes a real quick glance my way.

"Know what else?"

"What, Mama?" I can tell she still don't believe me.

"I met your baby there, Retta."

Henrietta swallows hard and cranes her neck at me.

"Keep your eyes on the road, child! You're gonna get us both killed." When she's looking straight ahead again, I say, "Retta, honey, I know all about your baby. I know all about you and Ray Fines."

All a sudden, Retta slams on the brakes and cars screech up to us, honking all the way! I grab my safety belt and stare at Henrietta. Her head's down on the steering wheel. She's bawling like a baby, and here we are, like a scared turtle right in the middle of Highway 17.

After a minute or two, I coax her into moving again. Maybe telling her that mess while we was driving weren't the best idea. EJ comes up behind us waving his arms, wondering what in tarnation's going on. I roll my window down to him and tell him everything's okay, and just to go on to the house without us for a minute.

Retta pulls on over in a Hardee's parking lot. There's folks pulling in and out of the drive-thru window. I watch 'em go by for a while and Retta cries.

After a few minutes, she sniffles and looks at me like a lost puppy dog. "It can't be," she says. "How could you know? There's no way you could know about this. How did you find out? Is it true? Have mercy! Is it true?"

"It's true, baby. I was there. And that little girl of yours is somethin' else," I say.

"It's . . . she's a girl? Oh, have mercy."

"She's the prettiest thing you ever saw. Looks a lot like you, you know, 'ceptin' she has bright green eyes."

Retta looks at me, pained. She knows they're Ray's green eyes.

It seems like the longest time that we sit there talking. She wants to know all about Eliza. I tell her that's her name now. I tell her what she looks like and how she's a better weaver than I ever hope to be. I tell her about her sweet smile and the way she loves to pick flowers in the field and skip in the sunshine. But I never ask her how come that baby ended up in heaven. That's 'tween her, Liza, and the good Lord now.

Retta holds my hand tight and asks me not to say a word to nobody, 'specially Eddie. I tell her my mouth is shut long as I'm living and it's up to her to tell him, if'n she ever wants to. That, I reckon, is 'tween her, Eddie, and the good Lord, as well.

Epilogue

THE FIRST THING I DONE when I got back home to my lime-green house on Rifle Range Road was to go in the bathroom, lean down, and pick up that loose floor tile. I grabbed that old diary of Auntie Leona's, tore out each and every page, and flushed 'em down the commode, one by one. I breathed a good sigh o' relief when they was all done and gone.

EJ's still working at the li-berry. He and Felicia live in a little old house not far from me up the road. They check in on me a lot, sweet things. And my sugar, Mister Jeffrey Lowes, comes to see me and says he's putting together the flowers for a big ol' wedding downtown—for none other than the daughter of Jackson Hemmingway, of the Isle of Palm Hemmingways, don't you know. Well, I was so tickled I call Jackson up from out the blue, and he's right happy to hear from this old lady after so many years. He's terrible upset to hear 'bout the poor state o' things for the sweetgrass weavers in Mount Pleasant. Yes sir, I smile from here to heaven when Jackson offers to stop over and see how he might help us ladies out. I got me a good feeling he'll be able to do a whole lot o' good. In fact, I've already cleaned out my back room to make space for a little office, just right for lobbying and organizing, if'n that's what we intend to do.

And Retta weaves with me nowadays. We sit here at my lime-green stand, just like I used to, weaving and talking 'til the day is long. Course, some things is different now, like we got three chairs set out 'stead o' two. That's right—Jim comes and sits with me still. Glory hallelujah, praise God! He come to me first day we was out here, little booger. And Retta even pulls out his pink plastic chair every day. She can't see him or hear him like I can, but she don't make fun no more. That's the truth. And we don't sit up where I used to be. No, developers come and put up buildings and such 'round there. So Retta and me, we moved over by Miss Nancy and Georgia, over yonder from the new fancy grocery store.

I got to say, life is good as far as living goes. I got my Retta back. That's all I ever wanted. I got my EJ too. And Daddy Jim. And now, we're all expecting a baby soon—Miss Felicia's got just a few more days to go. Miss Cassandra Mae ain't born yet, but I got a sneaky feeling that's what they're gonna name her.

While back, I asked Henrietta if she'd had a big falling out with EJ while I was gone. 'Course, she said she ain't, 'ceptin' they had a little struggle when he first introduced Felicia. So I warned her. "The time is now, baby. Go on and clear out any prejudice you got inside 'cause it don't go 'way on it's own, no sir. Whatever happened with Ray Fines or any other white folk ain't got squat to do with Felicia or this grandbaby you 'bout to have." I told her to be real sweet to EJ, too, 'cause he's stubborn just like her. "Ain't nothin' worth losin' family over," I said.

And I tell you what, I can't explain how I went to heaven and then ended up alive again, but I thank the good Lord for it. Things are changed now. I got a whole new view on life I ain't never had before. And the best thing about it is, Retta's actually listening to what I got to say these days. And she's happier. I can see she's changed too. When I told her 'bout Liza and we talked things through, I went on and on about Jesus and forgiveness. I reckon that's what she's gone and done now—forgiven Ray Fines or forgiven herself—whichever one she really needed to do.

I'm thankful to Retta for saving my house on Rifle Range. I love being in it, but it ain't so nice as when Jim was there. I had my blue trim painted all green like the rest of the house just for Jim. But for some reason he still don't come home with me—even though he ain't no haint.

And even though I've lived here my entire life, it's funny, 'cause Mount Pleasant don't feel like home to me no more. No sir, home is something you feel deep in your bones, way down in your soul, and now that I've been to heaven and back, I know heaven was home to me all along. Lord, I'm mighty happy to be here, but I look forward to going on back someday. Maybe after I see my new great-grandbaby grow up, then I'll be ready to go.

I wish all folks would act right so's they can go up to heaven one day, 'cause not everybody gets to go, no sir. Can't understand why, 'cause in the book o' John third chapter, Jesus tells you how to get there plain as day. Oh, did I mention John's up there? Yep, I met him. Real nice fella, too, 'long with Matthew, Mark, and Luke. There's lots o' good Bible folk like that up there, but even some folks who never even heard o' Jesus is up there too. I reckon He can be in your heart whether you know it or not.

See, it's stuff like that—since I been up to heaven, I understand so much more. Take for instance, I always felt invisible setting out there on Highway 17 all them years. Thought I had no power in me a'tall. I just watched as the powerful people rolled on by me, kicking up dust. Well, now I can see the Power all through me. And He was there, all along—in my mind, in my mouth, in my fingertips. And the folks I thought was so mighty? Turns out, they ain't so powerful after all.

No, true power comes in the way we treat folks. In the things we say. In the way we act. My Retta, my EJ, my family is the good I done in my lifetime. And it's real nice to know the doing good part don't end, even when we think we're up and gone forever.

See in my family we're all weavers, and we always will be, just like Jesus, I reckon. Don't matter what color skin we got or where we come from—He told me He weaves us all in and out, in and out, every day. We go 'round and around and get tighter and tighter 'til each one of us comes together like music, like a fine old Gullah spiritual humming deep down in your soul.

So I'm here to tell you, just like this here grass in my hands, that every word of this is true, mm hmm. See how this basket's all sewn up, this way and that, and you can't pull it apart if'n you wanted to? Yes sir, that's the sign of a good basket. See, we're stitched together like this—past, present, black, white, and purple. And let me tell you, sweetgrass don't lie. It's the realest and most honest thing I know. "Ain't that right, Jim?"

"Yes sir, Mama. You sure got that right."

Lord in heaven, I do love this man.

A Note to the Reader

SOME THINGS HAVE CHANGED since I first began writing this novel in October 2004. Many efforts of the fictitious "Grass Roots Society" have actually been achieved by caring local governments, individuals, and organizations. The first annual Sweetgrass Cultural Arts Festival was held in June 2005. In 2006, the Gullah/Geechee Cultural Heritage Act was approved by Congress, providing ten million dollars to preserve aspects of Gullah/Geechee Culture. Also in 2006, sweetgrass basket making was named the South Carolina State Handcraft, and a place to grow sweetgrass was proposed for a spot in the new Mount Pleasant waterfront park slated to be built at the foot of the old Cooper River Bridge.

In 2006 that "skinny little bridge to downtown Charleston," otherwise known as the Grace Memorial Bridge, was demolished along with the Silas Pearlman Bridge beside it. What replaced them is the new Arthur J. Ravenel Bridge, an impressive eight-lane cable-stayed bridge that opened in 2005.

The Spirit of Sweetgrass is a work of fiction, although some of the places exist and some of the characters and circumstances are inspired by people I've met along the way. Most inspiring is the Lowcountry itself and the beautiful basket makers and Gullah/ Geechee people who call it "home."

Millions of African-Americans can trace their ancestors back to the Gullah/Geechee Nation, an area encompassing all of the Sea Islands from Jacksonville, Florida, to Jacksonville, North Carolina, and thirty to thirty-five miles inland—also called "the Lowcountry." Nearly 40 percent of the West Africans brought to America in the eighteenth century arrived through Sullivan's Island located in present-day Charleston County, South Carolina. They were forcibly shipped here and enslaved because of their skills and knowledge of coastal life, and their contributions were many: agriculture (Sea Island cotton, Carolina Gold rice, and indigo), artisanship, domestic, culinary, and building arts, just to name a few. These West Africans affected the landscape and culture of the American South; and their descendants, called Gullah/Geechees, are still here.

In the U.S. Civil War, the Union army captured many of the Sea Islands after whites fled. As a result, the Gullah/Geechee people there were isolated from other ethnic groups, a solitude that lasted into the early 1900s as there were few bridges to the Islands until then. The Gullah/Geechees created their own unique language, an amalgamation of African and English, and kept many traditional spiritual practices, food ways, and customs such as net making and sweetgrass basket weaving.

The Gullah/Geechee people are becoming fewer and more scattered as new residential and commercial developments sweep over the Sea Islands and inland. Many treasured traditions must be passed down through generations for the Gullah/Geechee heritage to survive but oftentimes, today's youth are too busy or disinterested to learn time-consuming crafts. Sweetgrass basket making is the most visible of these customs and is now considered an art form in the coastal region of the South. Many Gullah/Geechee descendants in Mount Pleasant still weave and sell their wares at roadside stands on Highway 17 and in the Charleston market nearby. But developments are pushing these men and women further and further north, and the precious resource of sweetgrass itself, Muhlenbergia sericea, is in jeopardy of extinction.

In recent years, progress has been made to protect the Gullah/Geechee heritage and sweetgrass basket making. But as a Lowcountry native, it saddens me to watch as encroachments upon the Gullah/Geechee people and their traditions force this important part of American history to become just that—history. There is much work to be done to preserve Gullah/Geechee culture and to ensure this colorful heritage remains a vibrant part of our Southern coast.

Visit www.nicoleseitz.com to learn more about the sweetgrass culture and ways to get involved. Or visit the Gullah/Geechee Sea Island Coalition at www.officialgullahgeechee.info for information on authentic efforts to keep the Gullah/Geechee culture alive and the people on their homeland.

Discussion Questions

1. Essie Mae is 78-years-old. Is she part of your generation, your mother's, or your grandmother's? What characteristics does she share with women of her generation?

2. The themes of home and homeland are strong in *The Spirit of Sweetgrass*. Why is heritage and paying homage to homeland important? What is Essie Mae's true homeland? What is yours?

3. Does Daddy Jim truly sit with Essie Mae and speak with her? What do EJ and Henrietta believe?

4. Why do you think Daddy Jim visits Essie Mae at her roadside stand? Why doesn't he come to the house on Rifle Range Road? If Daddy Jim truly loves Essie Mae, why do you think he won't go to Sunnydale Farms?

5. In what ways is *The Spirit of Sweetgrass* a love story?

6. The notion of "Power" or being "powerful" fuels this story. What is Power, where does it come from, and who has it? Does Essie Mae have power in the beginning of the book? In the end? Is there power in Essie Mae's "love baskets"?

7. The themes of life and death are threaded throughout this book. What are some instances of these events? How do these events affect Essie Mae, Jeffrey, and Henrietta?

8. Who or what is "the spirit of sweetgrass"?

9. Discuss the use of color in The Spirit of Sweetgrass. Are these colors symbolic in any way?

10. When Essie Mae is in heaven she says, "It's a wonder we understand

each other a'tall down on Earth what with us only seeing little snippets of folks every now and again." Does Essie Mae ever understand her daughter, Henrietta? Does Henrietta ever understand her mother? In any relationship, how important is it that we understand each other? What are some ways to foster better understanding?

11. How do you think Essie Mae feels when she learns Jeffrey is gay? Are her beliefs conservative or liberal? Upon learning his sexual orientation, do Essie Mae's feelings toward Jeffrey change? Is it possible to love someone unconditionally yet not accept everything about him or her?

12. Both Jeffrey Lowes and Jackson Hemmingway were cared for as children by Essie Mae. What do you think about nanny-child relationships? What does it say to you that a white family chooses a nanny who is African-American?

13. After the Soiree EJ thinks his mother, Henrietta, is a racist. Do you believe she is? If so, what is at the root of her prejudice? If issues of the past are fully dealt with, do you believe racial prejudice can be overcome?

14. In this book, Essie Mae has a strong spiritual connection to places: Mount Pleasant, the lime-green house, her roadside stand, Africa, heaven. What does it mean to have a spiritual connection to a physical place? Do you have a spiritual connection to a place? Explain.

15. Essie Mae feels she's found her calling in life. What is her calling? Have you found your calling in life? If so, how did you realize it? If not, what may be standing in your way? Do you believe everyone has a calling?

16. What do you think Essie Mae is most afraid of? How does she handle that fear? What about Henrietta? Have you ever considered what you're most afraid of? How might your fears impact your actions and your loved ones?

17. Essie Mae and her band of heavenly spirits are involved in a spiritual battle at the Sweetgrass Soiree. What are they battling over? Do you believe that spiritual battles between good and evil go on in our daily lives?

18. Heaven is an important setting in this book. Describe what you imagine heaven is like. What do you hope it will be like? Do you have any fears about heaven? Do you believe there's a connection between heaven and Earth?